CURVY GIRLS CAN'T DATE ROCK STARS

KELSIE STELTING

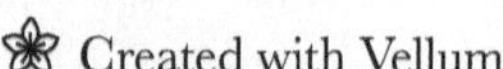 Created with Vellum

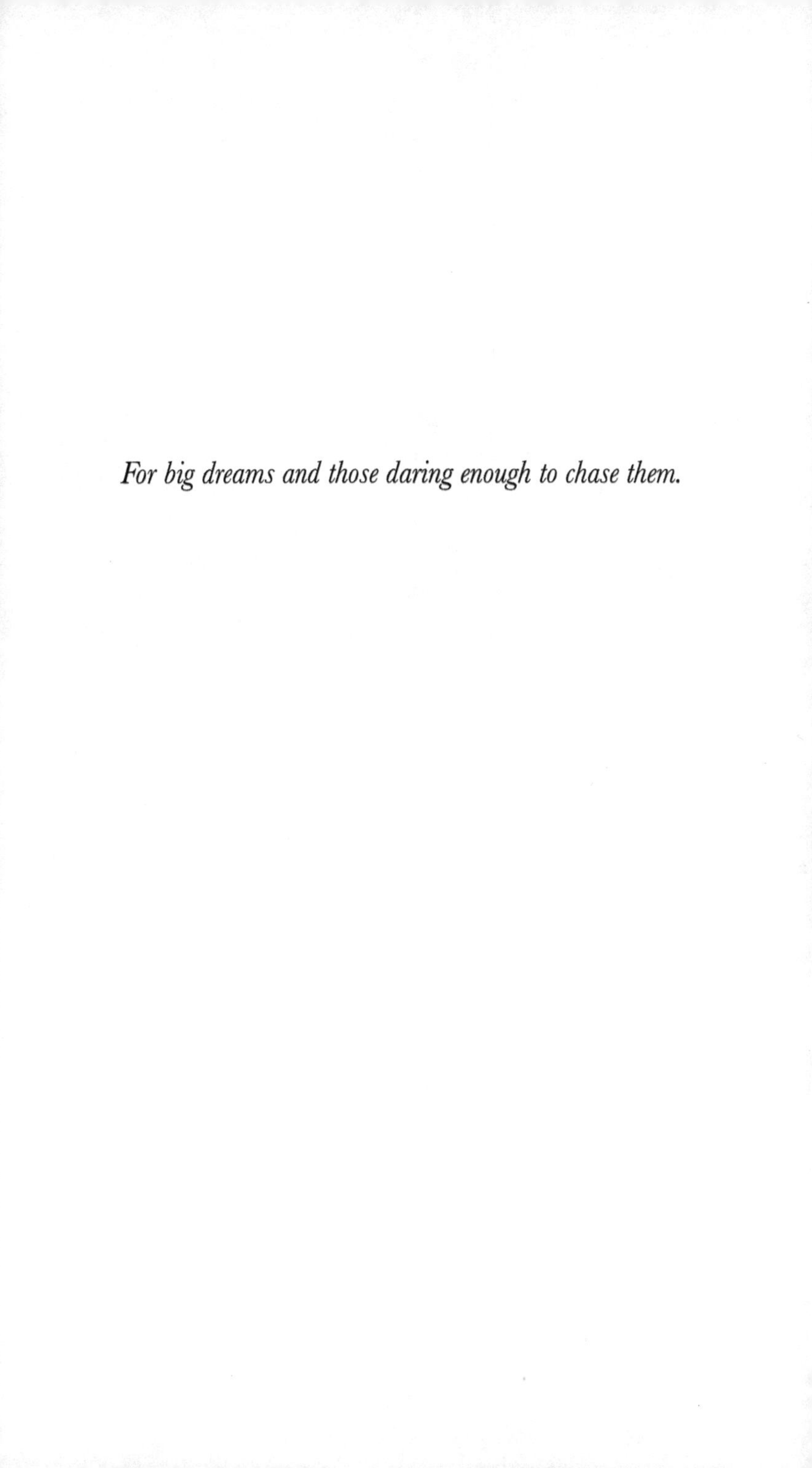

For big dreams and those daring enough to chase them.

CONTENTS

ONE

DES

THIS WAS the most important meeting of my life.

The meeting that could change everything.

The meeting that could make my dreams come true and turn me into a famous singer, performing in front of thousands of people. I'd finally show everyone who doubted me that plus-size girls deserve to be center stage, standing in the spotlight.

I was finally getting to talk with Natalie Maeler, famous agent with Songbird Agency.

Mom and I followed Natalie's assistant into a boardroom that had a massively long glass table with clear chairs and floor-to-ceiling windows showing a multi-million-dollar view of West Hollywood.

Everything about this room spelled luxury. *Success*. I could practically taste it.

Natalie wasn't here yet, because of course she wasn't. Important people had things to attend to. And Natalie was a *very* VIP. I was more than happy to wait.

So many performers had been exactly where I was now and had gone on to do incredible things. Jude Santiago, the latest pop sensation, for one. Sure, the record label he'd signed with made him into a plastic mannequin singing pandering nonsense, but I knew this agency could find the right label for me.

Natalie's assistant asked, "Can I get you anything to drink? A latte maybe?"

My mom instantly nudged my side. In our culture, it was rude to turn down food at a social event, but this wasn't a family barbecue. I doubted Natalie's assistant would care that I said no, but I still answered, "A caramel macchiato. Extra whip if you have it."

Mom said, "Americano, please."

"Absolutely." She turned on her four-inch heels and left us by ourselves in this beautiful room full of possibilities.

Mom squeezed my hand. "I'm so excited for you, *mija.*"

I grinned back, fully embracing the smile I'd been holding back. "I'm excited for us! Do you remember taking me to vocal lessons when I was eight years old? Or the karaoke machine for my tenth birthday? I wouldn't be here without you, Mom."

Mom pressed at the corner of her eyes with her short red nails and said, "Don't make me cry. The spots will show on this table." She hovered her hand over the glass top. "We could never have this at home."

I laughed. "Fingerprints everywhere."

"And fog," she said. "With little words drawn in it."

The door opened, and we both jumped, just a little. Mom stood, and I stood beside her, feeling strangely formal as I took in the woman walking through the door.

Natalie Maeler looked exactly like her photo on the company website. She had short blond hair cut into a severe bob. Her eyes were icy blue, her lips thin, and her jawline just as sharp as the manicured points on her fingers.

I barely even noticed her assistant following her

in, carrying two fancy cups of coffee. But now that I did, I wondered if they had a café inside the building or if she was also a trained barista.

She handed them to us and then sat a few seats away from Natalie, a notepad open and pen poised over the page.

Natalie looked across the table at me, her eyes glinting under the pendant lights. "It's nice to meet you, Desirae. I've heard great things about you."

"That's good to hear." I tried to keep it cool, even though I felt like flying. After all the song covers posted on YouTube... After singing every national anthem humanly possible... My dreams were coming true.

"Let's get to it," Natalie said, all business. "We're going to have to pass."

The words hit my ears, but that's where the processing stopped. I couldn't have heard her correctly.

"Excuse me?" my mom said quietly. "Didn't you ask for the meeting?"

"I got your name from one of my clients. I listened to some of your songs a few minutes ago, and you have an amazing voice, but something's missing." She pressed her hands to the table as if to stand, but I spoke fast.

"Missing? What's missing?" I asked. "Because I'm a quick learner and a hard worker, and I'm sure I could fix it."

Natalie pressed her lips together, sitting again in her chair, but on the edge. "Songbird is an agency that creates superstars, not midlist artists. We pride ourselves in knowing what sells and what doesn't."

Midlist sounded just as dirty to my ears as any cuss word. "Why would I be midlist?" I asked. "I've grown my social following to a hundred thousand people within a year. Jude Santiago had half that when he signed with you."

Natalie gave me a calculating look. "You did your research."

I nodded. I knew what I wanted, and I knew I was worthy of having it.

"You're young, so I don't want to give you false hope and have you waste your time." She leaned forward, elbows on the table, hands laced together. "There are thousands, millions of people out there with good voices. To be a star, guys have to want you, and girls have to want to be you."

"Why wouldn't they?" I asked, still confused.

Natalie's cold eyes scanned me up and down. "You don't have the look."

Mom went rigid next to me, but my temper was

already through the roof. "So you're saying you won't sign me because I'm too fat?"

Natalie let out a disappointed sigh, like I was wasting her time. "This is a business, Desirae. One where your body is onstage and your face is on screen. Your looks are a major part of a package that we have to sell."

Fuming, hot behind my ears, I said, "I'll have you know plenty of guys have wanted to be with me." I could practically feel my mom doing the sign of the cross next to me, but I couldn't stop. "I've sung every national anthem at my school, to standing ovations. I've gotten multiple offers to sing live at local venues. I have thousands of dedicated fans who would be very willing to pay money to see me in concert."

"That's good for you," Natalie said.

My fists clenched at my sides. "And you know what else I have?"

Natalie raised an eyebrow.

I held up my middle finger and stormed out of the room.

TWO

DES

ON THE WAY HOME, Mom alternated between chiding me and cursing Natalie, who she refused to call by name. No, Natalie would forever be "*la bruja*" in my mother's eyes.

And, to be fair, mine also.

I couldn't believe Natalie had the audacity to tell me that I didn't have "the look" to be famous when people like Lizzo and Adele and Meghan Trainor had found so much success in the industry. Sure, I was curvier than those girls, but who cared?

And as my mom had said, more than once, it was cruel to pulverize my dreams so thoroughly based solely on my looks.

As we walked through the front door, Mom

said, "I'll make you a *tres leches*, okay? It'll be ready soon."

"I'm going outside," I said in response. I didn't want to be taken care of right now. I wanted to be signing with an agent, getting a record deal, living the life I *knew* I was meant to live.

I probably pushed the door too roughly, but I let it close behind me and left our patio for the soft sand of the beach. I could hear the ocean waves crashing, and it echoed the tumult in my heart.

The closer I got to the water, the heavier my breaths came, and the closer I felt to crying. I'd gotten a meeting with *Jude Santiago's agent*, and it had gone just as poorly as it possibly could. Was my dream really over before it even had a chance to begin?

"How'd it go?" my brother Diego asked.

I jumped away from his voice, covering my chest. "I didn't see you out here, Diego!" And now I knew why. He was lying on his surfboard in the sand, completely still and quiet. Well, until he asked me how my meeting went.

"Sorry." He propped himself up, grinning and squinting against the sunlight. "So you didn't come out here to tell me good news?"

"Nope." I dropped into the sand beside him. "It was a complete failure."

He lifted his eyebrows. "Seriously?"

I nodded slowly. "She basically told me I was too fat and that she only took the meeting with me as a favor."

"Wow." He dug his fists through the sand. "That sucks."

"Yep."

"You gonna do anything about it?"

I gave him a look. "I'm not about to lose weight just to get her attention."

His eyes turned back toward the water, where he spent most of his time in the summers. "I didn't take you as the kind of person who gave up so easily."

"What is there to do?" I asked. I'd seen Jude Santiago go down that road. When he started YouTubing, he was a cute guy from some small town in Arizona. Now? They were letting his talents go to waste. They'd turned him into nothing more than a cute face. But after that meeting, I understood why.

Diego sat up and shrugged. "Last I heard from Mrs. H. in health class, more than a third of the US population is overweight. Seems like a third of Jude Santiago's fans would be interested in hearing what his agent said about you."

He was right.

THREE

JUDE

I CLIMBED out of the pool and grabbed a towel to wrap around my waist. I couldn't believe I'd be leaving our house and living in a tour bus again in only a week. It would be a short tour—three months packed with shows so we could make the most of summer vacation.

I couldn't say I was looking forward to it. Tours were exhausting... and lonely. When we were on the road, I was surrounded by adults. My dad/manager, Francie the bus driver, Jago my security guard, makeup artists, hairstylists, publicists, not to mention my terrible agent.

The only people my age were in the stands, most of them girls who didn't exactly see me as a person. They screamed at me and cheered like I was made of gold. Like I wasn't a nineteen-year-old guy who'd gotten insanely lucky.

Through the large sliding door, I could see Dad pacing the living room outside of his office, talking on the phone. There was a deep crease between his brows that he always got when something bad had happened.

I walked inside just in time to hear Dad say, "She's just a YouTuber. How bad can it be?"

"What's going on?" I mouthed.

Dad covered the mouthpiece and whispered, "Natalie made someone mad."

Of course my heartless agent was behind the negative news. I couldn't wait until my commitment with her ran its course and I could find someone new. January wouldn't come soon enough.

Dad's voice rose. "Meteor backed out? We're five days from the tour!"

My mouth fell open. "My opening act?" I said. I'd only met them a few times, but they'd seemed so excited to go on tour with me.

Dad ignored me, pacing faster. "There have to be a million people who'd love to take their place." He listened for a little before hanging up and rolling his eyes. "Well, Natalie's lack of empathy got her in trouble with some YouTuber."

"Which one?" I asked. "What did she say?"

"Some girl named Desirae De Leon. Natalie told her she was too fat to make it big." Dad pinched his nose like he always did right before popping some aspirin for a migraine. "Now Songbird's looking bad, which makes you look bad, which is why Meteor pulled themselves from the tour."

Trying to keep my expression neutral, I said, "What's she going to do to fix it? Did you call my publicist?"

Dad gave me an exasperated look. "Of course I did. Samantha thinks you should write this Desirae. Endear her to you again. Maybe even get her to take the video down."

"I'll take care of it," I said.

"Let Samantha read over anything before you send it, okay?"

"Dad." I gave him a look. "If I can speak in front of thousands of people live, I can handle this."

He raised his hands in surrender. "Fine. Just take care of it."

"I will." I clenched my towel and jogged up the stairs two at a time, desperate to know what Des had said. Dreading what Natalie had told her.

I'd been watching Des's channel for the last year, getting lost in her voice. Someday, when she made it big, I wanted to sing a duet with her. Face her across the microphone, the crowd fading out until it was just her and me and a melody.

My heart beat quickly as I tapped to her page, and even faster when I saw her face.

Des De Leon was one of a kind, that was for certain. Her lips caught my attention first. Full and painted with bright red lipstick that demanded to be noticed. Her eyes were angled, with dark lashes and glittering brown irises. Her high cheekbones made her look regal. And the spark in her smile, the fire she put behind everything she did online... it was... captivating to say the least.

Her latest video was titled TOO FAT TO BE FAMOUS?

My stomach hardened to a heavy pit. What was this about?

I clicked play and watched her come to life.

"Sorry, guys, but there isn't a cover today. No, I'm pulling *off* the cover instead. I've hinted that I had a big meeting today. It was with an agent. The same agent representing Jude Santiago.

"I went into the meeting hoping she would help my dreams come true. What I got instead was a fatphobic rejection saying I didn't have the 'look' to make a real career in music."

Her voice shook with anger. With hurt. "But you know what? I'm better off without them. They take people like this..." Her face was replaced by a clip of one of my earlier original songs.

I remembered how many hours I spent writing it, wondering if people would ever even hear it onstage. Now, a few years later, I could see the flaws in my performance, but there was something so raw about it. So real.

The clip of me singing ended, and Des said, "They took absolute beauty, pure talent, and turned it into this."

My latest music video played on the screen. The video director had girls feeding me grapes from the vine, and I cringed. If she only knew how much I'd gotten them to tone it down from their original vision.

She came back on screen, shaking her head. "Jude Santiago sold out to put cash in his pockets."

I bristled. How could she say that?

"But I'm not going to do that," she continued. "If Lizzo can become an icon exactly as she is, then you can bet I'm going to do the same. I don't care if it takes five years or fifty. When I make it to the top, it's going to be as me."

As she signed off the video, I sat back in my chair, feeling like I'd been sucker-punched. I'd only ever tried to be myself onstage. Being in business with other people required compromise, sure, but I'd always fought for the things that were most important to me. I'd even argued with the label on lyrics the songwriters presented.

It was hard to be mad at Des though. I imagined her walking into a meeting with my agency, with Batty Natty herself, and being told she was wrong for the business. Not only was Natalie wrong about Des, she was cruel, making the rejection about her weight.

One of my favorite things about music was the ability to close your eyes and hear the soul of a person through a song. It didn't matter how someone looked, only how they made you feel.

I clicked to my own YouTube page. I hadn't made a video in more than a year, but it was time to change that.

I'D BEEN CRYING EVER since I posted the video. First angry tears. Then tears of defeat. For as long as I could remember, I'd wanted to be a singer. I'd even given up going to college so I could stay home and focus on growing my following and hopefully land a record deal.

But what if Natalie had been right? What if Songbird not wanting me meant no one else would want to work with me either? Had I been foolish to devote all of myself to a dream that didn't want me?

A big commotion sounded in the kitchen but was quickly silenced, and I sat up in my bed.

Crap.

I'd already told my friends they should come

over and celebrate. Well, all of them except Faith, who would have to join via video since she was in DC training for her volunteer assignment in Peru.

In my mom's super-loud whisper, I heard her tell the girls about the meeting gone wrong. At least I wouldn't have to repeat the story again. Saying it out loud just made the horrible truth that much more real.

The talking quieted, and a knock sounded on my bedroom door.

"Come in," I called.

Four of my best friends filed in, concerned and sympathetic expressions on their faces.

"Des," Cori said. Her bright red hair was pulled up into a wet bun like she'd just came from working out. "Are you okay?"

"Okay?" I asked, my voice thick. "It's been the worst day of my life."

Adriel walked around my bed, sitting on one side, while Nadira and Cori sat on the other, surrounding me.

Nadira reached out, rubbing my knee, her black and white hand standing out against my white sheets. "Your mom told us what happened. That woman sounds evil."

Tatiana nodded in agreement.

I looked up at them. "You want to know the worst part?"

They were quiet, listening.

"I really thought I had a chance." My voice broke on the last word, and I stifled yet another sob.

Adriel pulled me into a hug, cradling me against her chest. "You do. This just wasn't the time."

My phone began ringing, and I sniffed, "That's probably Faith."

Cori grabbed my phone from my nightstand, answering it, and Faith appeared on the screen.

"Have you seen it?" Faith asked, her blue eyes wide.

"Seen what?" I asked.

"The video!" she cried.

My eyebrows drew together. "Of course I saw it. I posted it."

Faith shook her head, making her loose curls swing about her face. "Des, it's all over the news... Jude made a response."

I snapped up to a sitting position. "No way."

Faith said, "Go look at it!"

My friends made space as I climbed out from under my crumpled blankets and grabbed my laptop from my desk. As soon as I opened it, my YouTube screen came to life, and I covered my mouth. I had more notifications than I'd ever had before. But instead of checking them, I searched Jude Santiago. A new video was at the top of his channel.

As soon as I clicked it, he appeared on the screen. He was dressed casually, his dark hair damp, but he still looked like a million dollars. I spent far too much time taking in the intricate shape of his cheekbones, following the curve of his lips.

And now... he was speaking to me, with my friends gathered around watching.

"This video is for Desirae De Leon." He tilted his head to the side, his smile both charming and subdued. "I heard you loud and clear."

My cheeks immediately warmed. I had called him a sellout to a hundred thousand followers... even if it was true.

"This is a tough business, but it doesn't have to be cruel. I think you know, the fans know, and I definitely know that quality music is what matters most. So I have a proposition for you."

My lips parted. What was I hearing right now?

"Meteor recently dropped out of the Summer of Santiago Tour. And that means we need an opening act. The tour bus leaves in a week. I hope you'll be on it."

His earnest smile lit the screen just as surely as the light coming through his bedroom window. He looked away from the screen for a moment and then back. It was almost as though his green eyes were staring straight into mine.

"Oh, and for the record," he added, "I'm not a sellout. Once you come on tour with me, you'll see. If you still think I'm a sellout by the end, it'll be my last tour." He kissed his hand and waved at the screen. "You have an email in your inbox to set up the details, Desirae De Leon. I hope to hear from you soon."

Squealing erupted from around me.

Cori shook my shoulders, yelling, "JUDE FREAKING SANTIOGO INVITED YOU ON TOUR!"

Faith clapped her hands together. "You HAVE to go!"

Adriel nodded, her smile wide. "This is your big break!"

Nadira smirked. "And a chance to crush the competition."

I shook my head, blinking. "Why would he do that?"

"Who cares!" Tatiana said. "This is huge! Do

you know how many people you'll be singing in front of?"

"But the agent—" I began.

Adriel cut me off. "Who cares about one person's stupid opinion? Galina had worked with me for eight years and *still* thought I wasn't good enough. But look what I got." She smiled. "I'm going to *Juilliard*."

"Exactly," Cori said. "I can't believe *I'm* telling *you* this, but the only opinion that matters is yours."

Nadira lifted an eyebrow. "Where's Miss Confident with her cherry lips and self-love mantras? Huh?"

I shook my head, the reality of the situation sinking in. "I'm going on tour with Jude Santiago."

They cheered.

Then I remembered one hitch. "If my parents agree..."

"*Desirae Delante De Leon Desantis!*" Mom called from outside my room.

I shut my laptop and looked at my friends. "Looks like we're about to find out."

"Now!" Mom yelled.

I got off my bed and walked to the door, wiping my face. I knew I looked like an absolute mess, but the longer I chewed over the idea of going on tour with Jude, singing in front of all his fans... the more I knew I had to go.

I walked through the door to see her arms folded over her chest, her foot propped out, ready to begin angry tapping at any minute. Speaking to my friends first, she said, "Sorry, girls, you'll have to come back tomorrow."

They gave me hugs and promised to call me, then as soon as they were out the front door, Mom spoke quickly in Spanish. "Why did you create that mean video? Matilda called me and said it's all over the news!"

"I..." It was the last thing I'd expected her to yell about. "I was angry."

She shook her head. "He did nothing to you. It was that horrible woman. And now he wants you to go on tour with him? Is he okay in the head?"

"I don't know," I replied, "but isn't this amazing? I could have a chance to see what it's like to go on tour and perform! Maybe I'll even get picked up by a different agency!"

She pressed her lips together. "I don't know, Des. It's fishy to me. And I won't be able to come with you—I still need to watch your siblings, and your father needs to work."

"I'm eighteen, remember? I can go on my own.

What would you have done if Natalie would have picked me up anyway?"

"This kind of thing usually takes time, honey. I didn't think you'd sign and immediately be traveling around the country without me. I thought there would be time to prepare. To find a way to protect you."

"Protect me? What do I need protecting from?"

She unfolded her arms and put them on my shoulders. "Boys who have more power than you, for one. What if he tries something? You'll be alone with no one on your side."

The front door opened, and Dad came inside, pulling his tie over his head. He'd been in meetings a lot this week, looking to invest in other inventions like the food production piece he'd patented well before I was born.

Reading the room, he backed up slightly. "What did I just walk into? And where are the other children?"

Mom rattled off her list. "Diego's in his room, Mateo and Adelita are at the Watsons, Marisol is with the Ragnors, and Marco is making a 'creation' in the garage."

Dad nodded. "I'll be out there."

"Wait a minute," Mom said, looking to me. "We

have a lot of catching up to do." She filled him in on the meeting—emphasis on horrible woman—my video and Jude's response.

Dad scrubbed his face, like all the news had come too fast, and sat at the expansive kitchen island. "That's a lot."

Mom nodded. "And Des wants to go on tour with this stranger."

"He's not a stranger," I said. "I know his favorite color, and I listened to all his songs, even before he was famous."

She gave me a look. "That's not the same thing as knowing a person. What if you get on the road and he makes a move on you? Huh? What if his manager is just as cruel as that woman? What if you're attacked by one of the *Fantiagos*?"

I cringed. I hadn't even thought about how mad his crazy obsessed fan club would be about me riding on a tour bus with him.

"So the issue is," Dad said, "that you don't want her going alone?"

"Exactly," Mom said.

"And we can't go with her," Dad said. "We need to watch the younger kids, and I can't be away from work right now..."

My heart clenched on itself. Was I really this

close to my dreams and my parents weren't jumping up and down for joy? There had to be something we could do.

From behind me, my brother Diego said, "I can go."

I turned to see him casually walking up the stairs. "What?"

"I was coming up for some cake, and I heard the last part..."

At the word cake, Mom jumped and rushed to the oven. She pulled out the pan, setting it on the counter. "That was a close one."

I eyed the cake for a moment—it did smell amazing. But was Diego really offering to give up his summer to babysit me? And how did I feel about being chaperoned by my little brother?

Dad nodded slowly. "This could be good. A chance for Diego to see more of the world before he graduates next year. And Des would have someone in her corner."

"Why would you want to be on a tour bus all summer?" I asked him. It wasn't that I disliked Diego; we were just different. He spent all of his time outside on a surfboard. Never went to parties or really even hung out with girls. "You're going to miss out on so much surfing time."

He shrugged. "The ocean will always be there. This tour's only for a summer."

If this was my chance, I would take it. I looked between Mom and Dad. "So?"

Mom slowly broke a smile. "Tell Jude you're going."

FIVE

JUDE

NATALIE CAME into my house at suppertime without bothering to knock, followed by my publicist, Samantha. Their high heels clacked angrily over the stone tile as they walked into the dining room. "That was some stunt you pulled," Natalie snapped at me.

Samantha grinned. "But it worked."

Dad wiped his mouth with a napkin, seeming just as stunned as I was. "Excuse me?"

Samantha grinned, making the differences between her and Natalie that much more apparent. While Natalie was tall and commanding, Samantha was approachable and always had a hint of a smile in her blue eyes with creases around the corners.

"Not only did Jude help Songbird's reputation,"

Samantha said, "but his popularity has gone through the roof. 'Carry Your Books' has moved to the number-one spot in the charts. It was at twenty this morning! And you should see the way girls are talking about him now."

Natalie sat at an open seat and drawled, "Chubby girls everywhere are now wondering if they're his type."

Through clenched teeth, I said, "Enough with the fat shaming, Natalie. I did it because it was the right thing to do. Not that you'd be familiar with ethical conduct." Not to mention, Des De Leon was *exactly* my type.

Natalie rolled her eyes. "It's caused quite a bit of extra work for us."

"Worth it," Samantha said, sitting opposite Natalie. "Des riding on the bus with you? Genius. The press will eat that up."

"As long as Desirae doesn't eat it first," Natalie snorted.

"Natalie," I snapped. "*Enough* with the fat shaming."

The coldness in my voice must have shaken her because she was actually quiet for a moment. Then her eyes narrowed, and she said, "I think you're forgetting the person who made you a star."

"My fans did that," I replied. "And I won't be bringing Des on tour if she's going to be treated this way by you the entire time."

Samantha said, "Natalie, please behave yourself. For the sake of all our paychecks."

Natalie put her hands in the air as if surrendering. "Fine. I'll do better. Cross my heart."

There was a touch of sarcasm, but I'd take it. At this point, I'd do just about anything to have Des on tour with me. To hear her voice every night before I went onstage, and not just through my earbuds.

My email notification went off, and I hurriedly looked at my phone. One new email from Des De Leon.

Dear Jude,

Thank you for your offer. I would be happy to accept, with one condition. My younger brother comes with us. He's seventeen, and you'll hardly notice he's there.

Do we have a deal?

Des

Before even checking with Dad or Natalie, I typed back a response.

Deal. My manager will get details to you shortly. See you Monday. :)

"So?" Dad asked. Everyone was watching me now.

I couldn't help my grin. "She's in. And her brother's coming too."

Dad rubbed his face while Natalie said, "What? This isn't a family vacation; it's a music tour."

I shrugged. "We have an extra bunk in the back of the bus. I don't really see why not."

Samantha shrugged. "Family bonds is always a good angle."

Natalie narrowed her gaze and pointed her finger at me. "This better be the best tour of your life. Any more difficulty with you and you'll be on the street in two seconds flat."

I folded my arms across my chest. "I'd be careful if you want your contract renewed."

She laughed sardonically. "You're talking big now, but have you ever heard how things work out for child stars? Everyone's just waiting for you to mess up. And when you do, it won't even come as a surprise." With that, she turned and left our house, the door slamming behind her.

I turned to Dad and Samantha, demanding an explanation. Why would my own father let her talk to me like that?

"She's just fired up," he explained. "She cares about her work, and she's used to dealing with flaky artists."

"You're *excusing* her?"

Samantha frowned. "She's probably overwhelmed, and I'm sure the other partners at Songbird aren't thrilled with the bad press today."

Dad nodded. "See it from her side, Jude. She's got an entire company's reputation on the line, and what? It's resting in the hands of some nineteen-year-old kid?"

I grit my teeth. I hated that he referred to me as if I were a child. I'd been on tours with performances every single night, meeting thousands of fans after singing and dancing for hours. I put in more hours than most people worked, and it took so much out of me. But they treated my work like it was nothing. Like I was nothing more than an ATM to pump out money for them.

Instead of arguing with my dad, I grabbed my keys and walked out the door.

"Where are you going?" Dad called after me.

"Out."

The dumb thing about leaving my house was that I had nowhere to go. We lived in Beverly Hills, hours away from the small Arizona town where I grew up. My old friends got weird when I became famous, and my new "friends" were more like business acquaintances than anyone I could really connect with or confide in. Everyone had an angle here. Or maybe they were just more up front about it than the people in my hometown had been.

I loved singing, loved performing, but sometimes I missed my old life—going out to eat or to the mall without being seen and chased by one of the Fantiagos.

Maybe it was nostalgia or maybe just pure stupidity, but I decided to go to a movie like I would have done back home. I pulled off alongside the road, put on a hoodie from my backseat, a baseball cap, and sunglasses, then drove the rest of the way to the movie theatre.

It was later in the evening now, so the dark sky and movie theatre should be good enough to shield me from being noticed. I knew I looked ridiculous, and the glances I got from the ticket register workers only confirmed that fact.

Still, I got inside, sat in the back of the theater and watched my movie in peace. It was strangely liberating just to be a normal guy for a while... That was, until I walked out of the movie theatre to flashing cameras.

SIX

DES

THIS MIGHT HAVE BEEN the biggest barbecue my parents had thrown yet. All of our family who lived locally and almost all our friends were on our private stretch of beach, singing, dancing, talking, and eating the best barbacoa Dad had ever made.

News had spread quickly about my impending tour with Jude, and everyone wanted to celebrate. Which my family did well.

Dad kept telling anyone who would listen that I was going to be bigger than Selena. (As if.) Mom and all her friends talked about how happy they were to see a curvy Latina getting time in the spotlight. And of course all my cousins wanted me to remember them when I made it big.

After dancing with one of my uncles, I sat in a

chair around the fire with Cori, Adriel, Nadira, and Tatiana. I wished Faith could have been here too, but she was already in DC living her happily ever after with a real life prince charming.

Adriel handed me a can of soda. "I didn't know you could dance like that!"

I snapped my fingers. "I've been training my whole life. And our school doesn't exactly have a lot of Latin dancers."

Nadira, one of the few other people of color at Emerson Academy, smirked. "Or much of anyone who's not white."

I hoped that would change with time. "What am I going to do without you girls for the next three months?" I didn't even want to think about what would happen when I returned from the tour. The way it was scheduled, they'd all be ready to leave for college when I got back.

Cori gave me a look. "What are you going to do? Fall in love with Jude and become the next major pop duo, that's what!"

Tatiana nodded. "I could *totally* see you two making headlines."

I raised my eyebrows. "I just broke up with Devon like two weeks ago. No one said anything about falling in love."

"Except for me," she teased.

Adriel raised her hand. "And me."

Nadira grinned. "Me too."

"Not you!" I said to Nadira. "You're supposed to be the cynic!"

She shrugged, sucking her teeth. "Guess I'm a changed woman now, thanks to the soldier."

I couldn't help but smile as I shook my head. "Well, here's to hoping Jude makes me a changed woman. Wink, wink."

Adriel snorted, nearly spilling her soda, and I laughed out loud.

Cori patted Adriel's shoulder. "You'll get used to the innuendos... eventually."

Nadira shook her head. "I'm still not used to it."

Cori had been my friend for as long as I could remember, and Nadira had been my friend since she moved to Emerson in middle school. Adriel and I had gotten closer this year, but it still felt like forever. "It's going to be so weird being around guys all the time."

"Who's riding with you on the bus?" Adriel asked.

I ticked off my fingers. "Jude's dad, who's also his manager, Jude, of course, his bodyguard, the driver, then Diego and me. And they have an assistant who will be at the shows and be my 'mentor', but I don't even know if that will be a girl or not. I like guys but... I need my girl time."

Cori waved her hand. "You'll have them eating out of the palm of your hand in no time."

"Exactly," Adriel said. "And if you need some girl talk, we're just a phone call away."

Just then, my phone began ringing, and the girls around me laughed, their eyes dancing with humor and the light of the fire. I pulled out my cell and saw a video call from Faith. I swiped it open, saying, "Hey, girl, hey!"

"Des! Have you seen the news?"

"No, why? Is everything okay?" Last time she'd called like this, I was finding out my video had gone viral.

"Go to the TellAll app. They're interviewing Jude."

"Okay, talk to you soon." I hung up and tapped through to the news app that reported on younger celebrities. At the very top was a live video of Jude Santiago. He was dressed in a hoodie and a ball cap, and I felt for him because he clearly hadn't wanted to be seen.

"Jude," one woman said, jabbing a microphone

in his face. "Is it true you're bringing your girlfriend on tour?"

"Jude," a man called, "is this all a publicity stunt to save face?"

Yet another reporter yelled, "Jude! Are you using her to promote your next album?"

Jude held up his hands, silencing the crowd. It was amazing, the way he drew command just with a wave of his fingers. I had so much to learn from him.

With a winning smile, he said, "Desirae has a stunning voice and a smile that's just as beautiful. I'm honored she accepted my offer to come on tour with me. We're going to have a great three months."

Just then, mall security surrounded Jude and helped him make his exit. The screen cut to a reporter commenting on the story while my friends were doing the same.

Tatiana hit my shoulder. "Did you hear him say your smile is stunning?"

I rolled my eyes. "He has to say that. It's obviously a PR move. I wouldn't be surprised if Song-bird told him to be complimentary. Either way, I'm not about to look a gift horse in the mouth."

"What does that even mean?" Nadira asked.

"Heck if I know," I said.

"Actually," Cori replied, "it's a way to tell how old and healthy a horse is. If they're missing teeth, they're not likely to live as long." When we looked at her in shock, she said, "What? My sister's boyfriend is a cowboy! We talk sometimes."

"Either way," I said, "I'm going to prove *la bruja* wrong." I grinned. "And when I'm rich and famous, I'm flying you all right back here to Waldo's Diner, so we can celebrate."

SEVEN

DES

THE NEXT DAY, I had an appointment with Jude's publicist and costume designer to select a wardrobe for the upcoming shows. On the ninety-day tour, we were to perform eighty times, which seemed insane but also exciting.

That meant eighty towns, eighty stadiums full of fans, and eighty outfits good enough to be on Jude Santiago's stage. I couldn't wait.

My mom dropped the younger kids off with a cousin because there was no way she'd let me walk into a business meeting alone. Not after what happened with Natalie. No matter how many times I told her I'd be fine.

And this time, she put on her power outfit—a black tailored dress with black spiky heels, a bright red lip, and hair perfectly curled in loose waves. That look turned her from my sweet, *tres-leche*-making mama to a baddie in two seconds flat. When she walked up to our school in that outfit, Headmaster Bradford shook in his italian leather shoes.

I put in the address Jude's publicist sent me, and we drove the hour to LA from our home. Eventually, I found myself in a set of corporate offices. It was a tall building, not too different from the one Songbird Agency was in, with massive reflective windows stretching all the way to the sky. When we walked inside, there were security guards in front of the elevators.

I cleared my throat, pretending I was confident even though this was totally new territory. "Desirae De Leon. We're here to meet with Samantha Stone PR."

"Of course," the guard said, waving us past. "Floor twenty-four."

We got on the elevator with several other people and pushed the button. I could see some of the guys in suits checking out my mom, and I wanted to punch them all. She was my mom, not to mention married!

Mom nudged my arm. "No thirteenth floor.

That's a good sign."

I smiled, laughing quietly. "You're so superstitious."

On my right, the same middle-aged guy who'd been ogling my mom said, "Most buildings leave it off so people feel safer."

The elevator pinged the twenty-fourth floor, and the doors opened to a posh reception area. I took it in with stars in my eyes. Everything was sleek and shiny and glamorous. It felt right—like I was exactly where I belonged. And this time, I knew Natalie wouldn't take it all away.

The receptionist held up a finger, talking into her earpiece. When she said goodbye, she gave my mom and me an apologetic smile. "Some people won't stop talking. Let me give Samantha a call. She's excited to meet you."

I smiled and waited while she pressed a button and said, "Desirae and her mother are here to see you." She clicked the button again and said, "She'll be here shortly."

The receptionist, Penny, according to her name plate, answered another call, and I walked to the floor-to-ceiling windows, taking in the view of LA. It was amazing, being all the way up here. Everyone below looked so small.

How had I been down there only moments ago?

"Desirae?" someone said from behind me.

I turned to see a woman dressed sharply in a charcoal-gray pant suit and a baby-blue silk top. But instead of being severe like *la bruja*, she was my height and had plenty of curves too. Her blue eyes gave away her wit, but her smile gave away her heart.

"That's me," I said. "And this is my mom, Delfina."

"Nice to meet you," she said. "I'm Samantha Stone, Jude's publicist, and yours too for this tour. Come on back."

I grinned. "This office is incredible."

"We think so too." She gestured at the office spaces we walked by with dozens of people working in half-height cubicles.

It struck me that Samantha must have built this business, brought all these people together, and created a service that people like Jude Santiago felt was valuable. I wanted to learn as much from her as possible.

As we walked across the office space, she said, "Alma has set out several looks for Desirae, and we'll have you try them on, take some test photos, and be sure your look is ready for the tour. I also want to get some quick clips of you for our PR campaign and for new posters, since we had to nix Meteor from the design." She rolled her eyes, obviously annoyed by them flaking out.

I was just trying to keep up with her quick steps over the tile and all the news she was throwing at me. Luckily, I had enough practice in front of the camera for my YouTube videos that making a few quick statements wouldn't be hard.

Samantha opened the door into a spacious room filled with racks of clothes and... the woman I couldn't stand.

Natalie flipped through one of the racks, looking just as severe and heartless as I remembered her. Another woman with spiky hair, wearing an outfit with thigh-high leather boots, flipped through a rack farther down.

Mom and I froze in the doorway, taking in Natalie. No one had told us she would be here.

"Hello," Samantha said, oblivious to our discomfort. "Our star has arrived."

I saw Natalie cringe. That just made me smile. Revenge was going to be so much fun.

Mom said, "We remember *la br*—Natalie. And who is this?" She walked past Natalie, completely ignoring her. "You are so beautiful. And these clothes?" She looked to the racks beside her. "Amazing."

The woman with pink hair said, "I'm Alma. It's so nice to meet you, Mrs. De Leon."

"Nonsense," Mom said. "Friends call me Delphina. Let's see what you're working on?"

I smiled between my mom and Natalie, who was clearly offended at the snub. Good. Mom hadn't gotten in much of a word in the meeting, but she was being heard loud and clear here. She would not tolerate Natalie messing with her daughter, and neither would I.

Alma held up a red sundress and said, "This is going to look so good next to Jude's outfit."

"Onstage?" I asked. "I thought I was only going on before him."

Samantha explained, "For the shoot today. He's coming in to take some photos and film with you."

My lips parted. Jude Santiago was coming here?

Mom grinned. "I can't wait to meet him."

Maybe that's what the knots in my stomach were. Excitement. Definitely not nerves. No. Not one bit nervous.

I was meeting Jude Santiago. Today.

EIGHT

JUDE

DAD PARKED in the closest spot to the entrance of Samantha's building. She and Batty Natty had requested our presence today. I was to do a costume run and take a few photos with Desirae for tour promotion.

It was all completely normal...

So why did I feel so nervous?

The sound of Dad's door opening echoed in the garage, drawing me back to the present. I got out of the car and straightened my jacket. We walked in silence to the elevator, and Dad used a swipe card to the private elevator that would take us up to the proper floor.

I remembered my first time here two years ago,

walking through the front doors and facing security guards. They'd seemed so big back then. We'd gone up the elevator, looked out the tall windows at a city that had only existed on TV to me back then. And then Samantha sat across from me in her office, silhouetted by this incredible view, and told me she'd make me a star.

She'd followed through on her promise, but I was still far more nervous today than I had been then.

At the twenty-fourth floor, the elevator pinged open, and Penny grinned at us, silently waving us back while she continued her phone conversation.

She always seemed to be on the phone when I saw her. I wondered what it was like to have someone talking into your ear all day long. Hearing directions in my earpiece at concerts got over-whelming, and that was just a couple of hours at a time.

Dad and I continued back into the room where Samantha always put us to arrange costumes before a tour. Natalie said most publicists weren't so hands on, but Samantha was the best in the business for a reason.

Dad opened the door to the room, and I barely kept my legs moving.

Des stood in a sparkling red dress that perfectly hugged her curves. A slit in the dress rose up her shapely leg, and I found my eyes fixated on her bronze skin, the curve of her calf. When I looked back up, I found her eyes on mine.

Busted.

Samantha put her arm around me and said, "What do you think? This will be great for the last leg of the tour in LA. Totally red carpet ready."

"Definitely," I agreed.

Des didn't blush. She smiled at me like she already knew how beautiful she was, and that made her even sexier in my eyes.

She extended her hand and said, "It's nice to meet you, Jude."

The way she said my name. I wanted to hear it again. "It's nice to meet you too."

She gestured at the woman beside her, an older version of herself. "This is my mom, Delfina."

Delfina extended her hand. "All the kids' friends call me Mamá De."

I shook her hand. "Am I a friend?"

She gave me the kind of smile that told me she could either be the best woman I ever met or the worst, all depending on how I treated her daughter. "Time will tell."

I laughed along with everyone else, although I wished I could tell her she had nothing to worry about. Des was getting taken care of on my tour. I'd make sure of it.

Dad stepped forward, introducing himself, and then stepped aside, talking with Natalie about tour logistics that had already been hashed and rehashed a million times over.

Samantha turned back to Des. "Now that everyone's introduced, let's put on that red eyelet dress and get you both through makeup." She shuffled me to a makeup chair in the corner of the room while Des went to the dressing area. She had this place set up for last-minute press conferences, quick clips for promo, and of course the odd bits of bad press. Not that I'd ever had any before Natalie was so mean to Des.

The closest I'd ever come to a media nightmare was the time a Fantiago snuck into my studio and undressed. Luckily, a crew member had gone in before I did, and security was able to get her dressed and gone before I went back into my room.

Samantha stood behind me as the makeup artist worked on my complexion. "I have a good feeling about this, don't you?"

"I do," I said, trying not to move my lips too much. "I think the fans are going to love her."

"Even the ones who are jealous," Samantha agreed. "Ah, here's our girl."

Des slid into the chair next to mine. And even though I was situated a few feet away from her, I felt her presence like we were only inches apart. I shoved down my nerves and said, "How's the first day going?"

When the other makeup artist finished powdering around her mouth, Des muttered, "Fabulous. Would be even better if Natalie wasn't here."

I laughed out loud, earning a look from my own makeup artist. I stilled and said, "Can't say I disagree."

Des gave me a sideways look, which I returned with a grin.

"Any tips for filming the content?" she asked.

Performing in front of the camera came so naturally now, I had to think about what advice I would give. Especially to Desirae. "Just be yourself," I said. "They're going to think you're made of gold either way."

She looked down, then back at me through the mirror with a smirk. "I guess being myself is what got me here in the first place."

That temper, I thought with a chuckle to myself, mixed with her confidence and good looks? They would definitely take her places.

She had to quiet while they finished her lips. Her makeup took far longer than mine. While we waited for her, Samantha and Natalie whisked me away to do a few clips in front of the camera.

"Great," Sam said, then glanced over her shoulder. "Ah, looks like Des is ready!"

I followed her gaze, and I quickly clamped my jaw together. If she'd captivated me before in that red dress, she completely took me under her spell now. Instead of a sexy red gown, this cherry sundress showed off her legs and bared her shoulders with thin straps. Her lips were full and pouty, and all I wanted to do was see how long it would take to kiss it all off.

Instead of giving myself away, I sent her a practiced smile and said, "Ready?"

She nodded, full of an intoxicating confidence.

Behind the camera, the director said, "Introduce yourselves."

I lifted my chin and said, "I'm Jude Santiago." I put my arm around Des's shoulders, feeling the softness and warmth of her skin. "And this is my new opening act, the amazingly talented—"

"Desirae De Leon," she finished, making sure her voice was heard. "I can't wait to meet you and sing for you on Summer of Santiago tour!"

Samantha clapped her hands together, laughing. "I love it!"

Mamá De gave us a thumbs up and a smile.

"Right," Natalie said wryly. Giving me a pointed look, she said, "A little less familiar this time, Jude."

Samantha shook her head. "Absolutely not. This is going to be great. Imagine all the speculation around the two of them."

Natalie seemed to tense. "Hinting he's off the market could slash our market share, not to mention the chaos the Fantiagos will cause."

Des spoke up. "Don't you think a little competition will make him that much more desirable?"

I raised my eyebrows, amazed by her willingness to stand her ground amidst a room of powerful people.

Samantha tapped her nose. "I like the way you think, Des."

Narrowing her gaze, Natalie said, "You're forgetting the gay population."

Des smirked. "Who said Jude isn't bi?" She looked at me. "That's possible, right?"

Standing next to her in that sundress, I thought there was no way in the world I could even consider a man—or any other girl for that matter. But out loud, I said, "Natalie, I think you've been outnumbered."

And let me tell you, I watched her *implode*. It was glorious.

"That settles it," Samantha said with a grin. "Let's try another couple takes where Des cuddles into your shoulder, and then we'll try one with you giving her a kiss on the cheek."

My stomach dropped. "Are you sure?" This was not the way I imagined kissing Des for the first time. Not in front of a bunch of people, and certainly not on the cheek.

"Of course," Samantha said.

Something evil sparked in Natalie's eyes. "Unless you don't want to kiss her. We'd understand, of course."

Mamá De narrowed her eyes at me.

"That's not it," I said quickly. My wandering thoughts could confirm that.

Des gave me an easy smile, drawing my attention back to her. "I won't bite."

"What if I want you to?" I teased.

She laughed out loud. "I'll have my people call your people."

I couldn't help but laugh with her.

Seeming delighted, Samantha clapped her hands together and said, "Let's get this rolling!"

I nodded and centered myself again in front of the camera. Des walked in her heels to stand beside me. As she flipped her hair over her shoulder, a hint of her perfume filled my senses. It was incredible—a blend of cinnamon and something sweeter I couldn't quite place.

"Ready?" Samantha said.

I nodded.

I lied. There was no way I could be ready to kiss Desirae De Leon.

"Hi," I began. "I'm Jude Santiago."

"And I'm Desirae De Leon," she said in her clear and throaty voice.

Maybe it was the movement of her lips, the subtle shift of her throat as she spoke, but I couldn't help myself. I leaned closer until my lips brushed along the space between the arch of her cheekbone and the soft edge of her jaw.

The feel of her skin against my lips sent my pulse racing.

But the camera was running too.

"I'm thrilled to have her joining me on tour," I said and ended with a smile that didn't have to be forced at all.

NINE

DES

FOR MY LAST night in Emerson, I sat on my bed with Cori, Nadira, Adriel, and Tatiana. Faith was on a tablet propped on a pillow. Even though she was in DC, I still wanted her to be a part of it all.

Since the tour bus was set to leave in the morning, my friends and I were supposed to be having a packing party. Instead, we had ended up on my bed, eating my mom's amazing *churros* and talking about the kiss.

I still couldn't get the way Jude's lips had felt against my skin out of my mind. "It was just a kiss on the cheek *for an advertisement*," I reminded both my friends and myself. "It wasn't even real."

Adriel narrowed her eyes at me. "Can't you let a girl dream?"

Cori added, "Don't you mean it's not real *yet*?"

I smirked. "It doesn't have to be real to be fun."

Nadira hit me with a pillow, laughing. "Leave it to you to plan a fling with a rock star."

Tatiana laughed. "Someone should have fun with him!"

I shrugged with a smile. "I wouldn't mind one bit." Besides, I didn't do relationships. Not long-term at least. Guys were fun, but you could hardly count on them to be there when you needed them to be—especially guys my age. "Devon didn't take the breakup that well. I'd rather not have another guy screaming at me any time soon."

Cori raised her eyebrows. "You never told me he yelled at you."

Adriel said, "Why would he yell? You never even put labels on it."

"He said he felt used," I answered. "Not that it gives him an excuse to act like a toddler throwing a tantrum. I'm free to end a relationship any time I choose."

"Preach," Nadira said.

I nodded. "He said he wanted to be more serious, but why would I want to tie myself down when I was busy reaching for the stars?"

Faith said, "With the right person, it won't feel

like tying yourself down. It'll feel like you're both working toward something incredible."

"Well, I definitely haven't felt that yet," I said. I doubted I would for a really long time, if ever. "We don't need to talk about Devon anyway. I dated him for like a minute, and I'd like to leave him in the past where he belongs."

"Agreed," Tatiana said. "What about the tour? Are you nervous?"

I shrugged. "I think I'm more afraid of being disappointed than anything. What if I get out there and nothing happens? What if this isn't the big break I think it will be?"

Nadira frowned. "Do you hear yourself? Where's my confident friend?"

"Exactly," Adriel said. "You believed that Carter and I could win a *national dance competition* even though he'd never danced competitively a day in his life and my own coach said I wasn't fit for the sport."

Cori nodded, reaching across our small circle to put her hand on my knee. "You've reminded us, and now it's our turn to remind you. You're too incredible to miss, babe."

I smiled down at my lap. They were right. I knew my voice was good. I knew I could engage a crowd. All I had to do was wait for the right eyes to see me. It wasn't a matter of if, but when.

"Thank you," I said. "For reminding me. Now help me find the right outfit for the trip tomorrow. Apparently, the stylist only does my outfits for public appearances." I dusted the cinnamon sugar from the *churros* off my fingers and got off the bed. "I want to be sexy but not look like I'm trying so hard and also be comfortable on the bus."

As I flipped through my closet, sorting through options to have the girls choose from, Cori told us about the training program Brentwood U's basketball coach had given her to work on during the summer. "I feel like my arms are about to fall off."

Nadira shook her head. "At least breaking a mental sweat doesn't incur physical injury."

Cori laughed. "They're paying for my college, so it's a little late now."

"True," Nadira said. "What about you, Faith? How's lover boy?"

Her smile was clear on the tablet, even from more than a thousand miles away. "Feels like happily ever after."

I held a blouse to my chest. "I love that for you." I was so happy for Faith that she'd found

Prince Charming. That he'd seen her worth and she had too.

"What about you, Des?" Tatiana asked. "How many broken hearts are you leaving in Emerson?"

I laughed. "Not a one." I hadn't really gone out since breaking things off with Devon a few weeks ago. "You know, except for you girls," I said, only half-teasing. "I feel like you're the loves of my life and I'm just having fun with everyone else."

Adriel blew a kiss at me. "We love you too."

Cori leaned forward. "Let's make a promise."

"What?" I asked, walking back toward my bed.

She sat up. "No matter what, no matter how far we go, we'll always be best friends. The Curvy Girl Club 2.0, forever."

I grinned. "Promise."

The sentiment echoed throughout the room.

No matter what happened in my relationships, I knew, these girls were my forever.

My phone rang, and I glanced at the screen. It was a number I didn't recognize. "Probably a scam."

Tatiana said, "What if it's Jude?"

I looked between her and the ringing device. I'd risk a thousand calls about my car's extended warranty before missing a call from Jude Santiago.

I quickly swiped to answer and said a tentative, "Hello?"

"Hey, Des, it's Jude." He must have mistaken my shocked pause for not knowing who he was because he added, "Jude Santiago."

"Right, of course," I said, switching my phone to speaker and putting a finger to my lips to keep my friends from squealing. "What's up?"

"Well, I, um… I gave them my list of snacks for the bus, and I realized I never asked you or your brother if there was anything you wanted."

Cori covered her heart, mouthing, *That's* so *sweet.*

It was pretty thoughtful; I had to give her that. "My mom is definitely going to send snacks with us. But if you want to earn your way to my brother's heart, pizza rolls will do the trick."

Jude laughed, and the sound was just as musical as his voice. "Pizza rolls are my favorite. The freezer's going to be full of them."

I smiled. "Awesome."

"And nothing for you?"

I remembered my mom's rule about never turning down an offer for food. "I'm a huge fan of Twizzlers. If you want to bring some for me."

"Absolutely. If you think of anything else, you have my number."

"Thanks, Jude."

There was a smile in his voice as he said, "Absolutely. I'll see you first thing in the morning."

The call ended and my friends stared at me, open-mouthed.

"What?" I asked.

Adriel was grinning ear-to-ear as she said, "Jude Santiago has a crush on you!"

I rolled my eyes. "Girl, please. He's a rock star. His personality is automatically tuned to *flirt*."

"Nuh uh," Cori said, shaking her head. "That was so adorable. Is it just me or did he sound nervous?"

Nadira nodded. "And he was thinking of you."

My cheeks warmed a little bit at the fact that for however long, I'd been on Jude Santiago's mind, just like he was on mine.

TEN

DES

MY ALARM WENT off at an ungodly hour. Four times.

Because you know I couldn't wake up on the first alarm. Or the second or third.

When I finally got the willpower to stumble out of bed, I went to the bathroom and washed my face, then stepped into the shower. This was my first day on tour. Somewhere between minute five and ten, it started to sink in.

I was going on tour with Jude Santiago.

I didn't care how or why it was happening, only that it really was happening.

I finished my shower and got ready for the day, for the trip, for the moment that would change my life forever.

My hair was perfectly blow-dried and straightened, my makeup was on point, and I had on the outfit that signaled just the right mix of nonchalance and celebrity.

The only hitch, really, was my brother's attendance, and I couldn't even complain about that. We got along well, and if him coming along led my parents to agree, I'd take it.

A knock sounded on my bedroom door. Probably Mom making sure I was awake.

"Coming," I called.

Then I realized I'd miss that while I was gone. She'd been here every day of my life, making sure I was fed, clothed, taken to voice lessons, and above all, loved. I opened my door to see her holding a plate of burritos wrapped in plastic.

"Thought I could make extra in case anyone else wanted some too."

I took the plate and set it on a table along the wall, then I hugged her tight. "Thank you, *ama*."

She held me back tightly. "I love you, *mija*."

"I love you too." I stepped back. "Thank you for this."

She nodded, straightening her blouse and then picking up the plate. "The bus is outside."

My eyes widened. "He's here already? Why didn't you say something?"

She shrugged, mumbling something about him being early. I couldn't make it out clearly because I was too busy rushing the front door and looking out the window to see that Jude Santiago's bus was, in fact, parked in front of our house.

The sliding door up front accordioned open, and Jude Santiago himself stepped out. But instead of a pair of painted-on jeans and a black T-shirt that hugged toned biceps, he wore a pair of joggers and a sweater.

I'd dressed exactly right, in leggings that showed off my curves and a cropped hoodie, giving just a hint at my midriff.

His grin was so disarming, I almost missed the man walking behind him. I recognized him from the shoot as Anthony Santiago, Jude's dad. And then, I noticed the sleek BMW behind the bus and heartless Natalie stepping out.

Next to me, Mom muttered in Spanish, "What is *la bruja* doing here?"

I shook my head, not really wanting to know. If I never saw Natalie again, it would be too soon.

Jude said, "Having an early going-away party?"

I glanced behind me, realizing all of my siblings

and my dad had come outside as well to see the spectacle. "No, this is just my family." A lot of people in Emerson had small families, two or three kids, but I loved having so many siblings around. Our home was never quiet or boring.

I went down the line, introducing Jude to each of my siblings and my parents. Adelita had the biggest grin on her face, but Marisol was paler than the white guy my auntie married a few years ago. Her eyes were wide brown saucers, taking him in. They were ten and completely starstruck.

And if I was being honest? Girl, same.

Dad stepped forward, his arms folded across his chest and his eyes intense. "I want to have a word with you two." He was clearly talking to Jude and his father.

My stomach dropped. Dad reserved that expression for when someone crossed a line, and I'd only gotten that look twice in my life. Once, when I'd stolen money from Mom's purse, and another when I'd stayed out all night without letting anyone know where I was or who I was with.

But Anthony stayed cool and nodded. "Of course."

Dad spoke in a regular tone, but the strength behind his words couldn't be missed. "*Mis hijos* are everything to me." He nodded toward Diego and me. "I expect you to watch over them just as you would your own."

Anthony extended his hand, as if he'd ever had any choice but to listen to my dad. Dad examined Anthony for a moment before shaking on it. The exchange felt binding... sacred.

Then Dad turned his gaze on Jude. "My daughter *es una reina*. A queen. And I expect her to be treated as such."

Jude nodded. "Absolutely, Mr. De Leon."

Dad seemed to appreciate it and shook hands with Jude just like he had with Anthony.

Completely oblivious—or irreverent—Natalie said, "Desirae, a word?"

Mom started to protest, but I said, "It's okay. I can handle this."

Natalie sent my mom what I could only assume was supposed to be a reassuring smile. It looked more like a snake baring its fangs.

Mom nodded at me, not at Natalie. I stepped onto the front lawn, away from my family, where they were now quizzing Jude about his next song coming out and what it was like to be famous. I wanted to hear his answers, but Natalie was already speaking.

"Des, I wanted to lay down a few ground rules for this tour, and it's imperative that you follow them. If you don't, you'll be off the tour bus faster than you can blink."

I tensed, getting ready for a fight. Was she seriously threatening me already? We hadn't even left Emerson yet!

"First, this tour is called the Summer of Santiago, not the Desirae Show. Your time onstage should get fans ready for his performance, not promote your own agenda."

"Obviously." I shrugged. "What else?"

She seemed annoyed, and I realized she didn't like me keeping my cool. She wanted to make me mad. Well, I wouldn't give her the satisfaction.

"You signed the NDA," she continued, "but I wanted to make sure you remembered the highlights. You will not post negatively about Jude, Songbird Creative, or anyone affiliated with this tour."

"Anything else?" I asked, keeping my voice chipper.

A dark light shined in her eyes now, and she nodded. "Under no circumstance are you to have a romantic relationship with Jude Santiago. A little flirtation on screen is one thing—a relationship disappointing all his fans is another entirely. This is non-negotiable."

The instant she made the rule, I wanted to break it. Who was this woman to think she had any amount of control over who I liked or loved? "And what if I date Jude? What are you going to do about it?"

"I'll take away his record deal and reach out to all my contacts in the industry to tell them not to sign him." She said it easily, like reading the lunch special off a menu. Not like she was threatening to destroy someone's entire life and livelihood.

"Why would you do that?" I asked, not even able to hide the horror on my face. "He's your client."

She narrowed her eyes. "I don't like being made a fool by hot-headed little girls and hormone-ridden boys."

I glanced across the lawn where Jude was chatting easily with my family. I wanted to tell him what Natalie was threatening, but the terms of the NDA had been clear. No talking about my dealings with Songbird with anyone outside of my immediate family. Even my parents had to sign NDAs for themselves and Diego.

"Don't think I won't do it," she said.

It wasn't her vindictiveness I doubted. Natalie had already proven herself merciless. And even though I was sure she didn't want to lose the money Jude made her... I didn't want to risk it.

Jude was nice and attractive and living the kind of life I aspired to, but I hadn't agreed to this tour to for a shot at love with a rock star. Boys were fun, but fame, a career, friendship, that was the stuff that lasted forever.

"Fine," I said easily.

"In showbiz, it's not official until you shake on it," Natalie said, extending her hand.

Feeling like I was making a deal with the devil, I shook it.

ELEVEN

DES

AS I WALKED BACK to my family, I heard Jude's dad say, "The bus needs to leave in five minutes! We've got a long drive ahead."

We did have a long drive across the country. This was the last time I'd be in Emerson for three months. The last time I'd eat my mom's breakfast burritos or hear Adelita and Marisol argue in the morning or watch Marco and Mateo race for the first spot in Mario Kart.

At least I was bringing a piece of home with me —although I'd never tell Diego how happy I was to have him. (It would make his head bigger than it already was.)

I gave my siblings one last hug, and then Mom and Dad faced Diego and me. Mom put her hand on Diego's cheek, looking between him and me. "Take care of each other."

"We will," Diego and I said at the same time.

Dad patted my shoulder, then pulled me into a hug. "*Cuando la voluntad está lista, los pies son livianos.*"

I smiled at the familiar phrase. "Only because you showed me how to chase my dreams."

He kissed the top of my head, then gave Diego a hug.

Soon there were no more excuses to stay. No more goodbyes to deny what was coming. My family was staying here in Emerson, and Diego and I... we were going on an adventure.

Our bigger bags were loaded into the storage hold underneath the bus, and we walked up the steps into... luxury.

The inside was so much bigger than I could have imagined. There was a living area with a couch, a dining table, a full-sized kitchen, and a big-screen TV. My eyes landed on a gaming console, and I immediately felt more at home. Maybe he even had Mario Kart.

Stepping onto the bus behind us, Jude said, "This is it. Our home on wheels."

I glanced over my shoulder at him. "It's incredible. Is it okay if I video some for my YouTube?"

"Of course," he said.

I got out my phone and recorded as he walked us through the bus, showing bunks on either side that had TVs over each bed. In the back, there was another room with two beds where he and his Dad slept. There were even two bathrooms on the bus, one for "guests" like us, and one for Jude and his dad.

When I finished recording, Jude rubbed his hands together and said, "Good enough to call home for a few months?"

"Definitely," Diego said.

I nudged my brother. "Diego would be happy sleeping on the beach all summer, but it is incredible."

Jude smiled. "Being on the road gets tiring after a while, but it's nice to have a place that's all your own."

I wondered if it would ever get old for me, performing onstage, traveling for the sole purpose of singing in front of more and more and more people. I could see it wearing on Diego though; he practically lived outside in the summertime.

The bus door shut, and the engine fired to life, and I looked around. It was all becoming so real. As the wheels slowly pulled us farther from the only life I knew, I walked to the window and waved.

This was goodbye, sure.

But it was also hello, to everything I'd ever imagined.

TWELVE

JUDE

DIEGO SET his backpack in one of the upper bunks and said, "What happens now?"

Honestly? I wanted time to ask Des what Natalie had wanted. It couldn't have been anything good or pleasant, but I didn't want to make things weird by pulling her aside. So I gestured to the couch and said, "Usually I watch a movie or play video games for a while. Sometimes I go back to the room and work on lyrics if I'm feeling inspired. Sleeping on the bus is actually pretty nice—it's like being rocked to sleep."

Des said, "I think I'm going to try that out. It's way too early to be awake."

"Fair," I said. "Help yourself to one of the

bunks. The remote should be attached to the shelf at the head of the bed."

She nodded, walking back toward the bunks. I enjoyed watching her go far too much to be standing in front of her brother.

I focused my attention on Diego and said, "Want something to eat?"

"Sure," he replied.

As I walked to the freezer, I could hear my dad up front, talking with our driver, Francie. He was telling her how much he wanted to show her the ice cream shop in Winslow.

Just the thought of visiting my hometown brought up uncomfortable feelings that I quickly shoved down. I pulled a bag of pizza rolls from the freezer. "Sound good?" I asked, holding the bag up so Diego could see it.

"Yeah." He feigned confusion. "But what are you going to eat?"

I laughed. "The freezer's stocked. I think we're good to go." I spread the frozen food on a plate and popped it in the microwave before walking back to the couch. I handed the remote to Diego and said, "You pick the show."

While he flipped through channels, I tried not to

focus on Des's presence. I thought I could hear her voice, maybe talking on the phone, but I wasn't creepy enough to go back and check. Still, I wondered who she was talking to this early in the morning. What she might say to them about the bus. About me.

The microwave went off, and I pulled the plate out, splitting the rolls on two separate dishes. As I handed one to Diego, I sat down next to him and looked at the screen. The characters were all speaking Spanish, and there weren't any English subtitles.

He glanced at me, three rolls already in his mouth. "This okay?"

"I don't speak Spanish," I admitted.

He lifted his eyebrows, swallowing hard. "Sorry, bro, I just assumed."

"No worries," I laughed. "I got made fun of in school for being a brown boy who couldn't speak Spanish. I forgot everything I learned my freshman year."

"My parents only speak Spanish at home. The second we leave the house? English. That way us kids learned both." Diego changed the channel to something I could actually understand, and we sat quietly for a while. That was until crazy loud snores came from the bunks.

Diego and I exchanged a look. "Is that..." I asked.

He grinned, grabbing his phone. "Let's prank her."

"She won't be mad?"

His grin turned that much more evil. "That's kind of the point. Come on."

He flicked to his camera, and when we reached her bunk, he gently pulled back on the curtain, making the snoring even more audible.

Des looked adorable with her mouth wide open, like a chipmunk yawning. Although, I'd never say that out loud. I may not have had a mom or sisters, but my grandma taught me enough about girls to know they didn't like being compared to woodland animals.

Diego whispered, "I'm going to start filming. You cover your ears like you can't take the noise."

I stifled my laughter as he began filming and I pretended to be protecting my eardrums from her snoring.

Diego's phone dinged with the end of the recording, and we hurried back to the front of the bus, snickering like little boys on the playground.

"She's gonna kill me," Diego said gleefully.

That made me laugh even harder.

"And..." He tapped his fingers over the screen. "Sent."

"Who'd you send it to?" I asked, worried.

"Des." He shoved his phone back in the pocket of his shorts. "I'd never send that kind of thing to the press."

I immediately liked Diego more for his loyalty. And for his humor. Was this what it was like to have siblings? Someone to laugh with and lean on?

Someone to prank?

"What happens when she wakes up?" I asked.

"You'll see," Diego said with a lopsided grin.

Just then, a scream broke out in the bus.

From the driver's seat, Francie yelled, "Everyone okay?"

"Fine," I called back. Although we might not be soon, judging by the way Des rolled out of the bunk and was currently storming toward Diego and me.

"You." She pointed at Diego. She had her phone clenched so tightly in her other hand that her knuckles were white.

In the most inflammatory response ever, Diego laid his head back, opened his mouth wide, and made a big snoring sound.

Des pounced.

She jumped onto his lap, wrapping one arm

around his head and rubbing her knuckles over his curly hair. He tried shoving her off, but her grip on him was bulletproof.

So instead, he stood, bringing her with him, and flopped on the ground, getting on top of her and tickling her sides.

She let out an angry cry and freed him. They both stepped away from each other, their chests heaving, bloodlust in their eyes.

I worried what would happen next... until they started laughing.

Des hit Diego with her phone. "I hate you."

"You love me," he retorted.

She pointed her finger at me. "And you. I thought you were better than that."

I suppressed a laugh, shrugging instead. "Guess I can still surprise my fans from time to time."

She rolled her eyes. "Are you sure I'm a fan?"

"If you're not now, you will be soon."

With a sly smile, she said, "I wouldn't be so sure."

Dad stood in the doorway between the driver's seat and the living room. "Des, if you want revenge, I suggest you get it now. We're almost to Jago's house."

"Jago?" she asked. "That's your bodyguard, right?"

"He prefers security detail," I said with a grin. I couldn't wait to see Jago. It had been a while since I'd had a public appearance, and I missed him. Never mind the fact that I paid him to be with me.

"Where are we?" she asked.

"Palm Springs," Dad answered.

The bus slowed, and we went to the windows, seeing the outside of Jago's nondescript home. He owned the house but had a roommate so the place would be taken care of while he was out of town.

The front door opened, and Jago came out the door, looking just as I remembered him. Way too pale for all this California sunlight and ripped enough to intimidate even the most zealous Fantiagos.

We pulled up, and the bus had barely stopped before Francie opened the door. Jago came on the bus with his duffel bag full of clothes. I used to ask him why he didn't bring more, but he said with a cell phone and laundry service, he had everything he needed.

I admired that.

Dad greeted him first, shaking his hand. "Nice to have you back, Jago."

"Good to be back," Jago replied, only the hint of a German accent in his voice.

He gave me a fist bump, then took in Des and Diego. With half a grin, he said, "Someone introduce me to trouble."

A more accurate description for the duo couldn't be found. "Desirae and her brother, Diego."

Jago said, "Nice to meet you both." Then he grinned at me. "This tour's going to be fun."

I couldn't agree more.

THIRTEEN

DES

WHILE THE BOYS gorged themselves on pizza rolls, Jude's dad, Francie, and I sat at the dining table with chicken salads. Francie had parked in a rest stop, but we couldn't exactly get out or we'd be swarmed by other travelers.

I looked out the crack in the blinds and said, "Anthony, I think that car's following us. The one with the camper."

Anthony tracked my gaze and said, "That's Vanessa Cooper, the head of the Fantiagos. She gets to follow us on tour in exchange for posting on social media and her blog. She usually tags on somewhere around Palm Springs."

I raised my eyebrows. "I didn't know Jude had *groupies*."

From the living area, Jude called back, "She's not a groupie; she's a stalker."

I raised my eyebrows. "What?"

Jago said, "He's just mad she got his name tattooed on her—"

"Don't remind me," Jude said, shuddering. "The day Samantha decides to stop giving her backstage passes will be the best day of my life."

I laughed, looking away from her cute SUV and teardrop trailer and back to my chicken salad.

"What do you think of the tour so far?" Anthony asked, dabbing the corners of his lips with a napkin.

"You mean besides the boys pranking me?"

Anthony laughed. "Besides that."

"It's amazing so far," I said honestly. "I can't imagine what it would be like to have my own tour bus."

Glancing around the bus, he said, "It was just a dream for us a few years ago."

Knowing I was sitting with a family who had gone from mild notoriety on YouTube to living my dream life... it was incredible. I could feel the buzz of possibility in my core. "What advice would you give me?"

He chewed his salad for a moment and swallowed. "Keep your fans happy. Focus on serving them first. After that, do your best not to make any enemies. This is a smaller world than you'd think."

I cringed, knowing I'd already had an arch nemesis in Natalie. But speaking my mind had gotten me on a tour bus with *the* Jude Santiago. It couldn't be that bad of a mistake, right?

From up front, Francie called, "We'll be at Mama Santiago's in ten!"

Anthony clapped his hands together. "I can't wait!"

"Mama Santiago?" I asked. I knew enough about Jude to know Winslow was his hometown, and it was small. Less than ten thousand people lived there. Also, it was mentioned in an Eagles song, which is pretty cool. But I'd never heard about his mom. Why wasn't she on tour with us?

Jude answered, "That's what we call my grandma. You're going to love her. She's the coolest person I know."

Coming from a rock star, that was saying something.

"Agreed," Anthony said. "And we have to stop by the Sipp Shoppe with her. They have great drinks and ice cream. We can grab a picture of you and Diego on the corner to send to your parents while we're there. They have it decorated up like the Eagles song. You've heard it right?"

Diego grinned. "How could I not have heard it? Des only played it five times yesterday."

My cheeks heated. "He's exaggerating."

From up front, Francie said, "This is it!"

Jude was already at the front of the bus, and we followed him out, seeing the quirkiest house I'd ever encountered in my life. It was almost like two houses smashed together. The front was a small white clapboard home that could only have been one or two bedrooms. But the back part? There was a two-story adobe mansion with extensive land-scaping.

Standing beside me, Anthony explained, "Mom refused to move out of her house. So Jude brought the mansion to her."

I didn't have time to think on how much more that made me like Jude because a fabulous little woman walked out of the house. She had short brown hair permed into sweeping curls, bright red lipstick, and a silk floral outfit that must have also been supplied by Jude.

She took Jude into her arms and kissed both of

his cheeks and his forehead. "My sweet boy! I've missed you!"

He had to bend at the waist to hug her, but he didn't seem to mind the awkward position or all the extra makeup he was now wearing. "I missed you too, Mama," he said, hugging her and rocking back and forth.

"What am I?" Anthony asked, stepping forward. "Chopped liver?"

"Oh hush," she said, releasing Jude and giving her son the same treatment. Then she moved on to Jago, kissing both his chiseled cheeks.

She soon turned on us and said, "You must be Desirae!" She kissed my cheeks and then stepped back, examining me. "My, you're a beautiful girl!" She glared at Dad. "I told you I didn't like that Natalie woman. Clearly doesn't have brains or eyes in that plastic head of hers."

Oh man, I *loved* Mama Santiago already.

"And you?" She looked at Diego. "Why, if I weren't eighty and you weren't a boy."

Diego flipped his hair and said, "Back at you."

She giggled, batting her hand at him. "Oh, I like you. Come inside. I have cookies and peanut butter fudge waiting."

I exchanged an open-mouthed smile with Jude,

following them inside. "Peanut butter fudge?" I whispered to him.

He nodded. "It's the best. She made it for all my school bake sales, and it's a favorite at every potluck in Winslow."

We walked through the front door, and I stared around. It looked nothing like it had from the outside. There were marble floors, modern fixtures, and even a glass fountain on the wall.

We walked through the front entrance, and I realized the kitchen must have been where the addition started. It had been expanded to allow for a table that could easily seat at least ten people, if not more. Plus, there were double ovens and a range with what looked like eight burners and a skillet.

"This is an amazing kitchen," I said.

Jude nodded. "Fit for a queen, just like Mama deserves."

I smiled between him and the woman serving Diego and Jago from a platter of way too many sweets. "Did she think you were bringing an army?"

"Oh, no," Jude said, "she'll be sending us with enough to make Dad start a diet again."

I laughed, loving this side of Jude. He seemed so at home here, and it made sense because Mama was already making Diego and me feel welcome, and we were complete strangers. I had a feeling my mom would adore her too.

Mama waved me over and said, "Des, you have to try some."

"You don't have to convince me," I said back with a grin. She handed me a cookie and a slice of caramel-brown fudge, and I tried the fudge first. It melted in my mouth, and I moaned. "Oh my gosh, you have to give me the recipe."

"Absolutely," she said, already going to a tin I recognized as a recipe card holder. She took out a fresh sheet and began writing in sweeping cursive. By the time she had the whole thing written, I'd eaten both of my sweets and was reaching for more.

Diego, who had wandered across the kitchen and was standing by a wall in the dining area, said, "Is this baby Jude?" He pointed at one of the frames.

"It is!" Mama Santiago said happily. "He was three there. I'm pretty sure he ate more dough than we baked."

I peered closer, and my eyes widened. "Oh my gosh!" It showed Jude completely naked in an apron and a chef's hat, covered in flour and grinning at a younger Mama across the counter. There was a bowl with some type of dough between them and so much love in their eyes. "Jude, you should wear that outfit for a concert. Your fans would love it."

Everyone laughed, except Jude, who said, "Har, har, har," with very red cheeks.

Mama smiled and said, "There's more where that came from."

FOURTEEN

JUDE

I THOUGHT I was embarrassment proof.

I'd tripped onstage.

I'd forgotten lines to songs I'd written.

I'd even taken prom pictures with my grandma's lipstick on my forehead.

But this? This was a level new to even me.

Grandma and Dad at the table with Des, Diego, and Jago, flipping through baby photos of yours truly.

"Why was I naked all the time?" I demanded of Dad and Grandma. "Did you forget to put me in clothes?" And more importantly, did they not know a very cute and cool girl would be sitting here someday giggling about the freckle on my butt?

Grandma looked up at me, grinning like a

Cheshire cat. "You would never wear them! From the time you were two to the time you started pre-school, you wouldn't keep a pair of clothes on to save your life. We had the hardest time taking you to restaurants."

Des said, "I like a free spirit."

Okay, now I was even more embarrassed.

"Hey, Diego?" I said.

"Yeah?" he asked, looking up from the photo album.

"When we drop you off, I'm getting payback, yeah?"

He grinned evilly. "You know it."

Des smacked his shoulder and gave him a threatening stare, but I could tell he wouldn't be deterred.

Payback would be mine, eventually.

Dad was strangely quiet, looking at his album for a long time, and when I followed his eyes, my heart stopped. It was a photo of him, my mom, and me.

I'd seen the photo before. She was young with a big smile and perfectly straight hair that dusted her shoulders. I hated that my nose had a bump in the center just like hers. That our teeth were shaped the same.

But most of all, I hated that Dad still looked at that photo of her like he was twenty years old and she was the love of his life.

"Hey, I don't want to run out of time for Des and Diego to see the corner," I said.

Dad closed the book, blinking his misty eyes. "Right, we should head that way. You're coming, right, Mama?"

Mama nodded and said, "Absolutely."

We left the house, the albums, and started walking.

Des asked, "Is it nearby?"

Dad said, "Less than a quarter mile."

I fell into step beside Grandma, putting my arm around her. She was slower than she used to be on our afternoon walks.

She patted my stomach. "It's great to see you, honey."

I smiled down at her. "You too. It's strange to be back here though. It feels like a different town every time I come back."

"It's the same," she said. "You're the one who's different, and that's exactly how it's meant to be."

The others were far enough ahead of us that I whispered, "Dad's going to see her after this."

With sadness in her eyes, Grandma nodded.

"She was his first love. Your mother. That's a love you never get past, no matter how much time has gone by." She reached up and patted my cheek. "You'll understand someday."

Sadness tugged at my heart. "I hope I get a happy ending." It almost felt selfish to say.

"Your father did get a happy ending," she said. "He got you."

WHILE ANTHONY, Francie, and Jago walked ahead of us, Jude had dropped back with his grandma. I glanced over my shoulder, seeing them deep in conversation. He didn't look happy. In fact… he almost looked the opposite. "Do you think he's okay?" I whispered to Diego.

He shook his head slightly. "Did you see him walk out of the house? He seemed tense."

I looked down at my phone, and as we walked, I started searching for reasons why Jude wouldn't want to go back to Winslow. And found... nothing. Not really. It seemed like the town had somehow made a silent agreement not to talk about Jude at all.

How was that possible?

There were stories archived on the local paper's website—photos of Jude in a basketball uniform with a bunch of other guys, announcements of him winning talent shows or performing at a local festival. But nothing personal or revealing.

"You're being a little creepy," Diego said close to my ear.

I nearly jumped out of my skin, then quickly swatted him. "You're the creepy one! Why are you always scaring me?"

He shrugged, obviously pleased with himself. "He'll tell you when he's ready."

"I don't need to know," I replied, tucking my phone in the pocket of my hoodie. Ahead of us, Francie, Jago, and Anthony were already on the famous corner, the Sipp Shoppe visible across the street. "So are you going to get ice cream to go with all the pizza rolls? Mom would die."

Diego smirked. "What Mom doesn't know won't hurt her."

I wondered if they were worried at all about security, but they didn't seem to be with Jago walking at least twenty feet away from Jude.

We stopped walking, standing next to the others. There wasn't much to the "corner", but they had a statue and a sign that referenced the Eagles song.

Plus a giant painting of a Route 66 sign in the middle of the road.

As I took it all in, I wondered what it must have been like to be on tour with the Eagles. To create music like them. Jude must have felt so inspired growing up here.

"Let's take a selfie," I said to Diego. "You can hold the phone with your long arms."

He took my phone and held it out, cheesing so big his eyes almost squinted shut, and then snapped a picture.

"Okay, now a good one," I said.

He looked at me questioningly. "Are you saying that *wasn't* a good one?"

"What? Is it so bad that I want to remember this moment with my baby brother not looking like a goofball?"

He rolled his eyes but held the phone out again, smiling for real this time.

"Much better," I said, taking my phone and sending the photo to our family group chat, along with a link to the Eagles song.

Mom instantly replied.

Mom: I'm so happy you're having a good time!

Dad: That's a great song.

In a separate message, Dad texted only me.

Dad: Don't let her fool you. She's been crying all day about her babies being gone. Be sure to call her tonight before bed.

I showed Diego the text, and he rubbed his neck. "What's she gonna do when you're on your world tour?"

"Who says I'm getting a world tour?"

He gave me a look. "If anyone can do it, it's you."

My heart swelled. "If I go on a world tour, I'm bringing everyone with me."

Diego laughed. "You're going to need a bigger bus."

"Or two," I agreed.

Behind me, a cold voice said, "So you're Desirae."

I jumped, turning to see a girl who looked like Barbie come to life. She stared at me with her hands on her mini-skirted hips. "Do I know you?"

She seemed offended. "Vanessa Cooper? Ugh. You don't even deserve to ride with him if you don't know the head of his very own fan group."

Okay, now I understood what Jude had meant on the bus. Vanessa was not someone I wanted to cross. "Hi," I said, extending my hand. "My friends call me Des. And this is my brother, Diego."

She glanced between Diego and me, ignoring my hand all together. "You're on the bus with Jude."

I glanced at Diego out of the corner of my eye. What planet was she from?

"Meteor was going to take their own bus," she said.

"I don't have my own bus," I explained. Not that I needed to explain myself.

"Yet," Diego added.

Vanessa narrowed her eyes at him, then looked back at me. "You know, Jude isn't dating you."

I laughed out loud.

Which, judging by her pinched features, was the wrong thing to do.

"Sorry," I quickly added. "I'm not interested in dating Jude. Not even a little bit." Okay, maybe that was a teensy bit of an overstatement. "He's all yours."

Jude stepped beside me and said, "Oh really?"

HEARING those words come out of Des's mouth in her beautiful voice was like a sucker punch to the gut.

Was the idea of dating me really that repulsive?

I knew we wouldn't have much time for dates once the nightly shows started, but I'd thought maybe after...

Vanessa quickly changed her expression to a sickly-sweet smile. Her eyes widened, making them look like doll eyes instead of human. Her teeth were just a little too white. And she instantly perked her chest out, no doubt trying to draw my attention there. As if she had a chance of taking my attention away from Desirae. "Jude! How are you? Are you loving being back on the bus?"

I put my arms around Des and Diego, trying to ignore the heated way my body reacted to Des's curvy form. "It's great having people my age on the bus. We've been having lots of fun, especially in the bunks." I winked at Des, if only to see Vanessa's horrified reaction. Which I got.

But I won the jackpot with Des's slap against my abs. Not only was I happy to have her touch me (which was weird, I should probably get my head examined), but I also got the privilege of her surprised reaction at the firmness of my muscles. Now I was puffing out my chest just as much as Vanessa.

I turned to Vanessa and said, "Would you get a picture of us three in front of the sign?"

Seeming especially disgruntled, she took my phone and snapped a couple pictures of the three of us. "Now one of you and me? For social?"

Diego said, "I've got this one."

"Come on, Des," I said, already knowing what Diego wanted to happen. I stood on Des's left, putting her in the middle of the photo. It was the kind of thing that would drive Vanessa absolutely nuts, especially since she wouldn't get to put her hands all over me. "Now you'll get a photo with both of the acts in the show."

Diego drew out his photos, getting closer, then farther away, and saying, "Oh man, Des blinked. Vanessa, chin up—wouldn't want to make your neck look short. Jude, dude, hands out of your pockets."

Vanessa was very nearly red, and I was barely containing my laughter by the time Diego said, "I think I got a good one."

She snapped the phone from him and then turned a sweet smile on me. "Are we going to the cemetery this time?"

My chest tightened. I didn't like that my private life was on display for anyone to know—especially people like Vanessa. To them, my story was just words on paper, decorations for the paper doll they knew. In reality? All I got was a single father and an ache for a woman I never even knew.

"I'm not feeling great," I said. "I think I'm going to get some sleep on the bus. You guys go."

Seeming concerned, Des said, "Are you okay?"

I nodded. "Just got tired all of a sudden."

I went and tapped on my grandma's shoulder, interrupting her conversation with Dad, Francie, and Jago. "Hey," I said, "I'm going to go on the bus and rest."

With a far-too-knowing look in her eyes, she

gave me a big hug. She whispered in my ear, "Be patient with your dad, okay?"

"I will," I said. Then I got the keys from Francie and walked back down the empty Winslow streets to my grandma's house. I remembered being so proud the first time she let me walk to the soda shop with my friend next door. I'd been ten, but I felt like a full-blown adult with her trust in me.

Now I felt smaller than ever. Winslow was a small town, but the people here weren't my friends anymore. Not really. Even that next door neighbor had stopped talking to me after I got a record deal.

When I dreamed of performing for thousands, touching people with my music, I'd never imagined the cost that would come with it. If I could go back and do it all over again...

It was better not to think about what-ifs. Instead, I got on the bus, went back to the bedroom, shut and locked the door. With my noise-cancelling headphones on, I tried to go to sleep as the bus took off again down the road.

Unfortunately, my dad had other ideas. About half an hour later, probably after he'd gotten ice cream at the place where he and Mom went on their first date, he sat on the bed next to me and tapped on my shoulder.

I pretended to be asleep, but the tapping only became more persistent. Disgruntled, I sat up, pulling off my headphones. "What?"

"Tone."

I took a breath. "What?"

"I thought you might want to put flowers on her grave with me."

I shook my head and lay back down.

Dad looked like he wanted to argue, but instead he turned around and left the room.

I knew I was being a bull-headed. I could practically feel the questions Des and Diego were going to have. But I was tired of this routine. Ever since I could remember, Dad had been dragging me out to the cemetery and laying flowers on her grave. At this point, it was a shrine, decorated with the finest items money could buy. He'd even upgraded her stone from the one he'd been able to afford before as a single dad. Now it was a massive cross, inscribed with a personal note.

But no matter how many stories he told me about her, she was still a stranger. Like someone I'd read about in a book but never really laid eyes on. And that almost hurt worse than the loss.

The bus stopped, and I rolled off the bed and went to the window, parting the blinds just enough to see outside. From here, I had a clear view of Dad kneeling in front of the stone. It was taller than his kneeling height. He had one hand on his knee and one hand on the white marble.

He must have been saying something, telling her about me as though she were actually there and could listen. But she couldn't. She was gone. Away from me, just as she'd intended.

THE MOOD on the bus was tense as Francie drove down a paved road to a cemetary. Jude had locked himself in the room, and didn't come out even after Anthony went back to get him.

The bus parked and Anthony walked outside with a bouquet of fake flowers. After he left, Jago and Francie waited in the living area with my brother and me. Without either of the Santiagos here and no explanations given, I had to ask. "What's going on?"

Jago and Francie exchanged a look, and Jago nodded.

With a grim expression on her face, Francie said, "Jude's mom died when he was less than a year old."

"What happened?" I asked, horrified by their loss.

Francie shook her head. "I don't think it's my place to say." She patted my shoulder and got on the bus, going to her seat.

When Anthony came back, Francie drove another hour or two past Winslow and then stopped in a private RV park. Jude was still in his room, and Anthony sat at the dining table, his tablet open, headphones in, and a serious look on his face.

It was the most awkward couple hours of my life as I sat by Diego and watched TV, trying to pretend I didn't feel all the tension that existed around us.

My family fought, sure, but our arguments never came with this heavy kind of pain.

When we stopped at the RV lot, Diego and I got out to stretch our legs and call our mom. I cherished her now more than ever. More than I had before I learned Jude had lost his own mother as a little boy. He probably didn't remember her at all.

Diego and I walked down the blacktop since there were no sidewalks, passing Vanessa's teardrop trailer. I couldn't believe she was that obsessed that she'd drop everything and follow Jude around the country.

Would I have fans like that someday?

Would I want to?

Diego dialed Mom's number and put her on speaker phone.

"Hello?" she said. "How are you? Are they feeding you well?"

Diego and I exchanged a smile.

"Only the best," Diego said.

"Definitely," I agreed. "We stopped in Arizona for the night, but we should get to the Arkansas Winslow tomorrow. Apparently, Anthony likes to stop in two Winslows on the way."

"That's fun," Mom said. "As long as they're keeping you safe. What's security like?"

I said, "It's top-notch. Jude's bodyguard goes everywhere with us."

A pause on Mom's end made me worry she was about to dig deeper, but then there was yelling and something crashing in the background. "Your siblings just broke their fort," she explained.

I smiled, already missing them. "Tell them I love them."

"I will," she said, "but you better send us post-cards from all these fun places!"

I'd never even thought about postcards—they seemed so archaic when I could just text them a picture, but that could be a fun way to keep our family together on this trip even though we were so far apart.

"We will," I agreed.

"Good, and keep an eye out for *la bruja*. I don't trust her."

"Me either," I said.

"Same here," Diego agreed.

"Good." Mom paused for a moment, and I heard a sniffle. "Stick together, okay? Family's all we can trust in this world."

Diego said, "We've got each other's backs, Mom. Just like you taught us."

"Good, now get some sleep. It's way too late."

Diego and I smiled at each other. She was still mothering us from hundreds of miles away.

"Night, Mom," I said.

"Goodnight," Diego echoed.

"I love you both with my whole heart," she said.

We told her we loved her too and then hung up, turning back toward the bus.

"Hey," Diego said. "Look up. You can see so many stars out here."

When I turned my gaze toward the stars, my mouth fell open. There were so many of them twinkling brightly in the sky. More than I'd ever seen at home on the beach. "Have these always been here?"

"I guess sometimes you need the right perspective." He stopped, his head tipped back to take in the sky.

I admired that about Diego. He wasn't in a rush for anything, wasn't bothered about finding success like I was. He saw things I missed sometimes.

"Hey," I said, "I know I haven't really said it yet, but thank you for coming. I wouldn't be here without you."

"Well, someone had to keep an eye on you." He grinned at me and continued walking back toward the bus.

I rolled my eyes, following him. "I take it back. You're still a pain."

"Just the way I like it," he retorted, reaching the bus and pulling the door open.

The bus was mostly dark inside. Francie was in one of the bunks; Anthony sat at the table, his laptop open and headphones on. The door to Jude and Anthony's room was still closed.

Diego and I exchanged a look. "I'm going to take a shower first, then I'll hit the hay," he said.

I whispered back, "Goodnight."

While Diego got ready for his shower, I crawled

into my bunk and shut the curtain, not nearly ready to go to sleep. Instead, I opened my phone, finally ready to respond to my friends' texts asking me how it was going.

Des: It started great and then things got tense… We went through Jude's hometown, and he refused to go to his mom's grave with his dad. Why would he do that?

I waited as I watched the bubble with three dots within appear in the group chat.

Faith: His mom passed? I didn't know that. Was it recent?

Des: It happened when he was still a baby.

Adriel: That's awful. :(Carter lost his parents when he was seven, and it still hurts him eleven years later.

Nadira: No words or advice here. I'm just sorry. :(

Cori: Maybe it will make sense the more you get to know him. I didn't understand why Ryker treated people the way he did until I saw what his life was like at home.

I basically was in Jude's home now, and it was so small there wasn't much room to retreat, even though he could close himself in his room. He'd have to come out eventually, for pizza rolls at least, judging by how many he and Diego ate today.

Faith: How's it been other than that?

Des: It's been a pretty good trip so far. Except for the fact that Jude and Diego GOT A VIDEO OF ME SNORING THIS MORNING!

Nadira: Okay, I have to see this.

Cringing all the while, I sent them the video, and my phone quickly blew up with a string of laughing emojis, gifs, and memes.

Des: I hate all of you.

Cori sent a meme of a lion yawning and the words: Hungry or sleepy? Just Des.

Des: Goodbyeeeeee

Faith: Have fun!

Nadira: Love you!

Adriel: For the record, you look cute when you sleep.

Cori: Don't snore tonight. ;)

Shaking my head and smiling, I locked my phone screen and rolled over to go to sleep.

Jude didn't come out of his room that night, and when I heard Anthony twist the knob, it was well past midnight.

Life on the road was amazing.

But apparently not perfect.

I WOKE up to the rumble of the bus starting. The ache in my chest was heavy, but I couldn't hide in here forever. It was time to get up. To face the day.

I connected my phone to the bathroom speaker and listened to music while I showered quickly and got ready for the day. When I finished, I walked into the lounge area, and amazing music with lyrics in Spanish hit my ears.

"What is this?" I asked.

Des and Diego stared at me, similar looks of shock and horror on their faces.

Des paused the TV that was playing a music video. "What did you say?"

"I haven't heard this before," I said, slowly walking to the fridge to get a juice. "Who is it?"

She and Diego looked at each other. Sometimes it was like they had a secret language between the two of them, and I found myself jealous of Diego's closeness to her.

Diego said, "Dude, it's Mana..." At my lack of recognition, he added, "The greatest Mexican rock band of all time? They're on the Hollywood Walk of Fame!"

Des hit play. "We have a Mana virgin!" She turned the volume up and took my hands, swaying to the music.

I may not have known about Mana, but I knew how to dance. My choreographer had made sure of that. I pulled her to my chest and dipped her back. She let out an excited squeal that turned into a giggle, and I pulled her back up.

Diego clapped his hands together, laughing as we continued dancing to the music. Des sang softly as we danced, her beautiful voice sweeping across my skin and into my soul. I'd never felt so free on tour, so... *inspired*.

"Wait," I said, letting her go and reaching for a notebook we always kept underneath the TV, just in case.

"What?" she asked.

"Say the lyrics again," I requested, biting the cap off the pen.

She repeated them slowly in Spanish and then in English, and I scribbled them down. "Turn off the TV?"

Diego did, and the room went silent, sans the rumble of the bus and the quiet drum of Dad and Francie's conversation.

I hummed a melody a few times, trying to piece together the notes that sounded right. Des asked, "What about this?" She adjusted a few notes from my composition and made it even better.

"Yes!" I cried, so excited I was dizzy. I could have kissed her, but I held myself back. When I kissed her for the first time, I was going to make it right.

And there were my lyrics.

It felt vulnerable, raw, to scribble them on the paper for her and Diego to see.

When I kiss her, I'm going to do it right.
When I kiss him, I want to see the light.
Stars in the sky burst within her eyes.
When I kiss her, I want to feel it all.
When I kiss him, I'll be ready for the fall.

When we kiss, it'll be everything or nothing at all.

The words came to my mind, a duet playing in our voices, blending with guitar and tambourines like the music we'd just heard.

"Hold on," I said, going back to my room to get my guitar in a heady rush. When I came back, I said, "Sing it with me?"

Des stared in my eyes. "A duet?"

I began strumming the opening chords I imagined. "Please?"

She nodded, taking a deep breath. "Okay."

I played the chords slowly, trying to get them just right, and sang the opening line, putting everything I already felt for Des in the words.

Her voice poured from her like a waterfall that never dreamed of being anything else. The lyrics danced around my body, squeezing my heart as I sang in return.

When we reached the end of my scribbled words in the notebook, I stalled my fingers on the guitar, a giddy smile on my face as I looked at Des.

Her lips parted slowly, no words coming out.

Clapping came from the front of the bus, and I

saw Dad walking toward us. "That was amazing! Did you write that just now?"

I nodded, grinning at Des. "She inspired me."

"It's a hit!" Dad said, just as thrilled as I was. "A little rough around the edges, but maybe we can get it ready to record by the end of the tour. If we pull the right strings, I bet we can get a big name to duet it with you."

My eyebrows drew together. Everything Dad was saying was wrong. My body physically rejected even the idea of singing it with anyone but Des. "It's Des or no one."

Dad's lips pulled in a line, but I could tell he didn't want to argue in front of Des. "We'll discuss it later," he said, walking back toward the front of the bus.

"My answer will be the same," I called after him.

He didn't respond.

I continued plucking at strings, trying to identify the bridge. As I did, I made myself a promise—I'd sing this song with her, make it come true, by the end of the tour. I couldn't imagine performing it with anyone else. Or anyone better.

I'D NEVER BEEN MUCH of a songwriter, choosing to perform covers of songs that resonated with me instead, but writing with Jude was like stepping into an entirely new world.

One moment, we'd been dancing, he'd been taking my breath away, and then it was like a burst of lightening had shocked him into action. Watching the words pour from his heart through the pen and onto the page was like seeing magic in action. I wanted to be a part of as much of it as I could.

But Jude's confrontation with his dad had seemed to dim his eyes. He worked on the song for a little longer, but after getting nowhere, set his guitar aside and asked us if we wanted anything for breakfast.

The fridge was stocked with prepared meals, and I chose a fruit plate with the last of Mom's breakfast burritos. The farther I got from home, the better they seemed to taste.

I sat on the couch and checked the comments on the video I'd posted of Jude's tour bus while the guys played video games. I had fifty thousand more followers already, and tons of my fans were happy that I'd gotten to go on tour.

But I was also getting more hateful comments on my videos than ever before.

Fantiago327: I can't believe Jude would even want to be close to a girl like you.

Papapaul: You're just glorifying obesity.

Cheekooo: Ever heard of a treadmill?

Lobo41: Stop shoving things in your mouth, you fat cow.

Paws53: Choosing to be fat and hurting your body isn't self-love.

GretaGene: Not trying to sound rude or anything but where do we draw the line between body positive and delusional?

GetSwole: The fact is being plus size isn't healthy. It WILL reduce your life span.

RobertH: You could work out 20 minutes a day and be fit. Why are you complaining?

They flowed across my screen like a river of acid, threatening to splash across my feet and destroy me if I got too close.

Each one I read made me angrier until I wanted to scream. Who were these people to make comments on my weight? Assumptions about my health? They had no idea what diagnoses, personal hardships, or how much time and money I had available. They had no clue what my diet or exercise routine looked like.

And so what if I *wanted* to be fat?

Could a person not enjoy living life at a larger size without the whole of the internet weighing in on it?

I must have been making a face because Jude put down his controller and asked, "What's wrong?"

I looked up from my phone, trying to even my expression. "Nothing. It's just some of these comments on my channel."

"What?" he asked.

"Nothing..."

But Diego took my phone and started scrolling. I tried to get it back from him, but it was pointless.

Despite sharing the same DNA, Diego was way taller and stronger than me. The more he read, the redder his face got. "What the hell?"

"What?" Jude asked again.

"Just some trolls," I said at the same time Diego said, "A bunch of jerks commenting on Des's weight from behind their freaking phones. They're even saying you shouldn't want to be around her."

Diego finally handed my phone back, looking disgusted, and Jude said, "No one talked crap about me on the internet before I was famous."

I drew my eyebrows together. "What does that mean?"

"It means..." He shrugged. "The only reason they even know to talk bad about you is because you're visible. But you're the one visible. Not them. Here..." He took out his phone, snapping a selfie of us I barely had time to smile for. "For the record, I'm more than happy to be sitting next to you."

Small butterflies danced in my stomach, despite the fact that they should not have been there. This was strictly business, and I needed to remember that.

He began tapping on his phone screen, and I asked, "What are you doing?"

"Sharing the photo online." He grinned at me. "You make me look good."

I gave him a grateful smile. "You're sweet." He didn't have to be nice about this—honestly, he didn't have to talk to me or Diego at all. We could have just been strangers riding on a bus together, but instead he'd chosen to be our friend.

On the other side of Jude, Diego said, "I still feel like I should beat someone up."

I rolled my eyes. "You mean more than you're beating Jude up in Mario Kart?"

"Hey!" Jude protested. "I've been letting him win."

Diego narrowed his eyes. "You wouldn't dare."

Jude smirked. "Rematch? I'll beat you this time, just to prove it."

The two of them got busy playing each other, and my anger slowly faded. Jude was right. Those trolls were only there because I was visible. Because I wasn't playing small and keeping myself hidden from the world.

I hoped bigger girls like me would keep playing big, putting their faces out there, and showing everyone (including *la bruja*) that we belonged in the spotlight if that's where we wanted to be.

WITHIN HOURS of posting the photo of Des and me, my notifications had blown up. The Fantiagos wanted to know why I hadn't dated one of my most devoted fans. The rest of my fans wanted to know if we were dating. And some of them even made similar comments to the horrible ones on Des's social media.

I spent more than half an hour replying to as many comments as I could. Making vague responses about my relationship with Des to create mystery. Telling those jerks that I was beyond grateful to be in Des's presence.

And soon, my phone lit up with a call from Batty Natty.

"Hello?" I said, taking it back to my room so I

wouldn't disturb the epic race Diego and Des were engaged in.

"Jude." She cut straight to the chase. "What's going on with you and Desirae?"

Glad I'd stepped away, I shut the bedroom door behind me. "Nothing, why?"

She was quiet for a moment—a rarity for Natalie. "Are you interested in her?"

What was she getting at? "Of course I am. She's a beautiful girl. And so far, she's been great to be around."

"Interesting."

"What?" I tried not to let my frustration with the comments and now Natalie bleed into my tone, but I was getting tired of this conversation.

"I have a question, and I want you to be honest."

"Go on."

"Did you ask me to have a meeting with her because you wanted to get with her or because you liked her voice?"

I clenched my jaw at the insinuation. "She has an amazing voice, Natalie. I can't believe you didn't even give her the time of day."

"I told her exactly what I told you. This is a business."

"And so far, inviting Des on tour has been great for business," I argued.

"Because she's an underdog now. People lap that up."

"She's only an underdog because you made her one." I let out a sigh. "Was that what you called about? To ask my feelings for her?"

"No," she said. "That wasn't all. Samantha told me your social media interactions are trending up with photos of her. If you did like her, I was going to say to go for it, if only for the extra attention. Surely she'd love to date a rock star."

I glanced over my shoulder as if I could see through the closed door to where she and Diego sat in the living room. Dating Des would be amazing but... "I don't think she's like that."

"Like what?" Natalie asked.

"I don't think she's impressed by my fame," I said simply. The few times I'd tried flirting with her, she'd hardly reciprocated. Hardly been impressed.

"I don't know about that. When I talked to her at the house, she asked me if you were single."

My eyebrows rose, and I had to clear my throat to keep from stumbling over my words. "She did?"

"Absolutely. I think you should go for it. For your career."

My interest in Des went far beyond growing my career, but Natalie didn't need to know that. "Thanks."

With a smile in her voice, she said, "I'll see you in New York for the run-through."

I hung up without saying goodbye, but I couldn't get Natalie's words out of my mind. Had Des really asked if I was single? And why did that possibility make me so giddy?

I'd dated before, but never someone who was on tour with me. Never a girl I could see in the morning and before bed.

Never a girl like Des.

I felt the bus slow to a stop, and I walked back out of the room. "Where are we?" I asked no one specific.

Dad said, "Fuel stop."

"Where?" I asked.

"Some backwoods town in Virginia," he answered. "You should be good to get out and walk around a little if you want."

"Awesome." I grinned, thankful for a chance to get out of the bus. I turned to Des and Diego. "Want to go with me?"

Diego got up and began walking toward his bunk. "I'm going to run. I need to get a workout in."

I looked at Des, raising a questioning eyebrow.

"Sure," she said as she tied her jacket around her waist. "Let's check it out."

Stepping out of the bus was like entering another world. This town must have had a population of five, including the goat I saw grazing someone's front yard across the street.

Francie was brilliant. She always tried to stop in places where I wouldn't be recognized and swarmed by fans. Not so brilliant, though, was Vanessa's voice calling, "Yoo hoo! Jude!"

I stifled my cringe and turned, lifting a hand. "Hey. Des and I are going on a walk."

"Mind if I join?" she asked.

I glanced at Des. "Actually, we're working on a song together. We want everyone to be surprised. Right, Des?"

"Definitely," Des agreed. "Sorry."

She didn't sound sorry at all.

Vanessa frowned and said, "Fine then. I was about to write a post for the Fantiago group anyway." She turned on her heel and stormed back toward her car and trailer.

"Thank you," Des said quietly. "I have the

distinct feeling she would cut me if she had the chance."

I laughed. "Not a problem."

I kicked at a rock in front of my foot and continued walking over the worn-down blacktop. The air felt thick and humid, and the heat made my shirt stick to my back. Des had little beads of sweat forming on her forehead, making her skin glisten.

"That was a beautiful song, by the way," she said.

My chest swelled with pride, but my cheeks heated with humility. I loved that she liked my work, even before it was perfected. I usually didn't write in front of anyone. The process felt so raw. But then I asked a question that made me feel even more vulnerable. "Will you sing it with me for the album?"

She stalled for a moment, and then resumed walking again. "Your dad said..."

I waved my hand. "He just gets excited about the possibilities of collabs with big names. He thinks I'm going to be the next Justin Bieber."

She laughed. "I wouldn't want to get in the way of that."

I shook my head. "Really, it was your voice I heard in my head when I was writing the lines."

Her cheeks were full of color, from the heat or my words I wasn't sure, but eventually she tucked a strand of hair behind her ear. "I'd like that."

My smile came easily, and my eyes followed her hand as it dropped by her side. We were only inches apart, but something stopped me from trying to hold it.

She caught her lip between her teeth and said, "I'm sorry about your mom."

It was like a shadow fell across the sky, just at the mention of my mom. But we were already out of town, at least five minutes away from the bus. I couldn't hide away in my room so easily now. And besides, she'd only offered condolences. She wasn't trying to pry like someone else might have.

"It's okay," I finally said.

"You act like it's not," she observed.

And man, I couldn't argue with her. "It's not."

She looked over at me with a half-smile, then kept walking.

For some reason, I wanted to explain to her, show her I wasn't just some moody kid holing up in my room for no reason. "My mom overdosed on my first birthday." The words hung between us, heavier than the humid air. And despite the fact that I couldn't remember her, that I'd lived my whole life without her, my throat still felt tight.

Des stopped on the side of the road, just looking at me, her hands at her sides. "Was she an addict?"

"Dad said she started 'self-medicating' when I was six months old. That she'd had a lot of pain after my birth and wasn't herself." Now that the words were coming out of my mouth and landing on someone new, I couldn't stop myself. "But he doesn't remember her like that. He remembers his high school sweetheart he got ice cream with at the Sipp Shoppe, and the girl he took to senior prom, and the woman he married after high school, and the person he tried to have children with for years before they finally got me." My voice was shaky and so were my breaths. "But all I know about her is that she left him. Left me."

Des covered her mouth with her hand, her eyes shining. "I'm so sorry, Jude."

I shook my head, swallowing hard. "She took my mom from me. I could have had siblings, like you. My dad could have given his love to her instead of taking all her pain. And instead of being a grandma, Mama had to step up and be a mom. What was so wrong with me that she didn't want to stay?"

She tilted her head. "Nothing was wrong with you, Jude."

"What do you mean?"

"I mean, she probably had a really bad case of PPD."

"PPD? Prescription pill dependency?"

She tilted her head, her eyes full of compassion. "Postpartum depression. It's really common for women to struggle after having a baby. Their hormones are out of whack, and they're losing sleep. My mom had a really hard time after Adelita. She had to hire a nanny—wouldn't get out of bed for weeks. It was scary."

Her words hit me one after another. Grandma had mentioned something called the "baby blues," but I'd always thought it was just a way to describe my mom struggling to be a mother. Why hadn't I learned about this in health class when we learned about pregnancy, or rather, pregnancy prevention?

I clung to the diagnosis I didn't even know my mom could have had. My tongue felt thick as I said, "I thought it was me. Something wrong with me."

"Have you ever seen a baby?" Des asked.

I scoffed at her, barely masking my frustration. "Have I seen a baby?"

"I remember all of my siblings being born,

except for Diego. They all looked the same. Squishy with these small fingers and stubby toes and chunky thighs. But no matter how they looked or how much they spit up or pooped or made a mess, everyone in my family treated them like they were made of gold."

"What's your point?" I asked. Just hearing about how special she was treated as a baby made my chest ache with jealousy.

"Hold on." She got out her phone and pulled up a collage of baby pictures. "Look at them."

My eyebrows drew together, but I did as she asked, taking in their chubby cheeks and toothless smiles and diapered bottoms. "Okay."

"Which one of them deserves to lose their mom?" she asked. "Which one deserves to be told they're ugly or stupid or not good enough?"

My eyes stung, and my throat tightened over the answer I couldn't bring myself to say out loud.

None of them deserved any less than the very best in life.

"Jude, all of these babies are six months old. I could swap one of those cute naked pictures of you in here, and it wouldn't change a thing."

I nodded, then wiped at my eyes. Despite the tears, my chest felt lighter.

I hadn't deserved it.

She reached for my hand, her fingers holding mine for a fraction of a second. For a million seconds too short. "Jude? Are you okay?"

"Maybe?" I took her in, the sheen of sweat on her forehead, the sweep of her bangs across her forehead. The tenderness in her expression. "You're amazing, you know?" I said.

She smiled. "I think you are too."

And for some reason, that felt like the best thing of all.

TWENTY-ONE

DES

"LOOK OUT THE WINDOW," Anthony said. "It's the Big Apple."

I practically sprinted to the window to lift the blinds and look through the glass. Instead of the countryside we'd driven through for the past few days, we were surrounded by city. I'd only been to New York once before—on a family trip as a child—and it looked so different now.

Skyscrapers rose around us, so tall I couldn't even get the right angle out the window to see to the top.

Beside me, Jude pointed at one and said, "I heard there are fifteen hundred apartments in that one."

On the opposite side of me, Diego said, "We

could fit all the students at Emerson Academy in there and still have a thousand spaces left."

When he put it like that, the scale truly hit me. In Emerson, I'd been a big fish in a small pond. Now? Welcome to the ocean.

Somehow, being surrounded by this concrete jungle, sitting next to Jude Santiago, my dreams felt more possible than ever before.

"How much longer until we're at the venue?" I asked. Now that we were in New York, everything felt so real. I couldn't believe I would start my career as an opener for Jude Santiago tomorrow.

From his spot at the table, Anthony said, "We should get there in about half an hour. We have lunch being delivered, and then we'll start rehearsals."

Even though I'd been dreaming of this moment my entire life, it was hard not to feel overwhelmed. My nerves racketed up higher and higher until we reached the venue.

There were fans lined around the building, and the second they saw our bus, they started jumping up and down. Some waved hand-painted signs.

Jude waved at them through the windows, although I wondered how much they could see through the tinting.

Security let our bus through, and then Anthony said, "It's showtime."

I smiled at him and followed Jude and Jago out the bus. Diego walked beside me, down the wide hallway. There weren't windows here, just cinderblock walls and cement floors. Eventually it let out into a spacious room with tables set up for lunch. The smell of food hit my nose, and my stomach quivered.

"Eat up," Jude said. "You're going to want your energy today."

Diego helped himself to food from the buffet pans, but I could hardly find it in me to want any of it.

Diego looked between me and my empty plate. "You okay?"

I nodded jerkily. "Just nervous."

He lifted a serving spoon full of pasta salad and dumped it on my plate. "Eat something. We don't want you to be nervous *and* hangry."

On the other side of me, Jude snorted.

I whacked him with the back of my hand, which made him laugh more. But the comedy had eased some of the pressure out of my chest. I followed Diego's advice and filled my plate, eating a little once we were at the table.

Jago and Diego occupied the conversation, talking about bodyguard strategies and things we might encounter while on tour. Apparently, the venue's security was supposed to watch me, but Diego said he wanted to be ready to help out if needed.

Jude caught my eyes across the table and mouthed, *You're going to be great.*

I blushed, not really wanting him to know I was nervous. I didn't usually get nervous, but this felt like the big time. For as long as I could remember, I'd dreamed of singing on big stages with stadiums full of fans. Someday, I wanted to sell out Madison Square Garden.

Today was just the beginning of a long path, but I felt closer than ever before.

A woman with brown hair held back by a claw clip approached our table. Anthony said, "Angelina! Great to see you."

"Same to you," she said, speaking quickly. She had this air about her that told me she was always just a little busier than she wanted to be.

Anthony said, "Des, Diego, this is Angelina, our assistant manager. She makes sure the show runs smoothly and keeps it all on schedule. When you're onstage, Des, she'll be the voice in your ear."

"I'm looking forward to it," I said.

She smiled briefly and said, "We're ready for your part of the rehearsal, if you'll come with me."

"Sure," I said, picking up my plate.

Anthony said, "We'll take care of it. You and Diego go ahead."

Diego and I walked with Angelina down the hall. Even Diego was working hard to keep pace with her as she rattled off things I would need to know about the show.

"You've practiced your set list, right?" she said. "Because the band is prepped to do those songs in order."

"Band?" I asked.

"They didn't tell you? We have a live guitarist, keyboardist, and drummer for you. They know what they're doing, so you shouldn't have to worry too much about them. Just sing the songs, and you'll be good."

Well, singing I knew how to do.

We reached the stage, and she said, "I have a recording set up for the background. Sing along at a quarter of capacity. Don't wear yourself out during the warmup."

She played the songs I would cover over the sound system and coached me through moving about the stage as I performed. She also gave suggestions for things I could say to the crowd to get them excited for Jude.

She reminded me, just as Natalie had, that this show wasn't about me. But I didn't care. I was going to do what I loved most in the world, forget the rest.

When we finished, it was Jude's turn to run through his show—which was a lot more intricate than my part of the performance. I video-called my friends and flipped the screen so they could see it all. Jude and his backup dancers ran through their choreography as his enchanting voice played through the speakers.

I'd seen videos of him performing onstage, but seeing all that went into the background was incredible. There were at least fifty people here now, buzzing around like bees in a hive, all working toward a common purpose.

Tomorrow, there would be even more work—with hair and makeup and wardrobe involved, along with security and ticketing and fans. So many fans.

It was late when the rehearsal ended, and instead of sleeping on the bus, they let us stay in fancy hotel rooms. Diego and I split a two-bedroom suite, and I had to call my family to show them everything.

Diego talked Mom through how to connect our call to the smart TV so they could see everything on a bigger screen. And for a little while, it was almost like our entire family was here, enjoying the room and the newness of it all right alongside us.

At the end of the call, Dad looked into the screen and said, "I'm so proud of you two."

And that meant the world. "I hope I make you even prouder tomorrow," I replied.

He smiled. "There's not a doubt in my mind. This is what you were made to do."

I woke to a knock on the door in the morning.

Diego called, "Can you get it?" His voice came in a huff, and I could hear him working out.

"You can't?" I grunted through my door. "You're already up!"

"I have fifty more reps!" he yelled back.

I rolled my eyes, getting out of bed. I probably wasn't getting back to sleep anyway. We had a couple hours before we needed to leave for the venue, and I wanted to call my friends before then.

I wrapped the soft hotel robe around my body and answered the door. Where all the blood quickly drained from my face.

Jude stood in the hallway, holding a bouquet with dozens of red roses.

I didn't know whether to be shocked by his presence or mortified by the way I surely looked. I hadn't even properly scrubbed the crusty bits from the corners of my eyes yet.

"Jude, I..." I looked from the flowers to his smiling face. No wonder millions of girls were in love with him. He had this genuine way about him that contrasted the smolder of his dark eyes. It was incredibly endearing and effortlessly sexy, all at the same time.

He held out the flowers, and I gingerly took them, the soft fragrance of fresh roses wafting to my nose. "What is this for?" I finally managed to ask, dipping my nose to brush against the petals.

"I wanted to wish you a happy first day of tour. I know you're going to do amazing," he said, sincerity evident in each of his words and even more so in his smile.

"Thank you, Jude." I covered my heart with my free hand, still looking at the delicate curls of petals. I'd dated around, but I couldn't remember the last time a guy had gotten me flowers, much less red roses. "This means a lot."

He nodded and turned to leave, but I didn't want him to go. "Hey," I said, stepping into the hallway but propping the door open with my foot.

He turned back, a hopeful look on his face. "Yeah?"

I wanted to kiss him, thank him properly for the gesture. But Natalie's threat flashed through my mind, and I knew I had to keep our relationship platonic. If she had meant it, anything more than friendship could destroy his career.

"I, um..." I looked back down at my flowers and back to him again. "Any tips for today?"

Pushing his hands in his pocket, he said, "Enjoy it."

I already was.

TWENTY-TWO
JUDE

AFTER A COUPLE YEARS of traveling the country and performing for fans, I was used to the hurry up and wait of a tour. I knew what to expect from hair and makeup. I understood people were going to demand a lot, pulling me from one place to another, but Des didn't.

On the limo ride to the venue, I asked Jago to brief Diego about the kind of things he might expect as Des's right-hand man. And then I gave Des another rundown of what she could expect.

It was good I had too, because the second we arrived outside the venue, I could hear the screaming.

Des twisted in her seat, looking out the deeply tinted windows. "Are those your fans?"

I nodded, bracing myself for the me I needed to be. I wouldn't be here without the fans, so I wanted to give them my all each second they saw me.

The car stopped, and Jago got out, holding the door open for me. The screams turned from a dull roar to an echoing din that filled my eardrums and clouded my brain. The first time, it had been so overwhelming. Now I knew to take deep breaths and focus in on one fan at a time. One *person* at a time.

We walked right past the fence holding back all the people cheering, some of them holding signs. I did my best to sign as many autographs as I could. To smile and shake hands and give them everything they expected Jude Santiago to be.

As soon as we got inside, the heavy metal doors swung shut behind us, and my ears rang in the silence.

Des and Diego were quiet too. When I swung my head back to see her expression, she looked a little shell-shocked. It made me smile—that's exactly how I looked when I walked past my first excited fans. It still felt unreal sometimes that all those people were cheering for me.

Dad led us all back to the giant room for makeup, hair, and wardrobe.

She paused in the doorway, her wide eyes taking in all the busyness of backstage.

I squeezed her hand. "You're going to do great."

She seemed stunned by the contact, her full lips parting slightly. Her features quickly reset, and she whispered a "thank you" before Angelina hurried Des to her own makeup station, set fifteen feet away from mine.

Gentry, the girl who did my makeup on every tour, stood by my chair, and I jogged to her, giving her a big hug. "It's been too long," I said.

She grinned up at me, her pierced dimples deepening. She'd been working with me since I started touring, and after hundreds of shows, you got to know and trust a person.

"We better get started," she said, turning my chair.

I sat down, and as Gentry began applying layers of foundation to my skin, I sneaked glances at Des.

I couldn't hear her, but I could see her and Diego joking with her makeup artist. They seemed to be having so much fun, and it made me realize how much I'd been missing out on. I wanted my tours to be full of fun and laughter like the last few days had been with them.

"Close your eyes," Gentry said. As soon as I obliged, she began painting a swath of eyeliner across my lashes. "Don't let Natalie hear me say this, but I'm proud of what you did, inviting that girl on tour."

I tried not to shift as I smiled—I'd learned long ago the consequences of not staying still while she worked. Gentry had three grown children and didn't take any nonsense. "Thanks, G."

We were quiet as she finished my look, and my hairstylist stepped in, wetting and drying and styling my hair for the stage. I'd long since given up on trying to tame my waves, but Freddie worked magic with his toolkit.

Since my costume designer, Alma, hadn't come to get me yet, I got out of the chair, walking toward Des. Her hairstylist was still working through Des's hair with a curling iron and plenty of product.

"How's it going?" I asked, looking at her in the mirror.

Diego said, "I'm going to need a gas mask next time for all the product. I don't know how George does it."

The hairstylist fanned his hand at Diego. "When you've been doing this as long as I have, you're practically made up of hairspray anyway."

I chuckled, still caught in Des's eyes. Her makeup was intense—it had to be to be seen onstage—but her eyes were still the most captivating part of her appearance. I was convinced they were meant to be seen with show lights in them.

Des said, "I feel so pampered."

I grinned, glad she was enjoying herself. I wanted her to love being on tour with me... and maybe even go on more in the future. But I couldn't let myself get that far ahead. As Dad always said, one day at a time.

Alma stood at my shoulder. "Ready, Jude?"

I nodded.

"Great," she said, then smiled at Des. "I'll be back for you soon."

Des replied, "Looking forward to it!"

I followed Alma away to the racks of clothing, shoes and accessories set up next to makeshift changing rooms.

My favorite color was red, so there were plenty of pops of red amidst the black fabric. She set me up with a pair of ripped black skinny jeans, an oversized red T-shirt, and a pair of black and red high-top sneakers and gestured toward the fitting room.

At this point, my outfits were easy—I wasn't flashy onstage, focusing more on my voice and mobility since a lot of my songs included dance routines as well.

When I came out of the fitting room, I said, "These jeans are a little loose on the hips, Al."

She hooked her fingers in the waistband, nodding, then grabbed something off the rack. "Try this pair."

I went back into the fitting room liking the second pair way more. "Feels good."

"Good." She grabbed a red bandana, weaving it through the rips in my jeans and tying it securely.

"Nice touch," I said, glancing at myself in the mirror.

She gave me a pair of earrings, a belt, and a jacket, and then I was done just as Des came over, her hair equally as stunning as the rest of her.

Alma went to a different rack, pulling out a red dress, thigh-high leather boots, and a leather jacket. I bit my knuckle. I could already picture her wearing that, and I knew it was going to look good.

Seeing her come out of the dressing room, all of my suspicions were confirmed. The dress wasn't too short, but not too long either, giving me a clear view of her thick bronze thighs. The neckline swung low, and I forced my eyes away from her cleavage. Mix that with the leather boots and jacket, and Des looked every bit as dangerously sexy as I already knew she was.

She grinned as she examined herself in the mirror. "I look good."

My smile matched hers. "Exactly what I was thinking."

She looked at me under her lashes and back to Alma. "Do you think it needs anything else?"

Alma tapped her chin, then went back to the jewelry stand. "This necklace." She pulled out a thick black chain with a blood-red ruby on the end and gave it to Des. She lifted it around her neck, trying to clasp it.

"Let me," I said, walking to her and brushing her fingers as I took hold of the necklace.

Des's skin was warm under my fingertips as I hooked the clasp together. Not quite ready to let go yet, I brushed her hair back in place.

Slowly, she turned back to me, looking into my eyes. "What do you think?"

"I think you're absolutely beautiful."

Diego said, "He's right." I'd almost forgotten he was here, but now I could see the look of admiration and respect in his eyes.

From behind me, Angelina said, "Jude, Des, time to warm up vocals."

I nodded and glanced back at Des. "Let's go."

We followed Angelina back to the locker room where steam billowed from the running shower. Luckily our hair and makeup crew knew to use plenty of hairspray and setting powder to make sure the moisture wouldn't ruin our looks. Near the shower was Shantelle, my vocal coach. "Hi, Jude!" Her smile was just as big as her natural curls.

I'd worked with her daily for my first year, and now she was coming once a week to work with me and consult as needed. I couldn't wait for her to meet Des. "Hey!" I said, giving her a hug, then turning to Des. "Des, this is my vocal coach. Shantelle's saved my bacon more than once. She's the best."

Shantelle laughed and held out her hand. "It's great to meet you. I've already heard a lot from Natalie."

At Des's cringe, I said, "Don't worry, Shantelle knows all about Natalie."

"Mhmm," Shantelle said disapprovingly. "But we should get started. Before you know it, it'll be time to go."

For the next half hour, we warmed up our voices. It was clear Des had worked with vocal coaches before. Definitely more than I had when I'd recorded my first album.

The door to the locker room opened, and Angelina poked her head back in. "Five minutes until Des is onstage. Time for the team meeting."

Shantelle turned off the water, and we followed Angelina down the hall, back to the open room beside the stage. There were about fifty people who worked on the tour, and most of them had gone on the last tour with me as well. They were more than show runners—they were family.

As we huddled into a circle, Dad started talking. "Today's the first day of our Summer of Santiago tour. It's great to see so many familiar faces and some new ones as well. Each of you means so much to us."

He looked to me, and that was the cue, my turn to address everyone. I thought back to the first time everyone had swung their heads toward me, waiting for me to lead. I'd been so nervous, worried I'd say the wrong thing. Now, I knew different. They each were better at their jobs, better than I could ever dream to be. They just needed to know that we were all on the same team.

I took a breath and said, "Our first show of the summer is today. It's going to be nonstop performing and moving and doing it all over again for the next three months. It'll be hard and fun and exhausting, and there's no other crew I'd rather do it with. Des, I can't wait to see you shine onstage with the help of the crew. They're the best there is." I smiled around the circle, thankful for each of them.

"Let's take a few moments of silence in gratitude for those fans out there. Close your eyes and listen. Can you hear them talking? Hear the joy in their voices? Picture each of them purchasing tickets to our show, wanting to be a part of the Summer of Santiago." I paused for a few breaths while we listened. Then I said, "Let's give them a great show! Hands in, everyone." I said, and we all packed as closely together as we could, getting our hands close to the center. "One, two, three, SantiaGO!"

TWENTY-THREE
DES

ANGELINA CAME to my side and said, "It's showtime."

She walked Diego and me to the wing of the stage and said, "We're mic-ing you up. Be careful what you say once they're on you. You never know whether they're switched on or not."

I swallowed and nodded, glancing to Diego as my support system. More than ever, I was glad Mom and Dad asked him to come—and that he'd agreed.

He gave me an encouraging smile, and I extended my arms so the audio engineer, a guy with more tattoos than skin visible, could work the cords through my outfit and secure the mic in my ear.

Angelina said, "I'll talk to you through that mic if we need anything."

The engineer said, "The mouthpiece is just there as a backup in case the mic onstage fails. Sing into the mic. Your mouth should be no more than two inches away. If you get too close to the speakers on the side, you'll get feedback."

I nodded, trying to remember every word they said.

"Okay," Angelina said. "You're on in three, two, one... go!"

She gave my shoulder a nudge and Diego said good luck, and... I was under the lights.

Purple and red and white lights panned over me as I walked onto the stage, and the crowd began cheering. My heart swelled—they didn't know who I was, at least most of them probably didn't, and they were cheering for me.

The biggest smile of my life stretched across my face.

I was made for this moment.

I was made to sing.

"Welcome to the Summer of Santiago!" I yelled into the mic, hearing my voice echo all around me and throughout the stadium.

The crowd *roared* with excitement.

"I was talking to Jude earlier, and he said he can't wait to see all your beautiful faces!"

Another cheer swept through the crowd, lifting me even higher. To keep from getting nervous, I kept my eyes unfocused, seeing a blur instead of individual faces. But I could feel myself growing braver by the second.

"While he gets his pretty voice ready, I thought I'd share a few of my favorite songs with you! Are you ready?"

They cheered again, and I waved my hands, growing the energy louder until all I could feel was the noise humming through my veins.

"Let's go!"

A drummer I'd only met yesterday pounded the beat, and a guitarist I'd met at the same time began strumming, and the keyboardist's music played through the speakers.

I sang the opening lines of "Unstoppable" by Sia.

Usually when I sang, it was something like the national anthem or at graduation, giving me only a small space to stand. But now, I had the whole run of a massive stage, and I made use of it, just like we'd practiced during rehearsals the day before.

And it was *fun*, singing close to the guitar player,

Randolph, and then pretending to bang on the drums with Gregory. It was like dancing in the bathroom, swinging my hair around and using my brush for a mic, but with thousands of people singing along.

I sang the last chords of the song, my breath heaving from the effort of singing and moving around, but my adrenaline carried me through to the next song and the song after that.

I knew I was doing exactly what everyone had told me to do: warm up the crowd for Jude's presentation. But there was one last song, and I wanted them to *remember* me. I wanted them to *demand* that I come back.

I danced to the edge of the stage, walking along and touching hands with every person who had their hands extended, and then I saw...

My parents?

They must have flown out here to see me for my first show, and that meant the world.

I smiled big, holding their hands and singing to them. My mom looked so beautiful with her brown hair sprinkled with gray in looping curls. Dad was dressed in his best shirt and dark jeans, gray hair gelled back.

Knowing I had more people to see, I moved on,

only to see my best friends from the Curvy Girl Club. Happy tears streamed down my cheeks as I sang to them and continued down the row, my song—and my time on stage—coming to an end.

"I have a confession to make," I said to the silent crowd. "This is my first time onstage like this, and I want to thank you for making it so incredible."

They cheered loudly, and my tears continued to fall as I took them in, including the people closest to me. They'd traveled across the country to be here, and I didn't even want to know how much front row tickets at a Jude Santiago concert had cost them.

"Thank you, New York! Now, let's see how loud we can cheer and let Jude know we're READY!"

The sound was deafening, but still I said, "He might be all the way back in the dressing room, and the walls are pretty thick! Let's yell louder!"

They began chanting, "JUDE, JUDE, JUDE!"

I grinned and began walking off the stage, but Jude's voice came just as loud over the speakers. "Not so fast, Desirae!"

My lips parted as I turned to the opposite side of the stage, but I didn't see him. Just then, I remembered to look up.

He descended from the air on a suspended platform and easily stepped off it, looking just as much the rock star he was. But he also looked like Jude, and that made butterflies dance in my adrenaline-filled body.

If I'd thought the cheering was loud before, it was earth-shaking now. It wouldn't be a surprise if people could hear the din all the way back home in California.

But Jude didn't have eyes for the crowd. No, with all the girls in the audience, he was looking right at me.

TWENTY-FOUR
JUDE

ON MY LAST TOUR, I listened to beginning singers online before I went onstage. Hearing people sing, who were exactly where I came from, was grounding and inspiring at the same time.

And then I heard her voice.

Des only had a few songs recorded at that time, but she quickly became the only singer I listened to before a concert. Show after show, I had her voice in my ear. That's why I asked Natalie to meet with her, because I knew Des had potential to be incredible. I knew she deserved to be heard.

And her show? Tonight? It proved I was right.

She looked so stunning before me, in a red dress that hugged all her beautiful curves, with her cheeks shining with tears and her hair damp at the roots with sweat.

You were amazing, I mouthed, so the mic wouldn't pick it up.

Her smile was that much brighter under the lights. *Thanks.*

In my ear, I could hear Angelina yelling at Des to get offstage, yelling at me to start the show.

Des began to walk away, but I held her hand. This was *my* show, after all.

"Let's give it up for Desirae De Leon!" I said, holding her hand in the air.

Cheers rang through the crowd, and I turned her shoulders so she could take it all in, see how amazed everyone was by her. Then I spoke into my mic and said, "What do you say Desirae sings, 'Diamonds in Her Eyes' with me? I've always thought it could be an incredible duet."

They yelled even louder, and I grinned at Des. "Do you know the words?"

She smiled confidently. "Of course I know them."

"Good. Let's go." I held her hand, bringing her closer to the front of the stage with me as I sang the opening line. The lightshow played over us, dusting us with sheens of red and purple and white. Out of the corner of my eye, I saw us together on the screen. It was like something out of one of my wildest dreams coming true.

She harmonized with me, her voice blending seamlessly with the music like she'd been meant to sing with me all this time.

I couldn't wait to see Natalie's face after the show. She'd made a *huge* mistake in turning Des down, and now the whole world knew it.

At the bridge of the song, Des and I broke apart, taking separate parts of the stage and engaging with the fans up front. I made sure to pay special attention to her friends and family before moving on.

As the song closed, Des and I came back together, singing the final lyrics. I drew my fingertips along Des's cheeks, feeling the moisture and heat on her skin.

She closed her eyes, releasing a note and a final, shaky breath.

My fans, now fans of her, of us, went *wild*.

In my earpiece, I heard Angelina say, "Okay, can she get offstage now?" Her voice was exasperated, but I could swear she was smiling.

I grinned. Sure, I'd let Des off the stage. As soon as I gave her a hug. My arms wrapped easily around her, but my lips found her cheek of their own accord. I pressed a kiss there and watched her stunned expression as she pulled away. Reveled in the slight smile that formed on her lips.

I wanted to kiss her for real as soon as this show was over, which meant I should probably get to the next song.

I spoke into my mic. "I think that's one of the best performances of 'Diamonds' I've ever done! What do you say?" As the fans cheered, I said, "Now let's get this party started with a dance song I like to call 'Slide Shimmy Shake!'"

TWENTY-FIVE

DES

I HELD my hand to my cheek as I walked offstage, my legs shaking with pure adrenaline and exhaustion.

Angelina patted my back, covering her mouthpiece and yelling, "Good job!" over the speakers.

I only had time to say a quick, "Thank you!" before Diego had me wrapped in his arms and was spinning me around.

"Des!" he shouted. "That was incredible!"

I grinned, feeling in my bones that it had been even better than I'd hoped for. "It was like I was meant to be onstage. It felt like coming home."

He grinned. "You should have seen Natalie's face when Jude kissed you on the cheek. She's pissed. Not that she wasn't before. The better you did, the more her nose scrunched up."

"How much did she see?" I asked, a sinking feeling hitting my gut. I didn't want her to think that I'd started a relationship with Jude. His career, this tour, it was too important.

"She got here and was talking to Angelina right after you went onstage," he said, brushing it off like it was no big deal. "Did you see Mom and Dad?"

I raised my eyebrows. "You knew they were here?"

"It was Jude's idea, but I helped him set up the whole thing," he answered. "I thought Cori was going to blow the secret."

I laughed; that would have been exactly like her. "She didn't say a word. None of them did." A fresh flow of happy tears spilled down my cheeks. I was so grateful my makeup artist had made everything waterproof, or I'd be an even bigger mess right now than I already was. "Thank you so much, Di."

He smiled. "*Con gusto.*" The phrase sounded better in Spanish than it did in English, and it reminded me so much of home. Made me thankful for the piece of home I had with me.

"Will they come backstage after the concert?" I asked.

He nodded. "They have VIP tickets. We'll see them right after, and when Jude finishes the meet-and-greet, he'll hang out with us too. He made late dinner reservations for all of us. Apparently, there's a dessert place in town we can't miss."

I smiled, thinking that plan sounded almost as amazing as what had just transpired. This whole night was like a fantasy.

Diego pulled a chair from a few feet over. "Sit, let's watch the show. Our seats are almost as good as Mom and Dad's." He winked.

I laughed, settling into the canvas chair. From here, it was a completely different experience. I watched all the people rushing around, carrying instruments and equipment on and off stage. Jude's choreography was much more elaborate than I'd ever thought, and I admired how good of shape he must have been in to do those dance moves and sing at the same time.

It seemed like minutes had passed, but soon he was singing his last song and coming offstage. I stepped to the side as everyone around us made to congratulate him on his performance, but soon the crowd became too loud to ignore.

They were chanting something... something that didn't make sense...

"JUDE AND DES! JUDE AND DES! JUDE AND DES!"

I sent Diego a questioning look. Surely I wasn't hearing them right. The speaker volume must have messed with my hearing. Or maybe I was so tired I was delirious.

But before Diego had a chance to answer, Angelina had me by the shoulders and was pushing me to the stage entrance. Jude was already out there, looking for me.

At the sight of me, he said, "Des, it seems like they are in awe of you just as much as I am."

My cheeks flushed as I walked toward him, still wondering how this could even be possible.

"Thank you so much," I said into my mic as I turned toward the audience. "I can't tell you how much this means to me. To every curvy girl who's ever been told she doesn't deserve to be in the spotlight."

They cheered louder for us, and then Jude said, "What do you say, Des? Will you sing one more song with me?"

I nodded. "Absolutely.

"How about we throw it back to my early days? Can you bring out my guitar?" He winked at me. "I'll show you the real me."

One of the stagehands brought out his guitar, and he put the mic in the stand before looping the strap over his shoulder. He used to play his guitar in almost every video he released, but he'd only used it for one song tonight.

A different stagehand gave me a mic and clipped an earpiece over my ear. Angelina said, "Let's give them some magic, you two."

Jude strummed his fingers over the strings. "Des?" he said into the mic.

I gripped my mic with both hands, drawing it to my lips. "Yes, Jude?"

"I'm not sure how long you've been watching me. Do you remember the words to 'Hopeful Hearts'?"

"I do." I almost hated to admit I did, that I'd listened to it enough times to remember each of the words as if they were my own.

His chest rose and fell under the guitar strap with his breath, and he sang the slow opening notes. Most of Jude's concert was upbeat, but there was something sincere about him now, something wholesome and... vulnerable.

We didn't move around the stage. Instead, it was the two of us, under a single spotlight, with ten thousand phone lights shining like stars in the crowd.

And then the song was over and the cheers were deafening, and Jude was leading me off the stage as the lights went dim.

As soon as we were offstage, he wrapped his arms around me and then pulled back, placing his palms on my shoulders. "Des, you were incredible!"

The high of performing had me smiling and blushing and gushing. "Me? You were so good, Jude!"

He smiled. "I've never performed with anyone and felt the things I did with you." His eyes flicked from mine to my lips, and I felt it. A pull inside like an invisible string drawing me closer to him.

His head tilted slightly and he leaned forward, his dark lashes coming together in a thick fringe as his eyes closed.

Every part of me wanted to feel his lips against mine, ride out the wave of this incredible night. Every part except one.

The voice of reason reminded me that Natalie was here and that kissing Jude would cost us both too much.

I turned my cheek, letting his lips fall against my skin in an awkward echo of the way he'd kissed my cheek onstage. When we parted, I barely had a chance to absorb his hurt expression, the way he tried to cover it with a smile, as we were being pulled on to the next part of the show. He had fans to greet, autographs to sign. And me? I had fans of my own to see, thanks to Jude.

TWENTY-SIX

JUDE

I WAS QUICKLY ESCORTED AWAY from the stage, from Des. Dad and Jago walked on one side, Samantha and Natalie on the other. They were taking me to the signing event for fans with special VIP tickets.

"That was a great show, Jude," Samantha said, handing me a bottle of water. "You and Des are going to be the talk of every single tabloid and gossip site tomorrow. Anyone want to take bets that there will be a hashtag with their couple name? Maybe #Desirude?"

"Samantha," Natalie said with an exasperated voice.

"You're right," Samantha said. "It's not right. Juderae? I love that!" She whipped out her phone.

"I'm sending that to my social media girl. It'll be trending by morning."

Dad said, "You two definitely had some stage presence together. Imagine what the fans will think of you with Jade."

"What do you mean?" I asked, swallowing and capping my water bottle. Jade was a mega popstar around my age who'd blown up after winning a TV talent show when she was fourteen years old. I'd never even met her in person.

Natalie clapped her hands together. "*Jade's* interested in performing your original song with you as long as you have final lyrics ready by the show in LA. This is huge, Jude! And can you imagine what fans will think of the two of you together? The number of albums you'll sell with a song featuring Jade..." She put her hand over her heart, as though she actually had one.

"I'm not singing with Jade," I said flatly.

Natalie raised her eyebrows. "And why would that be?"

"Her voice is all wrong. I've already decided I'm singing it with Des."

Dad grunted, clearing his throat. "Son, it's nothing personal against Des. It's about what's best for your career, and tapping into Jade's audience... that would be huge."

Samantha nodded. "Imagine the connections you would make, not just to her audience, but to her colleagues and acquaintances. It could benefit Des as well. Knowing someone like Jade could launch her career."

I bristled. "And knowing me isn't helping her?"

Samantha laughed. "It already is. Did you see her onstage? She was incredible."

"I was there," I said.

Dad patted my back. "Good call on bringing her along, son. You have an eye for what the fans want, and I think with more practice, you'll be well on your way to a lifelong career in this industry."

Gentry stood outside the door to the conference area where I'd be signing autographs and posing for pictures. She wore her makeup belt and had brushes in hand. She quickly touched up my makeup and then Dad said, "Deep breath."

My shoulders rose and fell. Back to business.

DIEGO and I approached a studio with my name hanging on the door. I'd barely gone in there the last two days, but Angelina told us that's where my family and friends would be waiting.

Diego pushed the door open, and we were greeted with our own personal cheering section.

Mom reached me first, nearly knocking me over with the force of her embrace. She hugged me close and kissed my cheeks and ran her hands over my curls. "*Mija. Eres increible.*"

I smiled, rubbing my nose against hers like we always did when I was younger. "I'm so happy you were here to see it."

She hugged me again. "You made us *so* proud." She stepped back, only to let Dad hug me.

He hooked an arm around my shoulders, pulling me close, and then said in my ear, *"Eres la mejor."* He kissed me on my cheek, scratching my skin with his short stubble.

After he let go, my friends surrounded me, trapping me in one big group hug. When we made our way to one of the couches, squeezing in all together, I leaned across them and said, "I can't believe you guys all made it here!"

Cori said, "It was crazy! One second, your brother's texting me and asking me how to spell Coriander, and the next second, we're on a flight—first class, with lie-flat seats, mind you—to New York! We even got picked up from the airport in a stretch limo, Des! It was incredible!"

I grinned, thinking about all the effort that Jude and even Diego had put in to make sure the people I loved most were here for me. "What about you, Faith? Did you ride the train here?"

She shook her head. "He flew me in too. I landed just a little before them."

I wiped at my face, which had been wet pretty much from my first moment onstage. "This night has been so perfect. I knew I wanted to sing, but this was so much... more than anything I imagined it would be."

Nadira said, "You were exactly where you're meant to be, Des. Seeing you onstage was like watching a fish swim. It was so *natural*."

Tatiana nodded in agreement. "I've never seen a dancer with so much stage presence. You could give lessons."

I smiled at her. "It just came to me to do it that way," I admitted. "I guess singing the national anthem two hundred times really paid off."

They laughed, and then Adriel said, "But what about Jude? I can't believe he was so generous to us."

Cori held her hands over her heart. "And that last song onstage? It was so heartfelt. That can't be acting."

My lips tugged down, and I glanced over to make sure my parents were still talking to Diego. They were, but I still lowered my voice and said, "He tried to kiss me, after the show."

The girls went nuts, effectively ruining our cover. My parents came over, and Mom said, "What are we excited about?"

Cori opened her mouth to speak, but I said, "Dessert. It's going to be so good."

Mom clapped her hands together. "It sounds like it. But I'm dying to know..." She sat on the coffee table in front of the couch. "How has Jude behaved? Has he tried making a pass at you?"

My cheeks went red. "Mom."

"What?" she asked. "I need to make sure my baby girl is safe."

Still feeling heat in my face and now neck, I said, "Jude's been a perfect gentleman, Mom. But there is something..." I didn't know why I hadn't told anyone up until now, but I needed advice.

"What is it?" Cori asked.

"When they picked us up, Natalie took me aside, and she told me that if I pursued a romantic relationship with Jude, there would be... consequences for him."

"Consequences?" Mom asked. Now Dad and Diego were listening too.

"She threatened his career."

Diego seemed horrified. "Des, I had no idea. I would have discouraged him."

"From what?" I asked, my eyebrows drawing together.

"Well, Jude, he kind of asked my advice," Diego admitted. At the questioning look in all of our eyes, he continued, "He asked me what kind of flowers you liked and wanted to make sure you answered the door so he could be the one to give them to you.

And I'm thinking he doesn't give every opening act the star treatment by flying in their entire family and giving them front row seats."

After the thrill of realizing that Jude could like me... I sagged. "This isn't good."

Dad put his hand on my shoulder. "We'll call Manuel. Have a plan in place in case Natalie decides to try something."

I nodded slowly. "Sorry, I didn't want to bring up any drama tonight. Let's just focus on the show." I flipped my hair over my shoulder. "Wasn't I amazing?"

Cori giggled and hugged me. "There's my girl."

MY HAND HURT like it always did in a meet-and-greet, but my chest ached more. I felt like Des and I had made a real connection onstage, but when I'd tried to kiss her, she just turned away. Had I misread the signs? Had being famous made me so bold I thought I could kiss whoever I wanted?

Either way, my pride was more than a little wounded, and we were scheduled to have dessert with her and her family at one of the most romantic restaurants in the whole of New York City.

I'd been so excited to spend time with her parents and meet her friends who Diego had described as "tighter than Charlie's Angels." But now I wondered what she had told them about me.

Did they think I was some kind of weirdo, coming on to girls who weren't interested in me?

I decided I would pull Des aside at the restaurant and apologize, promise to keep things strictly professional between us. And did I mention I'd apologize? Surely she'd understand, maybe allow me a little wiggle room since we were both coming off such an amazing show together.

It would be fine, I reassured myself, only half believing it.

I finished changing into jeans that weren't sweaty and a fresh shirt, then slipped on my sneakers and reapplied my deodorant and cologne. Dad and Jago met me in the hall, and we walked to the next studio with Des's name framed in lights. I could hear voices coming softly from under the door, and I had to fight the urge to listen for my name. Instead, I knocked.

Des answered the door, dressed now in a romper that showed off her legs. They were quickly becoming my favorite asset of hers.

"Hey," I said, my cheeks heating. Didn't my wandering thoughts know I was supposed to be keeping things professional? I awkwardly jerked my thumb over my shoulder. "Ready to go?"

She nodded and looked over her shoulder. "Can you grab my purse, Mom?"

Delfina picked up a purse from the desk and followed behind her. As soon as Delfina reached me, she gave me a tight hug. It dislodged something in my chest, made my throat tighten.

I wondered if my mom would have hugged me that way if she were still alive. If she would have been as proud of me as Delfina looked of Des tonight.

She backed away and said, "Thank you, thank you, thank you." Her eyes shone with tears. "We wanted to come, but the show was all sold out." She wiped at a stray tear and smiled. "Now I know why. It was *magnifico*."

I grinned, already feeling relieved. At least Des's mom didn't think I was a total jerk. "I'm so glad you could make it. Des deserved to be seen."

My dad clapped my shoulder and said, "Good to see you all again. I just got word the limo's ready for us!"

We all followed Jago out a back doorway surrounded by fences and security and got in the stretch limo. All of us fit comfortably and had plenty of room to move and talk. Des sat across from me, but she wouldn't meet my eyes no matter how many glances I sent her way.

I just hoped I hadn't ruined everything between us. It would be a long tour if I had.

As we approached the restaurant, Jago said, "The paparazzi are out. Put your heads down and keep walking."

I nodded, knowing I'd follow whatever instructions he gave me. Jago had my back, had protected me since I was a dumb seventeen-year-old riding around the country on my first tour.

The driver stopped the car and opened the door for us. Jago got out first, and he was right. I could already see cameras flashing around the roped entrance to the restaurant.

He ushered out Des's family and friends, letting them pass, then Diego and Jago flanked Des and me as we made the short walk.

Her shoulder brushed against mine, making my skin heat under my T-shirt. I liked being this close to her. I just wished she wanted the same thing.

All around us, the paparazzi shouted questions, wondering if we were dating, if we were in love, what to look out for in the future. At Jago's instruction, we continued through the front doors and entered a lit waiting area.

We rode an elevator up to the top floor, and when we stepped into the restaurant, the world was a different place.

Flickering votive candles lit most of the restaurant, a combination of tables and couches and chairs with a panoramic view of sparkling city lights out floor-to-ceiling windows. It made me feel like a small-town kid again, in awe of the big city and the places my music could take me.

A maître d' seated us at a long set of two-person tables right at the window. Dad, Jago, and I ended up in a middle table, surrounded by all of Des's friends and family. There was so much love between them. Being sandwiched in the middle of it all only reminded me how much I was missing this.

They all introduced themselves, and I did my best to remember their names. Cori was the redhead. Nadira had a contagious smile, Adriel carried herself like a dancer, and Faith had beautiful, big blue eyes. Tatiana was the only thin girl among them, but she didn't act superior to any of them.

Faith turned those eyes on me, and with a smile, said, "This view is absolutely stunning! Thank you so much for taking us here!"

I smiled back at her and said, "You're welcome. I try to come here every time I'm in town."

"I can see why," she replied.

A server came and took our order, cutting conversation short for a time. After Des finished ordering, I leaned over and quietly asked her if she could come speak with me.

She nodded, still not quite meeting my eyes, and whispered something to her mom before following me away from the table.

While she walked behind me, I tried to steady my nerves. I could perform live in front of thousands of people, but for some reason, when it came to Des...

We reached the hallway to the bathrooms, and there wasn't really anywhere else to go. No longer walk to give me time to figure out what I was going to say. So, I took a breath and decided to put it all out there, hoping we had a chance of clearing the air.

"Des, I'm sorry about earlier," I said quickly.

She blinked. "What?"

"The kiss—it was clear you didn't want it, and I absolutely didn't mean to force it on you. I... I shouldn't have."

She shook her head quickly. "Jude, it's not that."

Now I was confused. "What?"

"It's not that I didn't want you to kiss me," she said slowly, breaking her gaze from mine on the word kiss.

But my mind was tripping over something else. "You *wanted* to kiss me?" I'd felt so rejected and embarrassed only moments ago, but now? I was very aware of the fact that no one had walked past us. We were as alone as we could be in this restaurant.

"It's..." She paused, turning her eyes skyward. "Complicated."

"How so?"

She studied me. "I signed an NDA."

"And?" I said. "What does that have to do with us?"

"Everything."

TWENTY-NINE

DES

I WASN'T the kind of girl who stayed silent, not during the good times, and certainly not in the bad. But there was nothing more than I could say that wouldn't hurt us both.

Because the truth was, I *had* wanted to kiss him. I'd been so high after the show, flooded with adrenaline and joy and pure emotion over the guy who'd helped make it happen.

He didn't have to invite me on tour. He easily could have written me off as just another girl who didn't take it to the top. Instead, he saw something wrong, reached out, and pulled me to the top with him.

That was exactly the kind of guy I wanted to

date. (His incredible voice, beautiful eyes, and chiseled abs didn't hurt either.)

But Natalie had ensured that couldn't happen.

And that made me sadder than I cared to admit.

Instead of going right back to the table, I went to the bathroom and splashed my face with water. When I got back, the desserts and drinks were already on the tables.

I was worried about how Jude would react when I arrived at the table, but he was deep in conversation with Faith.

"And you all would hang out at your grandma's house and make quilts?" he asked.

Faith nodded. "The ladies made at least one a year for children in the hospital, and sometimes they would make some for their friends and families, and of course new babies."

"Of course," Jude said. "My grandma was a tailor for wedding gowns and bridesmaid dresses, so I was around sewing all the time. She used to make me put on the dresses so she could fit them on a body." He chuckled. "I'd make sure the front door was locked and all the curtains were drawn before I ever stepped on the podium."

Anthony laughed, love and joy in his eyes. "You

would have done it just to get those popcorn balls." He explained, "My mom made the best popcorn balls, and she put candy corn in them because Jude was the only one who would eat it. Every time he tried on a dress, he got one."

Jude smiled. "I miss her popcorn balls."

"Maybe when we get off the tour, we can ask her to mail some."

"Maybe," Jude said, looking down at his bowl of berries. I'd ordered the same thing, since Shantelle said we should avoid sweets or dairy while we were on tour to help save our voices. We had shows scheduled almost every night, with only a few days off. I'd never done anything so strenuous, but Jude said the effort wore on your throat over time.

"What about you, Cori?" Jude asked. "Des said you're playing basketball in college? What are you studying?"

Cori swallowed her bite of ice cream that looked a million times better than my fruit. "I have absolutely no idea." She shrugged, dipping her spoon back through her chocolate ice cream. "I don't really know what I want to do for the rest of my life. I have fun playing basketball, and I think a degree just gets your foot in the door. And most people change majors, so it might not matter too much right now."

"That's a good point," Jude said. "Dad, do you remember that one guy? Grant? He had a mental breakdown trying to decide which college to go to."

"Oh yeah," Anthony said, stroking his chin. "He went to some ivy league school, didn't he?"

"MIT!" Jude said. "You might see him, Nadira!"

Cori laughed. "Definitely. I bet he's the kind that hangs out in the library, just like Dira."

Nadira rolled her eyes at Cori, and I laughed.

I loved watching Jude with my friends. He seemed to fit with them so well, not because he was a rock star, but because he was kind. Here was a guy who'd probably been on every continent and worked with tons of famous people, and he was asking my friends questions about *their* lives. Swoon.

On my left, Tatiana nudged me and mouthed, *I like him.*

Me too, I thought. And that was a problem.

In the morning, my parents left on an early flight so they could get back to my siblings, but my friends came over to my suite, and we ordered room service for breakfast. A big spread was on our table now, full of eggs and breakfast meat, potatoes, and plenty of fruit. We sat in our robes and drank orange juice from champagne glasses while Diego was in the hotel gym working out.

Cori grinned at me and said, "I think I could get used to this."

"Room service is amazing," I agreed.

"No," she replied. "Being friends with a rock goddess."

I laughed, taking another sip. "You know I'll always be a California girl with stars in her eyes."

Adriel said, "It's inspiring, really. Seeing you onstage makes me want to chase my dreams too."

"Agreed," Nadira said. "Except I'll do it in the library. Not in front of a bunch of people."

Faith held up her juice and said, "Hear, hear."

Cori said, "Wait... what is that?"

I followed her eyes to the giant bouquet of roses on the coffee table in front of the couch. I was still sad I'd have to leave them here, since there was hardly room for them on the bus and I didn't want to draw attention.

"Who sent you these?" She got up and walked to them. "There have to be at least fifty here!"

I almost lied, but it was no use. She knew me better than I knew myself half the time. "Jude brought them over to wish me luck before the show."

Cori turned from the flowers, back to me, an overly pleased smile on her face.

"Stop looking at me like that," I said, my cheeks getting hot.

"He brought them to your room?" she said.

I became very interested in the fruit on my plate. "Yeah."

Tatiana leaned forward, eyeing me closely. "He didn't have them delivered? It's an important distinction."

I looked at her incredulously. "Yes, he brought them himself. What's the big deal?"

"That means he likes you! A guy like Jude could have paid anyone to bring them, no big deal, but he personally delivered them because he wanted to see you!" Tatiana clapped her hands together excitedly. "I knew you would fall in love with a rock star!"

I shook my head. "First of all, it's Jude, not just some rock star."

She smiled bigger.

"And second of all, there are a million and one reasons why we can't be in love."

"Like?" Cori pressed, and I could practically see all my friends lean in.

"Like the fact that I signed an NDA saying I wouldn't talk negatively about Songbird or Jude's future projects? Natalie threatened Jude's career if he started anything romantic with me. The only reason I'm telling you guys is because I'd trust you with my life."

Nadira frowned. "That's awful."

I nodded.

Cori said, "So if something goes wrong, you're really just expected to stay quiet about it? That's not you."

"It isn't," I agreed. "And neither is not going out with a guy I like. But I can't. I'd just worry the whole time that something could go wrong with Jude's career. And if Natalie's not bluffing, it's not just Jude I'd hurt. Trust me, no guy is worth all that drama."

An alarm went off on Nadira's phone, and she hurried to turn off the shrill noise.

"What's that for?" I asked, glancing at my own phone. I didn't need to leave the hotel for another hour.

"We need to get dressed and head for the airport," she explained.

Cori nudged Nadira. "She'd never let us get there late."

I laughed, despite the sinking feeling in my stomach. It had felt so good to have them here, to talk things out with them. But now it was back to business, back to the tour, back to my first taste of life as a working musician.

Back to the boy who could never be more than the person who helps me rise to fame.

THIRTY

JUDE

THE BUS PULLED in front of the hotel lobby, exhaust drifting out the tailpipe. Vanessa's car with the teardrop trailer idled behind the bus, ready to go.

Our crew got on the bus, saying hi to Francie as we did. Jago sat with Dad at the dining table, Diego and Des went to the couch, and I sat with them, still feeling confused and awkward about the night before.

Francie called back and said, "Everyone ready to go?"

From outside the bus, Natalie yelled, "WAIT FOR US."

We all looked as she and Samantha got on the bus. Natalie carried a stack of newspapers and magazines. She marched to the table and slammed down one at a time between Dad and Jago. I stood, walking closer to read the headlines.

WILL JUDE ADD TO HER BODY COUNT?

JUDE'S NEW ACT HAS AN ACT OF HER OWN.

WHO IS DES DE LEON? AN EX TELLS ALL.

JUICY DEETS ON JUDE'S NEW OPENING ACT.

My stomach quickly sank to new lows. The tabloids had gotten a hold of Des this quickly? I glanced over my shoulder, hoping she hadn't come over yet so I could shield her somewhat from the vitriol, but she was already looking at the table, scowling.

Natalie slapped the last one down and said, "That's not even the tip of the iceberg. All the gossip sites and the Fantiagos are raging about it on social. They're saying Des's just going to burn and turn Jude." Natalie lifted her gaze toward Des, not slowing her rampage one bit. "What do you have to say for yourself?"

Des raised her eyebrows, her expression dangerous. "What do I have to say for myself?"

Samantha stepped forward, holding her hands between Natalie and Des. "Hold on. I think the important thing here is that Des knows now, so she's not blindsided on social media or when friends call her." She faced Des, blocking Natalie fully. "Are you okay, honey?"

I held my breath, waiting for her answer.

Des was quiet for a moment. "I don't even know what's going on. What are they saying about me?"

"My media monitor says they got a few interviews with Desirae's ex-boyfriends. One was especially... vicious. They typically say things like Des didn't take their relationship seriously or that she was more focused on friends and school than she was on them. But the media is making it out like Des is loose and that Jude's in danger of falling for someone who won't love him back."

Samantha was as gentle as she could be, but her straightforward, simplified version was still a lot for someone to hear, especially when they weren't used to being in the public eye. I watched Des, trying to see how she felt. Behind her, Diego's face was pale and just as worried as mine probably looked.

Des shrugged and said, "I don't see the problem."

The entire bus was silent, and Natalie's face changed to colors of red never seen before.

A stunned Samantha said, "What do you mean?"

"I mean," Des said, her voice growing clearer,

"if I was a man, this wouldn't be a big deal to any of you, or the media. I would get branded as a playboy troubadour and the world would keep spinning. Honestly, Natalie, your misogyny's showing." There was a small smirk on Des's lips that made me like her even more.

Samantha laughed, clapping her hands together. "If you decide singing's not for you, you have a place at my firm." She pulled out her phone and held it to her ear. "I'm calling our press person, and we'll get that going. Maybe we can even get Des some interviews on sex-positive women's empowerment to help promote the tour."

Natalie's jaw was clenched as she said, "Great. Samantha, we should get off the bus so they can get on the road."

As soon as they left the bus, Jago extended his fist, and Des tapped her knuckles to his. Diego did the same, and I did too.

Dad said, "I'm impressed, Des. It takes a lot to stop Natalie when she's on a roll like that."

Des shook her head. "I knew I couldn't have such a great night without some skeletons coming up the next day."

Tapping his nose, Dad said, "Smart. We were caught off guard the first time it happened to Jude."

I remembered that. A reporter had crawled around our hometown, and when they couldn't find much of a story, they went to the newspaper archives, digging up information on my mother and how she'd passed. I'd thrown up after seeing the headlines. Dad's eyes had been red for days.

From the driver's seat, Francie said, "Everyone ready?"

We gave her the go-ahead, and the bus pulled away from the hotel. We only had a couple hours to drive, and then we'd be at the new venue, checking out the setup of the stage and doing a quick rehearsal before it was time to perform again.

Diego had started up the console, but Des walked to the stack of magazines.

"What are you doing?" I asked.

She held them to her chest. "If I'm going to have an interview, I need to know what they're saying."

"Do you want help?" I asked. I could have cared less what dirt the media had dug up on her —I knew first-hand that half the "sources" that came forward were just hungry for their fifteen minutes of fame—but I didn't want her to be alone in this.

She seemed to hesitate. "Fine." She held out

half the magazines, but when I grabbed them, she held on. "Don't you judge me," she said.

"Don't worry, I've seen it all before, mostly said about me." I took my half of the stack, and we sat cross-legged on the floor, flipping through the stack, while Diego played video games.

About five minutes in, Des muttered, "That rat."

I raised my eyebrows.

In response, she shook her head. "Devon. He was so mad I didn't want to be his *girlfriend*." She rolled her eyes. "How good of a girlfriend would I have been to him on this tour? Huh?"

"Exactly," I said. "It's hard to date when you're constantly traveling. And don't even get me started about meeting someone for long enough to develop a relationship, much less maintain it."

"Yes! I didn't want to be on this *incredible* tour and spend the entire time worrying about what's going on in Emerson. And *why* would I want to leave a guy at home who'd probably get bored and meet someone new in three weeks anyway?"

"You're wrong about that," I said.

"What do you mean?"

I smiled at her. "You're the kind of girl a guy waits for."

THIRTY-ONE

DES

JUDE'S WORDS were such a contrast to the ones on the page before me. I believed what I said to Natalie, but at the same time, reading about my history made me sick. How could they take a fun social life and twist it to be something gross? I'd gone from a girl who dated around to being slut-shamed on national media.

I gave him a grateful smile and faced the magazine again, reading the interview Devon had with *HOT BEATS* magazine.

Desirae De Leon has been making headlines as Jude Santiago's new opening act. Their chemistry onstage was undeniable, which makes us wonder if there's more to their performance than meets the eye. We got in touch with Desirae's most recent boy toy, and here's what he had to say.

Q: Hi, Devon. It's great talking to you today. We've heard that you dated Desirae De Leon recently. When did your relationship begin?

A: We started dating this spring, even went to prom together, and as soon as she got invited on the tour, she dropped me like old news. I guess she thought she could do better than me once she got to be around Jude.

Q: Interesting. And how close were you two? Casual acquaintances or... more, if you know what I mean.

A: Definitely more. Des was the best in, well, you know. It was like she had me under a spell or something.

Q: And you said she'd dated plenty of guys from your college before you?

A: Oh yeah, she was always at the house parties hanging on some different guy's arm. I thought maybe things were different with me, but apparently not.

Q: Did she ever talk about her career aspirations when you were together?

A: Not that we did much talking, but yeah. She liked to sing, and she was always replying to comments from her followers. It got annoying, like, put down the phone already.

Q: And did she talk about Jude Santiago?

A: She always sang his songs when they came on. She definitely has a thing for him.

Q: She broke it, didn't she? Your heart.
A: Into a million pieces.

The interview ended there, and good thing too because I was about to vomit in my mouth. They made it sound like I was some kind of sex-crazed hussy, as if that somehow invalidated my talents or my performance with Jude.

I got out my phone and began searching through the contacts.

"What are you doing?" Jude asked.

"Calling him," I said, standing up.

He reached for my phone. "Oh no you don't."

"Diego!" I cried, pulling it away. "Do your bodyguard thing."

With an evil smile, Diego quickly pinned back Jude's arms.

Jude glared between the two of us. "I hate you both."

"Uh huh," I replied, the phone already ringing.

Devon picked up within a few rings and said, "Miss me, baby?"

"Grow up," I said. "What the hell were you thinking, talking to the press about me?"

Some guys laughed in the background, one of

the many reasons I'd dumped him. He was always surrounded by his band of stupid meatheads.

"Am I on speakerphone?" I demanded.

More laughing.

"Devon, so help me, if you keep talking to the pre—"

Jude broke free from Diego and grabbed my phone, pressing end.

"Hey!" I protested. "I was just starting my lecture!"

He waved the phone. "Rule number one of being famous? Don't give them more material to work with."

I glared at him, but it only took me a few minutes to realize he was right. Next thing I knew, Devon would have a recording airing on *Good Morning America* of me chewing him out.

"Fine," I said, extending my palm.

He held the phone over my hand, but then wrapped his fingers around mine. "My advice? Find someone to call and vent to when you get mad. That way, your words don't go farther than you want them to."

From behind Jude, Diego said, "Not it."

"As if," I said, taking my phone back. The girls

would do that for me—if they weren't already on a plane back home.

Anthony's phone rang, and he nodded and then said, "Okay, I'll let her know." With a smile, he hung up and said, "Looks like we're going on the news."

As we drove through the outskirts of Philadelphia, my phone rang with a call from my mom, and I held the screen out to Diego.

His face went white. "She's going to be so worried."

I frowned. "It'll be okay," I said to him more than me and answered the phone.

"Mom?"

"Honey. Are you okay? I've seen the news. I'm so sorry. I would go and smack that boy if I knew where he lived. I—"

"Mom," I said, "slow down. It's okay."

"Let me talk to Anthony," she demanded.

Slowly, I extended the phone toward Anthony.

He glanced at it as if it were a snake, then painstakingly extended his hand. "I'll handle it."

He held the phone to his ear, and Mom's voice

was so loud I could hear her. "YOU WERE SUPPOSED TO TAKE CARE OF MY BABY. WHY IS SHE BEING SLUT-SHAMED ON NATIONAL MEDIA? WHAT ARE YOU GOING TO DO ABOUT IT?"

Wincing, Anthony held the phone away from his face. "I can see why you're upset, but this is a part of the job."

"UPSET?" Mom yelled. "I'M LIVID! DO YOU KNOW HOW PRECIOUS THAT GIRL IS TO ME?"

My cheeks were growing redder by the second.

Anthony said, "Just as precious as Jude is to me." Before Mom could respond, he hurried up and added, "We already have a plan on how to spin it in her favor. You'll be able to watch Des on TV!"

Anthony was quiet for a moment. "Yeah, you know Winnie Winters... She's having Des on to talk about body positivity, and Samantha Stone herself will prep Des for the interview. It's going to be great... Yeah, here you go."

He handed the phone back to me, and I gave him an impressed look. That was possibly the fastest I'd seen someone calm my mom down in my entire life.

"Mom?" I asked into the phone.

"Honey, I'm worried about you. I don't want to go back to how things were with Luke."

The name made my stomach drop. "Mom, they won't. I promise."

"I can get your therapist to do telehealth with you. Maybe a checkup would do you some good," she said.

I appreciated her concern, but I wasn't going back there. "I'll be okay...but did you talk to our lawyer yet?"

"We called him last night," Mom said. "Manuel says that Natalie's threat is within the realm of the NDA. I wouldn't tell anyone outside of your friends or our family."

"And the..." I walked back toward my bunk, hoping for some privacy.

Fortunately, my mom understood the meaning. "Manuel said she'd be crazy to tank Jude's career. Most agents have sunset clauses with their clients, so she'll earn a percentage for a year or two even after he finds a new agent. *La bruja* is probably just trying to scare you to keep you miserable. I wouldn't be surprised if she was the one who found Devon in the first place."

"But no one said she's not crazy," I replied. I

thought I'd be relieved to hear news like that, but when it came to Natalie... I didn't trust her.

"Des," Diego said.

"Yeah?" I called back.

"We're here."

"Mom," I said into the phone. "I've gotta go."

"I'll see you on TV," she replied. "Love you, love you, love you."

"Love you more." I hung up the phone and walked back to the lounge of the bus.

When we parked behind the concert venue in Philadelphia, a car was waiting to take Diego and me to a news station for my first interview while Jude walked through his portion of the show.

I got off the bus, walking toward the black car with tinted windows, but Jude gently held my arm. I turned, looking up at him with questions in my eyes.

"Don't look at the cameras," he said. "Just focus on the reporter. They'll try to surprise you, but you're too good for that. Stay focused on your message." A gust of wind blew my hair into my face, but before I could sweep it away, he reached up and brushed it off my forehead, tucking it behind my ear. "You're going to do great."

"Thank you." I smiled, trying to ignore the fluttering in my stomach at the simple touch. Guys didn't touch me that way, so gently, carefully, as if I were something that could be broken.

He nodded, then gave Diego a two-finger wave. "Take care of her."

"Jago's taught me well," Diego said, giving Jago a fist bump.

Samantha got out of the black car, still talking on her phone, and waved us in. Diego and I sat in the back, and as we drove away, I watched Jude walk with his team into the concert venue.

Samantha finished her call and twisted so she could see us in the back seat. She handed me a sheet of paper and said, "Here are your talking points, although I have a feeling you'd do just fine on your own."

I lifted the corners of my lips, then looked down at the sheet. It was filled with one-liners I could slip in during the interview.

I love working with Jude because he's been so supportive from the moment I first met him. I wouldn't be here without him.

The sex-positive movement is important to me. I want girls and women to feel comfortable in their bodies.

Men and women can both enjoy sex. It's time we stop

stigmatizing women for enjoying the same things men are lauded for.

"Some of it's a little over the top," I said, studying the paper, "but I'll be sure to stay on message."

"Good girl," Samantha said. "Diego, you'll stick with me off camera. Should be pretty straightforward."

He nodded. "We should probably tell Mom and Dad which channel to watch. They'd love to see Des on TV."

"Good idea!" Samantha said. "It's Winnie Winters's show. And they're planning on airing it live!"

I raised my eyebrows. "A live interview?"

Samantha nodded. "And she thinks she's the next Oprah, so she wants to give away some tickets for the concert at the show."

"There will be an audience?" I asked.

"Yeah, but you're not stage shy," Samantha said, sending a wink my way.

Of course I wasn't shy when I was singing—I knew what I was doing. But talking on body positivity and relationships to complete strangers? I'd only ever done that with my friends, and I just gave my opinion to them. Now it was going to be live on national television and to a studio audience?

I tipped my head down, paying more attention to the talking points than I had before. Too soon, we were pulling up to the news station and Samantha was leading me inside.

A receptionist told us to wait in the green room, but when we got there, the room wasn't green at all. The walls were white with a purple KWTN logo in a repeating pattern on the wall.

In the corner, there was a giant table of snacks, which Diego started picking over.

"Are you always hungry?" I asked, my nerves strung tight.

"Just between meals," he retorted.

How he could eat right now was beyond me. I paced back and forth, trying to picture myself doing well. It would be fine. Hadn't Samantha said she'd hire me at her firm? Maybe it was just an off-handed comment, but coming from her, that had to mean something.

Right?

Someone came in to do my makeup, and before I knew it, we were standing on the eaves of the stage, getting ready to go on.

Winnie Winters sat in her plush chair onstage,

two empty chairs beside her. She must be planning an interview with a couple after me.

She crossed her legs and had her cup of coffee in both hands. "Desirae De Leon has been gracing headlines since her appearance last night as the opening act for Jude Santiago's Summer of Santiago tour. They're traveling across the United States together this summer, sources say, on the very same bus, which has brought questions from the Fantiagos about who exactly Desirae De Leon is and what her intentions are with our sweet Jude Santiago.

"I'd like to welcome Desirae to the stage, along with Vanessa Cooper, the head of the Fantiagos."

My body froze, and I turned to Samantha. Had she known Vanessa was going to be here?

Samantha gave a slight shake of her head and nudged me onto the stage.

I STARED at my phone in disbelief. What was Vanessa doing on the interview with Des?

This couldn't be good.

Dad beckoned me over to the stage, signaling our water break was over, but I waved him to me. "What's this?"

Dad looked over my shoulder at the phone. "Want me to hook it to the screen?"

I nodded. "But hurry," I said, not wanting to miss any of the interview.

Dad tapped on the screen until the picture on my phone appeared in front of us.

A few of the other dancers and I gathered around the screen, staring at Des and Vanessa with

Winnie between them, set up like the announcer in a boxing ring.

I'd done an interview with Winnie before, back when I was just starting to break out, and I remember her being one of the bubbliest, fakest people I'd ever met. Now was no different. She sat on the edge of her chair with her legs crossed and her pointy heels showing like they were ready to stab someone with the spiky tips.

Winnie said, "So, Desirae, there's been quite a stir about you in the media." She tapped her finger like she was about to boop Des on the nose. Good thing she didn't, because Des would have snapped her finger off. "What do you have to say about the rumors?"

Des shrugged. "That they're true."

Murmurs sounded throughout the crowd, and with a predatory smile, Winnie said, "So it *is* true that you use guys and move on to the next like picking up a new piece of chewing gum. Things are so progressive these days. My mama would have had a heart attack."

Des kept a smile on her lips, but I could see the heat in her eyes. "I date around, yes, and there's absolutely nothing wrong with that. Men and women can both enjoy consensual sex. It's time we stop stigmatizing women for doing the same things men are lauded for."

The guy next to me clapped, and I put my hands together too. Des definitely won a point.

"Vanessa," Winnie said, "the Fantiagos have been very concerned on social media about Jude's heart in all of this. As you get a backstage pass to his shows, what do you see happening between Jude and Desirae?"

"First of all," Vanessa said, fluffing her ponytail, "it's so great to be in the room with another Fanti-ago! Fantiago cheer!"

Vanessa, Winnie, and every member in the audience did the cheer, "Fantiagos FOREVER!" There was a special dance that went along with the cheer that made me cringe every time.

Vanessa's ear-to-ear grin turned solemn, and she said, "You know, we're very concerned about Jude's heart. He puts his all into everything he does, whether it's music, interacting with us fans, or his love life."

The dancer on my left, Paul, teased, "What love life?"

I hit his side, waiting for the part of the train wreck coming next.

"Obviously they have chemistry," Vanessa

continued. "We've seen that onstage, but what the Fantiagos don't know is that on the tour, Jude and Desirae have gone on long walks *by themselves*. Who knows what's happening during those rendezvous."

An *ooh* went throughout the crowd, and I found my cheeks getting hot.

"And after the show, Jude tried to kiss Desirae, but she offered him her cheek."

Utter pandemonium was now breaking out, and the camera panned around the room, showing everyone's shocked faces.

Now the camera was back on Winnie, who was leaning over to Des and asking, "Are these things true?"

"Yes, but—" Des began.

"Wow," Winnie said. "There you have it. A spurned singer seeing Diamonds in Des's Eyes when all she sees is another notch in her bedpost. Tsk tsk tsk. When we get back from break, we'll ask Des more about her future in singing and things we can look forward to in the Summer of Santiago!"

The screen cut to a commercial for a pill of some sort, but I couldn't hear the words because I was livid. I turned to my dad, my vision clouded, and gritted out, "What the hell was that?"

Even Dad's usually calm face had an air of

confusion on it. "When Natalie called me about the interview, she didn't mention Vanessa would be there too."

"Natalie?" I said. "I thought Samantha set up the interview."

Dad shook his head. "Apparently Natalie pulled some strings with Winnie's network."

Dad didn't need to say anymore. With Natalie involved, no wonder Des had been played. I stormed away from the stage, knowing I'd need to have this conversation in private.

pp

I STORMED off stage as the commercials rolled, ignoring Vanessa and Winnie giggling together. They were clearly getting some sort of sick satisfaction about catching me off guard and making me out to be a sexual deviant bent on destroying Jude.

But when I reached Samantha to question her, Diego was already laying into her.

"What the hell was that?" he demanded. "There's no reason Des should have gone out there if they were just going to gang up on her like some kind of witch-hunt."

"I agree," Samantha said, her eyes troubled. "Natalie set it up, and this is never the kind of position we want to put our clients in. We always want to be more prepared than this."

From behind us, a cameraman called, "Ninety seconds to air."

"Let's go," I said. "We don't need to hang around for this."

Samantha quickly shook her head. "No, if you leave now, it'll just add fuel to their fire, make them think they're right."

"So, what?" I asked. "I'm supposed to sit around and let them cut me off and position me as Jude Santiago's downfall on national television?"

Samantha squared her shoulders, facing me. "Desirae De Leon. You are *done* playing small. You're going to get up there and do what you do best. You're going to put Winnie and that groupie in their place, just like you did with Natalie this morning."

"Thirty seconds!" the cameraman called.

Samantha turned my shoulders so I was facing the stage and said, "You can do this."

I glanced at Diego, and he nodded, then patted my arm.

They were right. I could do this. I marched back to the set where Winnie and Vanessa were yakking with each other like a pair of hyenas.

I gave them a smile just as big and fake as Winnie's and sat in my chair. I didn't cross my legs or fold my arms or touch my neck. No, I squared my shoulders and sat up and took up space, exactly like I deserved to do.

The cameraman counted down, and the crowd cheered. "Welcome back! We were just talking to Desirae about her past and our precious Jude's heart."

"Exactly," I said, standing up. I wasn't going to be cut off this time. "And I was about to say how thankful I am Winnie called me on her show today. It's not every day someone gets to talk about sex positivity. I want every girl in this audience, every girl watching in their living room, to know exactly how precious you are. How powerful you are. However you choose to express yourself is no one's choice but your own. But how you choose to treat other women is."

I gave Winnie and Vanessa a pointed look. The crowd began clapping, and Winnie tried to cut in, but I continued. "And because we women lift each other up, Winnie, Vanessa, and I are teaming up in the name of body positivity and female empowerment and gifting every member of the studio audience a ticket to Jude Santiago's show, in Philadelphia, tonight!"

The crowd grew even louder, and I grinned ear-to-ear. When I glanced to the wings, Samantha and Diego were smiling just as big.

Winnie clapped her hands together and said, "We're all Fantiagos today! Up next..."

As soon as I walked offstage, Diego wrapped me in a hug, picking me up and spinning me around. "You got her!" he cheered. "That was amazing!"

Samantha gave me a satisfied look. "That was exactly what I was talking about. Let's go. I have to get you to rehearsals."

I could hear the show continuing behind us, but as we walked farther from the noise, the win of what just happened settled in.

I realized I *could* do this. I could really be a star.

DAD FOLLOWED me and tried to call me back, but I wasn't stopping. "Natalie needs to explain herself."

"I'm sure she has a reason," Dad said, breathing hard to keep up with me. I was practically jogging now.

"A reason for what?" I asked. "Humiliating Des on live television? That's not okay." The more I talked, the angrier I became. Why would Natalie do something that could hurt Des and add bad press to the Summer of Santiago tour? Was she really that petty?

I reached the office space we'd walked past on the way inside and shoved the door open. It flew back, banging against the wall. And yeah, I hadn't really thought it would go that hard, but I couldn't take it back now.

Natalie and a few people I didn't recognize jumped.

"Natalie," I said through gritted teeth, "I need to speak with you."

"Sure," she said, closing her laptop and standing up. "Is something on fire?"

Just whatever was in my head making steam come out my ears. I turned and walked out of the office, standing in the echoing hallway.

As soon as the door was shut, I said, "Explain." My voice was deadly.

When Natalie feigned confusion, Dad prompted, "Des's interview with Winnie."

Just the sound of Winnie's name pissed me off even more.

Natalie smiled and said, "It was great, wasn't it?"

I glared at her.

"Didn't you see it?"

"Oh, I saw it," I snapped. "The whole world saw Winnie and Vanessa gang up on Des and make her out to be some kind of hoe. You might as well have sent her in there with the letter A embroidered on her chest."

"Jude," Natalie began in her most patronizing tone. (To be fair, it wasn't too different from her regular tone.) "Your job is to sing, and my job is to make sure you get bigger and better deals all the time, which means getting more people in these seats."

"And? You can't do that with integrity?"

"I know what makes good TV. Two enemies duking it out on Winnie Winters's show?" She grinned, her teeth flashing. "That's good TV. Not to mention every single Fantiago will be watching that interview, and you didn't even have to miss rehearsal time to be on it."

"You could have warned her," I said, hanging on to my anger.

"And lose the element of surprise? You and I both know Des is at her best when she's thinking on her toes."

No matter how much I hated to admit it, Natalie had a point. Des was brilliant when faced with adversity. But that still didn't mean my team had to be the one to stack the odds against her. "Imagine how well she could do if she actually knew what was coming," I grumbled.

Natalie said, "I'll keep that in mind." She

turned back to the office, but then she looked back at me. "Jude?"

"What?"

"I'd be careful where you place your allegiance. Des may have your heart, but Songbird has your career."

I leveled my gaze at her. "Is that a threat?"

"If you want it to be."

"Whoa," Dad said, lifting his hands between us.

"You're not the only agency in LA," I responded, ignoring him.

"We are to you until your non-compete runs out."

My jaw tensed as I bit back more angry words. "Six months is coming soon, Natalie."

Dad gripped my arm and began pulling me away. "Jude, let's go."

I fought against him for a moment, then gave in, muttering to him, "If you think we're staying with Songbird Agency after this, you're insane."

"Wait," Dad snapped, his tone firm. "We'll talk about this in your studio."

He kept his hand on my arm until we reached the studio, and I yanked myself away. "How could she do that? Can't she see how evil she's being?"

"Your feelings for Desirae are clouding your

judgment," Dad said, pacing back and forth. "I understand what it's like to be young. Everything feels so big—"

"Don't you dare compare Desirae and me to you and Mom," I warned.

Dad leveled an icy stare at me. "Throwing away your career on a girl you barely know is not something that's going to happen."

"Don't you mean *your* career?" I spat. "I'd be just fine going to college and figuring something else out."

Dad didn't call my bluff. Instead, he said, "Take a shower if you need to cool off. Clear your head. And leave Natalie to me."

He yanked open the door, but I said, "I'm not a puppet, Dad. I'm not going onstage if this is how my team is going to behave."

Dad clenched his jaw, then slammed the door behind him.

I HEARD the shouting before I saw the people yelling at each other.

We stood just inside the back entrance to the concert venue, hearing Anthony and Natalie's echoing shouts.

"YOU SHOULDN'T HAVE PUSHED HIM LIKE THAT. SHE MATTERS TO HIM. CAN'T YOU TELL?"

"JUDE'S A SPOILED CHILD, AND IF HE KEEPS ACTING LIKE THIS, HE WON'T HAVE A CAREER AS AN ADULT!"

"SPOILED? HE GREW UP WITHOUT A MOM, AND HE'S HANDLED THIS CAREER BETTER THAN SOME PEOPLE I KNOW."

With a troubled look, Samantha called, "Anthony? Natalie?"

The shouting stopped, and Samantha ushered Diego and me forward.

As soon as they saw us, Anthony turned to me and said, "Go talk to Jude."

My eyebrows drew together. "Why?"

Anthony tossed a glare at Natalie, who said, "He's refusing to go onstage."

"Because of your publicity stunt," Anthony added.

Stunned, I shook my head. "What am I supposed to say to him that you haven't already?" Besides, I kind of agreed with him. What Natalie had done was really crappy. Good thing she was just a bitter old woman and I could think on my feet. "Don't you think an apology from Natalie would mean more?"

Natalie said, "It wouldn't mean a thing because he'd know I was just doing it to get him onstage."

"And would you be?" I asked.

She didn't answer.

"Look," Anthony said. "We're about to have twenty thousand teenage girls descending on the stadium, and if Jude decides at the last minute to cancel, it's going to be a hellscape out there."

I looked between Anthony and Natalie, and it seemed as if everyone was holding their breath, waiting for my answer. "Fine," I said. "I'll talk to him."

At their relieved looks, I added, "I'm not doing it for you. I'm doing it for those twenty thousand girls. They don't deserve to have you ruin it for them."

I began walking away, and Diego came beside me while the arguing continued behind us—except now Samantha was in on it too.

As soon as we turned a corner, Diego said, "I don't blame him for taking a stand. Natalie's crazy."

"That's exactly what I was thinking," I replied. "They may have sent the wrong people to talk to him."

Diego chuckled. "We'll see about that. Jude would do anything you asked him to."

"What are you talking about? We hardly know each other."

"I have a feeling you and I know Jude better than most people do," he said.

"What do you mean?"

"Come on." He paused in the empty hallway. "How many people have you seen Jude talk to on this tour?"

I thought about it for a moment. Jude may have had millions of fans, but the people he interacted with on a day-to-day basis were... his dad/manager, his agent, his publicist, and now Diego and me. How lonely would he have been without us?

Diego said, "Even in his hometown, he didn't stop to talk to anyone. Don't you think that's strange?"

I shrugged. "Good friends are hard to come by. You only need a few."

"You're one of his friends," Diego said. "I hope you won't let him down if you decide to be more than that."

It was the closest Diego and I had ever come to a real conversation about my dating life, but the weight behind his words hit me heavy.

If I dated Jude, it would be more than just a fling. But I didn't like serious romantic relationships. I didn't want to date someone just to get distracted and have my heart broken. Or break his.

But whatever I had with Jude... it mattered to me too.

"I won't let him down," I said finally, and we continued to Jude's studio.

THIRTY-SIX
JUDE

A KNOCK SOUNDED on my door, and I yelled, "I'm not coming out."

I didn't care if it made me sound like a child. This was my career, and the way people were treated in my name mattered. What Natalie did to Des was wrong, and for my dad to defend her? I was disappointed beyond words.

But it wasn't my dad's voice that I heard on the other side of the door, and it wasn't Natalie's either.

"Jude, can we talk?" Des asked in that perfect voice of hers. She could have asked me to dress like a clown and chase a ball onstage and I would have done it. So I went to the door and opened it.

She was just as beautiful as she'd been on TV with her black tank top and speckled flowing skirt.

But now there was concern in her eyes. After that terrible display on television, she was worried about *me?*

"Come in," I said, swinging the door wider to let her inside. "Are you okay?" I asked, putting my arms on her shoulders. "I'm so sorry Natalie did that. I didn't know she was bringing Vanessa on, and I never would have cleared that." I pulled her into a hug. And when she put her arms around me, it felt like heaven. She was just short enough I could put my chin atop her head, smell the delicate scent of her shampoo, the slight spice of her perfume.

"I'm okay," she said, pulling back. "Did you see the interview? I thought I did pretty great."

I nodded. "Of course you did, considering the circumstances. As soon as it hit commercial break, I went to find Natalie."

"So you didn't see the second part?"

My eyebrows drew together. "There was a second part?"

Des nodded, grinning happily. "I totally turned it around. Winnie was *pissed.*"

"What happened?" I asked, reeling. I'd been so worried about Des, but she seemed thrilled.

"Here." She got out her phone and went to the internet, searching for her interview. It was already on social media, and she pulled up the video, pressing play. She shut the studio door as I sat on the couch holding her phone.

On screen, Des was completely confident, not letting Winnie or Vanessa shut her down for anything. She even stole Winnie's thunder, giving away tickets to the concert tonight. By the time the video was over, I was laughing.

"That was incredible, Des."

"All in a day's work." She sat next to me and pretended to brush lint off her shoulders.

I shook my head in awe. "You're amazing. How are you always so confident?"

Her body turned toward me as she drew her knee up on the couch. She looked up toward the ceiling, shrugging. "It's not like it's some sort of calculated thing. I just... let my heart lead."

How could she act like her confidence was no big deal? "Plenty of people could let their heart lead and not be so quick on their feet. I can't ever think so fast when it comes to my dad or Natalie. I just end up shutting down and running away."

Her dark eyes glittered, taking me in. "Is that why you told them you're not performing tonight?"

"You heard about that?"

She nodded.

I felt strangely vulnerable sitting alone with her, explaining why I'd refused to carry on. "I didn't like the way they treated you."

She placed her hand on my leg, and the heat was palpable. "Nobody asked you to save me."

I swallowed, trying to think. All I could focus on was the gentle pressure of her fingers on my knee, the way her cherry-red nails contrasted with my black pants. I looked up into her eyes. "You make me want to be a hero."

The truth in my words struck me. I was tired of being a puppet, placed in situations for the pleasure and wealth of others. I wanted to be myself, like Des was herself every single day. And maybe I didn't want her to have to be so tough. I just wanted her to shine like she was destined to do.

Her lips quivered, and she looked down.

Concerned, I asked, "What is it?"

She shook her head. "I'm not allowed to say."

"You can trust me."

"Can I?" I had a feeling she was asking herself just as much as she was asking me.

Either way, I nodded.

"I'm not supposed to like you," she said.

"But?" I asked. There had to be a but.

Her lips quirked slightly. "But."

I tilted my head, ready to kiss her, ready to discover what her full red lips felt like pressed against my own. I could feel her breath on my face, smell the mint of her gum.

And then a swift knock sounded on the door. "Jude! It's Shantelle! We have to warm up for the show!"

I let out a sigh, drawing away from Des. Our moment was gone, and when I kissed her for the first time, I didn't want to rush it. I didn't want to immediately leave for a show. I wanted it to be her and me and a perfect, lasting moment I could write about for the rest of my life.

Des said, "We should go."

So we did.

THIRTY-SEVEN

DES

AS SOON AS the show was over, I wanted more time alone with Jude to finish what we started.

What a selfish thought.

Natalie had threatened to end Jude's career over him having a relationship with me. And since I cared about him, I needed to put some space between us. It didn't matter how unlikely her revenge would be. It was a possibility, and that was enough.

But I couldn't help thinking about him almost kissing me.

How much I'd wanted to kiss him back.

As soon as the concert was over, I told Diego I was tired and retreated to the semi-privacy of my bunk to text my friends. I needed some outside perspective now more than ever.

Des: Jude almost kissed me.

My phone blew up with responses almost immediately.

Cori: AGAIN?!?!?!

Faith: Almost??

Nadira: Just kiss him already!

Tatiana: What she said ^^^

Adriel: EEK!!!

Cori: Please tell me you're going to kiss him for real soon. The suspense is truly killing me.

Des: If it's killing YOU think about what it's doing to ME!

Cori: I don't get it. Why hasn't it happened yet? Don't you like him?

Des: If I were to have a real, long-term relationship with someone, it would be Jude. But also... what would Natalie do if she found out?

Nadira: I think she's bluffing. There's no way she'd give up the amount of money that Jude is making her.

Des: I think that too, but she's done so much already, like with that television interview today. She's the one who surprised me with Vanessa. It's like I'm waiting for the other shoe to drop.

Adriel: What did your lawyer say?

Des: Basically that it would be very unlikely for Natalie to tank Jude's career.

Des: How pathetic am I? I need a lawyer and my friends' opinions to figure out if I can kiss the guy I like?

Cori: Can I say something?

Des: You're asking?

Cori: ...

Des: Cori.

Cori: Is the Natalie issue the only thing holding you back?

Des: What do you mean?

Cori: I've known you since second grade. You've never been the kind of person who listens to stupid rules. I have to wonder why you've gone along with this one?

I let out a sigh, resting my phone on my stomach for a moment.

There was a reason why I never dated guys for longer than a few weeks. Devon had been my longest "boyfriend", and that had only lasted a few months.

But Diego's words kept weighing on me. He didn't want me to let Jude down, and I didn't want to either. But what about me? What about my heart?

Des: Jude isn't the kind of guy you date for fun.

Nadira: Who are you and what have you done with Desirae?

Des: Seriously. He's not like other guys I've met or dated. He's kind. Deep. Handsome. Dedicated. Passionate. What if it doesn't go well? I've just lost the first guy I really liked. And what if it does go well? Natalie destroys him and he hates me forever?

Cori: What Natalie doesn't know won't hurt Jude.

I was hanging out in my bunk the next morning, like a good girl, trying not to think about how incredible it would be to kiss Jude, when a knock sounded on the frame of my bunk. I pulled the curtain back to see Jude. My cheeks felt a little hot, since I'd been thinking about him nonstop.

"Hey," he said, "I've been working on this song, and I think it's finished. Would you sing it with me?"

I propped myself up on my elbows. "The song you started writing on the drive here?"

He nodded, a small smile on his lips.

"Of course," I said, pulling myself out. It would be okay, right? We couldn't exactly do anything with everyone else on the bus. But when I got out of my bunk and looked around, I didn't see anyone. "Where did they all go?"

"Apparently, Diego bet Jago he could do more push-ups than him, so they're having a contest. Winner takes the other one out for a smoothie. Of course Dad and Francie wanted to watch."

I laughed. "Jago's going to have fun getting Diego a smoothie."

"That's what I was thinking."

"They're not worried about watching you?" I asked.

He shook his head. "We're already in the complex, and they had me lock up the bus. No one's getting in here except Francie with her key."

My eyes widened. We were completely alone?

"I know," he said, walking toward the living area, where his guitar case was open. "I feel like I'm always in a fishbowl."

"Same here," I said. "I think it's the only part of touring I don't like."

He picked up the guitar and set the case aside so I had room to sit next to him. Thoughts of what my friends had said and our almost kiss were swirling so fast in my mind that I was surprised when he handed me sheet music with the notes and words written in pencil.

I looked over the words, remembering the ones he'd quickly scribbled down and sang in a creative furor only several days ago.

They were more polished now. And I found I liked his handwriting. It was slanted and fast, like he didn't care so much how it looked as long as the message got across.

He began strumming and said, "I sing the first stanza, and then you, and we'll alternate until the chorus, which we'll sing together."

I nodded, following his notes on the page, the music hitting my ears, and he began singing.

"*When I kiss her, I'm going to do it right,*" he sang.

I closed my eyes, feeling the music, the lyrics. "*When I kiss him, I want to see the light.*"

"*Stars in the sky burst within her eyes. When I kiss her, I want to feel it all.*"

I opened my eyes at the emotion in his voice behind every word. This was the Jude I followed on YouTube before he became a star. This was the real Jude. And then it hit me... What if these words were real too, for us?

I almost missed my line, singing, "*When I kiss him, I'll be ready for the fall.*"

Our voices melted together, harmonizing

perfectly with his guitar. "*When we kiss, it'll be every-thing or nothing at all.*"

We sang through the lines, and I found my heart aching, wishing for that first kiss that would change everything. Maybe it was the words. Maybe it was me. Or maybe it was both, something I'd been longing for but holding back at the same time.

As the last chords faded in the small space, Jude looked at me, his dark eyes searching for an answer.

"Des?" he said.

I nodded, my throat tight with emotion.

He leaned closer, his eyes drifting closed.

But I said, "Wait."

He paused, close enough to make my brain fog. I could feel the heat of his breath, smell the spice of his cologne, see the small creases in his full lips.

"Natalie can't know," I whispered.

His eyebrows drew together. "Natalie? Why?"

I shook my head, knowing I was already pushing it. "Can you trust me?"

"Of course," he said without pause.

"And you're okay with keeping it between us?"

He looked at me, the corners of his lips turning up. "Just kiss me already."

I couldn't help but smile as I did exactly that.

THIRTY-EIGHT
JUDE

DES'S LIPS against mine felt like nothing I'd ever been bold enough to imagine. She was soft but strong, sweet but fierce, and most of all, she was *mine*.

A primal, possessive urge washed over me as I pushed the music away and put my arms around her. I'd been waiting on this kiss, this moment, for what felt like forever, and nothing was coming between us now that she'd finally confirmed what I'd only hoped was true.

She wanted to kiss me too.

I'd heard it in her words, in her voice, and now I could feel it in her touch.

She worked her fingers through the back of my hair, raking her nails gently over my skin. Her chest pressed against mine, making my heart beat that much faster.

The exposed skin of her calf crossed my leg. I reached for it, feeling her smooth skin, gripping her tightly and knowing I'd never let go, never be okay with anyone else touching her this way again.

And the way she kissed me? It was art. It was music. It was *life* in a way I'd never experienced before. And I was *living* for it.

I could have laid her down, could have taken the kiss as far as we could go, but that wasn't right. I'd meant every word in the song. When I kissed her, I wanted it to be the beginning, not just a means to an end.

So, no matter how much it sucked, no matter how much I wanted to fog every window in the bus, I pulled away from her. "I've been waiting for that," I admitted.

She looked up at me with those sparkling diamond eyes and smiled slightly, her lips full of color. "Me too."

Just those two words erased whatever doubt was left in my system, and I held both of her hands in my own. "I don't date often."

"I do." She chuckled. "Of course, you've seen

the news. But not like this... not when it means so much."

God, the things she did to my heart. "But I want to respect your wishes, all of them. If you want to keep it between us..."

"I do," she said quickly. So quickly it burst whatever excited bubble was forming in my chest. At my reaction, she cupped my cheek in her hand, making me look at her. "It's not that I'm ashamed of you, or I think it won't work out." She bit her lip—hard—and swore. "I want to tell you, but I—I can't."

My worry began to grow, the coldness of it creeping up my chest, my neck. But I had a choice. I could allow that feeling, that worry, or I could trust Des anyway. And of all the people in my life, of all the people on tour with us... I trusted her. And I hated the distressed look this was causing her.

"It's okay," I said, drawing her into a hug. She held me back, and it just felt... right.

And no matter how much I wanted to show Des to everyone, to tell them she was mine, I could keep our secret to myself. Because the realest part of what we had was right here.

As long as she was happy, everything else was fine.

"It'll stay between you and me," I promised.

The jangling sound of keys in the bus door broke us farther apart, and she looked at her reflection in her phone, checking her hair and makeup. I hurried about, picking up scattered music and positioning my guitar back over my lap.

I began strumming the song and whispered, "Let's keep singing."

When the others walked in to us singing, I could have sworn I saw a knowing smile on Diego's lips. I looked away, lest I give away the secret myself.

At the close of the song, Dad clapped his hands together. "That's going to be amazing with Jade."

"It already is," I said, keeping my eyes on the strings, "with Des."

THIRTY-NINE
DES

AFTER THAT NIGHT'S SHOW, Diego and I went to my studio so I could change and get ready for another night on the bus. But when we walked inside, the entire room was full of red roses and Mylar balloons.

I walked through the maze of flowers, a smile growing on my face.

"Man," Diego said, "he has it bad."

"Who?" I asked, already knowing the lie fell flat. I should have just kept my mouth shut.

He grabbed a balloon, sucking helium, and imitated me. "Who?"

I turned, rolling my eyes at him as I took out the heavy earrings I'd worn tonight. "You're ridiculous."

He sucked more helium. "You're ridiculous."

I tried not to laugh. "Shut up."

"Shut up."

"Diego!"

"Diego!"

I punched his shoulder. "You're the worst."

"You're the worst," he echoed, then flinched as I went to hit him again. "Really," he said, his voice returning to normal. "What happened between you two?"

I glanced toward the door, making sure it was shut and that no one had followed us in. "He kissed me, earlier on the bus."

Diego pumped his fist. "I knew it!"

I went to the vanity, removing the rest of my jewelry and using the makeup wipes to clear my skin. "You know you can't tell anyone."

"Who would I tell?"

"Jago?" I said. "You two are tight."

"You're my sister," he replied, as if that were explanation enough.

"Really. If Natalie finds out..."

"She won't." He walked behind me, looking at me through the mirror. "Des, I know this is your first real relationship—"

"It's not—"

"And I know you're worried about what could happen to Jude if it gets out—"

"It could be terri—"

"But I want you to know that I have your back. And Jude cares about you. Obviously. He was ready to cancel a whole concert because he thought Natalie hurt your feelings. So just relax. And enjoy it."

I smiled at him in the mirror. "When did you get so smart?"

"I have no idea. I definitely didn't learn it from you."

I made to swat him, but he quickly dodged out of the way and said, "I'll wait for you in the hall. All these balloons are giving me the creeps."

I laughed, waving him out, and then took a moment just to sit amongst all the flowers and balloons. My heart melted at all the shapes—squares and stars and circles, all in metallic red. It was the most thoughtful, over-the-top thing someone had ever done for me.

I reached out and gripped a thin ribbon, weaving it between my fingertips. How could I ever make it clear to Jude how much this meant to me?

Thinking for a moment, I got out my phone

and took a selfie amidst the balloons. Then I posted it on social media.

Being on tour with @JudeSantiago feels like floating.

I'd tell him thank you in person, but after leaving the studio and getting on the bus, we wouldn't have a minute alone. Jago was by Jude's side 24/7 at concert venues, and there were six of us on the bus at all times. We were surrounded.

So when we both went to our beds, I got out my phone and set him a text.

Des: The balloons and roses were so sweet. Thank you. <3

Jude: I hoped you enjoyed your first show as my girl.

Des: It was the best. Like I had a secret only you and I knew.

Jude: You were amazing, by the way.

Des: Aren't I always? ;)

Jude: Of course.

Des: I guess you were alright.

Jude: Hahaha.

Des: I wish we could talk. Or that I could hold your hand... I know you're only six feet away, but it feels like miles.

Jude: As soon as this tour's over, I'm taking you on a date.

Des: Oh really?

Jude: Absolutely. I'm going to rent a private house in Malibu and send a limo to get you, and we'll walk on the beach and eat dinner and watch a movie, you know, the old-fashioned way.

Des: Old-fashioned? You're an international icon, Jude Santiago.

Jude: But not a sellout. ;)

Des: True. :) What movie should we watch?

Jude: Something with tons of explosions.

Des: And girls in bikinis, right?

Jude: I mean, do you know a movie that exists without both?

Des: Not one that matters, amiright?

Jude: I knew you were perfect.

Des: :) What about the food?

Jude: Only the best for you.

Des: If you say pizza rolls...

Jude: It's like you can read my mind.

Des: Are you sure you don't want to date my brother?

Jude: Is he available?

Des: ._.

Jude: jkjk

Des: Sure.

Jude: I've always wanted a brother.

Des: Yeah?

Jude: Being an only child is lonely.

Des: Did your dad ever date?

Jude: Not that I know of. Grandma used to think Dad never wanted someone else to be my mom. But between you and me, I think he has a thing for Francie.

Des: !!!!!!!

Des: OMG that makes so much sense. He's ALWAYS up there with her!

Jude: I know! At first I thought it was just because he got bored watching Jago and me playing video games, but they went out to lunch a few times while they were in LA. Dad said it was to make plans for the trip, but I'm not so sure.

Des: Are you okay with him dating?

Jude: Definitely. It's been a long time coming. Sometimes I wonder what he missed out on all those years.

Des: Maybe it took that long for him to be ready.

Jude: To date?

Des: To have his heart broken again.

Jude didn't reply for a long moment, and it took all I had not to text him something light, to turn our conversation back to the happy banter we'd exchanged moments ago. I didn't like my relationships with guys to go deep. That's what the Curvy Girl Club 2.0 was for.

Instead, I waited. Within minutes, I was rewarded with a response.

Jude: Who broke your heart?

Des: That's a story for another day.

FORTY

JUDE

THE NEXT SEVERAL SHOWS, we continued the rhythm we'd established: rehearsal, makeup, hair, wardrobe, warmup, and performance. Most days, Des had interviews, and it was amazing to see her come into her own even more so than before.

We swapped kisses when we could. Shared smiles when no one was looking. Talked as friends when people were around.

But we'd yet to go on a date. Not that we could. I knew the second we snuck off the set, we'd be seen and the rumors would begin. I hated that.

So, I improvised instead.

I had little gifts delivered to her dressing room. Left notes in her bunk. Brushed her hand whenever I could.

And at night, when I lay in bed, I got out my phone and texted her.

We talked about what it was like for her to grow up in a big family. How she loved her siblings but knew she was meant to stand out on her own. I told her how lonely it had been growing up as an only child. How I hated that my grandma had to be a mom to me, instead of just a grandma.

We talked about after-parties and LA and how hard it was for me to be around all the drugs that got passed around. How lonely it was to be clean in this industry. How alone I felt on tour, no matter how many people were around.

I talked about how excited I was to find a new agent, one who really understood me. And she told me about her best friends, how they inspired her with all they'd overcome. How she knew she had people to fall on, no matter how many times she messed up.

How her friends could become my people too.

But she never told me who broke her heart. And I found myself watching her, trying to get a hint of what had happened to leave her so guarded. But there was nothing I could see beneath the glamor of her smile and the confidence she put forth.

It was like we were living two lives. The life of singers on tour and the life of *after*.

When our lives could come together as boyfriend and girlfriend.

We dreamed about walking on the beach, holding hands, eating cupcakes at this bakery she always raved about. Of what it would be like to go on separate tours, flying about to meet each other for romantic weekends. Or to attend movie premieres together, dressed to the nines, sharing popcorn from the same red and white container.

It was fun to dream.

To have someone.

And to have something to look forward to.

I couldn't wait for it to actually come true.

Since Des had a big interview today, she rehearsed onstage first, and I just got to hang out for a little while and sip coffee as I watched her.

She'd been a natural onstage from the very first show, but I could see how she'd grown. She was more comfortable in using the entire stage instead of portions. She was less stiff. And she was even more fun to watch.

I was proud to call her my girlfriend, even though no one knew.

As she was finishing up her final song, I wrote a note to her and folded it in the shape of a star. As she passed by with Diego, I slipped it into her palm. She flashed me a short smile and continued away from the stage.

Natalie called, "Jude! I have someone I'd like you to meet."

Standing next to her was Jade. No last name.

A cold feeling pooled in my gut. This was not good. I looked around for Des, but she was already gone.

Jade smiled at me, tucking a strand of electric-blue hair behind her ear. "Hi, Jude, it's nice to meet you!"

I nodded and gave her half a smile, trying not to be rude, but I had to ask. "Natalie, what's going on?"

Natalie brushed her hands over Jade's shoulders. "We sent Jade the song, and she said she'd love to collab with you on it. And since her family lives here in Denver, we thought this would be a great time to rehearse it together!"

Jade nodded enthusiastically. "The lyrics were so heartfelt, and I usually don't get a chance to work on songs like this since people see me as edgier. I'm so glad you thought of me."

That was the problem, though. I hadn't thought of her. Des had been in my mind the entire time I'd written that song. "Natalie, can I talk to you?"

Natalie gave me a cool smile and said, "After this rehearsal. We don't want to be rude and take too much time away from Jade and her family."

I couldn't believe I was saying this, but Natalie was right. At least partially. I didn't want to be rude to Jade and leave a bad taste in her mouth. This was a small industry, and people talked. If Jade had a bad experience here, it could cause problems for me down the road.

One rehearsal wouldn't kill me. And I could let Natalie know, privately, under no uncertain terms, that Des would be the one recording this song with me. Jade and I could collaborate on something else. This song was special.

"We have two chairs set up onstage," Natalie said. "Why don't you two try out an acoustic version?"

Struggling to stay calm, I walked to the stage and sat in the chair with my guitar in front of it, not looking Jade in the eyes. I needed to cool down, but all I felt like doing now was holing up in my studio and not coming out until things were better.

Until Des was here.

Until Natalie could see that I wasn't a marionette dangling from strings she controlled.

I lifted the guitar strap over my neck and played my fingers over the strings, making sure they were still in tune. I took longer than necessary twisting the tuning pegs, letting the feel of the guitar slow my heartbeat. Focusing on music instead of my problems was familiar territory.

That's what music had always been for me—an escape, an outlet, from pain that was older than my thoughts. It was hard to explain, but losing my mom so young... there was a part of me that ached but there were no words for the pain.

I tapped into that emotion, strumming a few lines from the song, and then looked at Jade. She sat comfortably on the other chair, one leg drawn up to her chest.

Jade was punk, edgy, in all the ways I was not, and I had to admit I was curious what she would do with my lyrics, how they would sound coming out in her deep, scratchy voice.

I began singing, wishing the entire time that Des could sing it with me. Jade belted the lyrics instead, tenderly at first, and then she put her own spin on them. With her, the song became something else entirely—aching and sad instead of hopeful like I'd imagined.

We finished singing, and Natalie clapped her hands together. "Match made in heaven!" I'm pretty sure I could see the dollar signs flashing in her eyes as she said it. Natalie approached us and said, "Why don't the two of you grab lunch and talk about ideas for the song?"

"Lunch?" I said.

Natalie nodded. "We have an extra hour or so in the schedule for you to eat."

Jade said, "I own this awesome vegan place a few blocks from here. Super discreet too."

"Own?" I said, eyebrows raised.

"One of my investments, you know, so I don't end up a broke former child star." She laughed as she said it, but crap, why did she sound so grown up? And why did I feel so unprepared? I didn't have much by way of investments, aside from our home in Beverly Hills and Grandma's home in Winslow.

I agreed to lunch, mostly so I could talk to Jade and get her advice. I wanted confidence that my future was taken care of, regardless of my performance schedule.

Jago walked us outside where a lime-green jeep sat in the waiting area. I didn't see anyone in the driver's seat though. "Where's your driver?"

She laughed. "You're looking at her."

I raised my eyebrows but then remembered this was her hometown. It was no different than me driving my car around Beverly Hills.

Jago and I got in her car, and she drove us the few blocks to her vegan restaurant. It was on the highest floor of a downtown building. We rode up an elevator, chatting genially, and then got seated at a corner table with an amazing view of downtown Denver. Jago took a table to himself, saying he wanted to get caught up on some work. I knew it was just so we could have some privacy.

Jade asked the server to bring us a sampling of everything. Once we were alone, she pulled a knee up to her chest and eyed me. "What made Jude Santiago, Jude Santiago?"

I glanced out the window, at the mountains that must have been so beautiful covered in snow. "My fans."

She smiled. "What got the fans for you?"

I looked back at her, seeing genuine curiosity in her eyes. "I was in this talent show in school, and Dad filmed it. Grandma said she wanted to listen to it again, and it was too hard for him to set up the video camera every time, so he had me upload it to YouTube and send her the link.

"But pretty soon, it wasn't just Grandma watching the videos. There were lots of people who said they liked me voice, so I recorded some more. I thought maybe I'd get monetized and make some money on ads. But then Natalie, my agent from Songbird, reached out to me. It all happened so fast after that."

The waiter returned with a big platter of different food, and we both thanked him. Jade said to me, "Sounds like the dream."

"It was," I agreed.

"Was?"

I paused, realizing I had used past tense. "I love my job. But the life that goes along with it? Sometimes it feels like I'm just a face for a machine, you know?"

"Oh, I know." She shook her head. "But try complaining to someone about being a rock star."

"Impossible. It's the dream."

She smiled, then took a bite of pita and hummus.

I tried some baba ganoush, eating it with a chip.

"How is it?" Jade asked.

"It's not pizza rolls."

She laughed, covering her mouth.

It was nice, I realized, talking to someone who understood what it was like to be famous, the pressures and the stressors and the joys as well.

"So, you wrote that song?" she asked.

I nodded. "Sometimes songs just come to me, and it feels like I have to get them out."

"Was it about someone?" she asked.

My smile gave me away.

Jade grinned back. "Des?"

"But keep it between us?" I asked.

She nodded. "I will, but you better practice your poker face. You're grinning like a lovestruck schoolboy."

I tried to wipe the smile, but I couldn't, so I tried to change the subject. "Are you seeing anyone?"

"No, but you know how hard it is to find someone who gets it."

"Definitely," I said.

My phone went off with a text from my dad saying I needed to be back pretty soon. We finished up our food, and Jade drove us back to the venue, leaving her number before driving away.

It was nice to make a new friend. And I hoped I

could introduce Jade to Des as well someday soon. Des would love her straightforward demeanor, the way she was unapologetically herself.

As I walked inside though, I realized I hadn't yet told Jade she wouldn't be singing the duet with me. Now I felt guilty. She had her hopes up, and I didn't want to let her down. It made me that much angrier at Natalie for putting me in this position.

One way or another, Natalie had to go.

MY INTERVIEW WITH DOTTIE PENCE, Denver's top daytime television host, was almost over when she pressed her finger to her earpiece. I knew it had to be bad news, judging by the calculating look in her eyes. I'd seen it in Winnie, and this was only déjà vu. I glanced to the wings, looking for Vanessa. There was no studio audience to sift through. In fact, offscreen it all looked really... basic. There were cement floors and cords taped to the floor and metal structures to hold up lights and cameras and more.

Dottie smiled at me and said, "Being on tour with Jude Santiago must be amazing."

I smiled back and gave her exactly what she was looking for. "Like a dream come true."

"Tell us, is Jude seeing anyone?"

My eyebrows drew together at this line of questioning. I didn't like it one bit, especially after that calculating look. "It's really not my place to discuss, Dot."

"You don't have to discuss it." She winked. "Blink twice if you knew Jude and Jade were out to lunch together right now."

The names didn't compute in the same sentence. Jude hadn't planned any lunches with Jade. He was supposed to be rehearsing for a show.

Dottie pointed to a screen showing a photo of Jude and Jade sitting together at a table framed by floor-to-ceiling windows. They were laughing, clearly having a good time.

Part of me hoped it was an old photo, that Jude hadn't planned a lunch with the person who was supposed to take my spot in *our* duet. But I recognized Jude's leather studded jacket, the ripped black overalls he'd worn over a fitted white shirt. He'd been with her today, while I was gone.

There were two possibilities—either he'd known he was going out with her and purposefully kept it from me. Or seeing Jade had been a surprise.

But they looked so friendly. Like they hadn't just met for the first time.

"Des?" Dottie said, and it was clear she was saying it for the second time.

I turned my smile on her, shoving down every feeling of betrayal that threatened to choke me. Jude was allowed to have friends other than me— even if they were successful girls. Cute girls. Girls with narrow hips and dimpled cheeks and bright blue hair.

"Jade is such an icon," I said. "She's definitely someone I look up to in music, and I love how she is always completely herself. Jade understood the assignment!"

Dottie laughed, her disappointment only showing in her eyes.

The segment ended, and a camera guy helped unmic me.

Samantha thanked Dottie for a great interview, and Diego handed me my purse. As we walked out, I whispered to Samantha, "Did you know Jude was meeting with Jade?"

"Oh yeah," she said. "I didn't know they'd get lunch though." Her phone went off, and she said, "Sorry, I have to get this."

She talked on the phone as we all went to the car. Samantha sat up front, and once Diego and I were in the back, he asked, "What's the deal with Jude and Jade? You didn't know?"

I shook my head. "Did you?"

"Jude didn't say anything."

I shook my head. "Jude wouldn't have lied. There was a misunderstanding." There had to be.

Despite my reassurance to Diego, I worried. And that worry made me miss my family and friends more than ever. At home, I knew I had people in my corner no matter what. Here? No one was who they seemed to be. I hated that I even had to question if Jude had told me less than the truth. It made me feel bare. Vulnerable. And I *hated* feeling that way.

When we got back to the venue, there was an air of excitement about. Jude was nearing the end of rehearsal. As I watched him, I wondered, would he ever betray me? There were countless girls who would die for a chance with him. And if he could pull someone successful like Jade...

I knew I was worthy of honesty, but that didn't mean guys always delivered that.

A tightness gripped my chest and wouldn't let go. I'd nearly worked myself into a panic when it was time to go back to the locker room and warm up our vocals.

On the way into the room, Jude smiled and said, "How'd the interview go?"

"Great," I said. "Until they surprised me with a photo of you and Jade."

His expression sobered. "Des, that wasn't—"

But I cut him off, not ready for some weak excuse. Jude could have texted me today, given me a heads-up.

But he hadn't.

I needed to bring my full energy to the show, and I couldn't do that with a betrayal wreaking havoc on my heart.

Shantelle wasn't here anymore, so I started the warmup, letting the steamy air soothe my vocal cords. Shantelle and Jude had been right. Singing almost every night wore on my throat, and I had to treat it right if I ever wanted a big break.

Jude slowly joined in. I knew we'd have to talk soon, but it would happen in private. After the show was over.

I had to perform.

He did too.

And that's what we did, like the professionals we were. We sang our parts, and when we got to the hotel, we went our separate ways, just as we always did. Him and his dad to his room. Diego and me to ours.

As soon as we were inside, Diego asked, "Do you want me to get Jude? See if I can create a distraction so you two can talk?"

Forcing a smile, I said, "I'm really tired. I think I'll just shower and go to bed."

Diego frowned. "Des, you guys have to talk it out. It's probably a big misunderstanding."

"Or maybe it's not," I said, trying to act cavalier and failing miserably.

Frowning, Diego said, "Jude's not like Luke."

That name was like a dagger to a barely closed wound. "Goodnight, Diego." Before he had a chance to reply, I went to my room and shut the door.

With my eyes feeling hot, I lay in my bed, scrolling through social media on my phone. Torturing myself. That picture of Jude and Jade was all over the internet now, especially in the Fantiagos group discussions.

I knew better now than to read the comment sections, but I did it anyway, seeking some information to make sense of this. But all I found were comments about my weight, how Jade would make a better partner for Jude.

And it made me feel like crap. It made me question myself, something I promised myself I would never do again.

I got undressed and stood in front of the bathroom mirror, looking at my body. Looking at every curve. My breasts were uneven. My chin had a double. My stomach hung over in the front, and there were dimples in my thighs.

The media would tell me it was all flaws that could be covered up with clever makeup or specially designed clothing. They could fix it with surgery.

But I looked at myself until I loved it.

There was no one like me. No amount of dieting or surgery anyone did could make them my double.

And there was beauty in the unique.

I was one of a kind.

Jude, or any other guy, would never have another like me.

The world would never see another like me.

A knock sounded on the door, and I called, "I'm fine, Diego, really."

"It's not Diego."

I SNUCK AWAY from Dad and Jago and was halfway to Des's room when I got the text from Diego.

Diego: Come fix this. Now.

The words standing out so starkly against the white background of my phone made my stomach drop. I paused in the hallway, texting him back.

Jude: What's going on? She's been off all night.

Diego: What were you doing with Jade?

I swore low and continued to their room, knocking lightly on the door. Diego answered, studying me with eyes that so closely resembled his sisters. He stood in the doorway, using his big frame to block my way.

"You didn't answer my text," he accused. "What happened with Jade? Des was completely blindsided at her interview today."

I instantly felt guilty, even though I'd done nothing wrong. Someone had probably grabbed a photo of us at lunch, but I didn't like Des finding out I'd been hanging out with another girl that way. Especially the girl my dad wanted to replace her with in my duet.

"Natalie surprised me with her on set today. It wasn't planned, and I didn't even think to warn Des about it."

Diego cussed and swung the door open. "I should have known Natalie was behind this."

I pressed my lips together. "No kidding."

He nodded toward one of the bedroom doors. "She's in there." Then he left the suite, shutting the door behind him. Giving us a gift we so rarely received: privacy.

I looked at Des's closed door, wondering what state she was in behind it. Taking a deep breath, I walked to the door and knocked.

"I'm fine, Diego, really." She was not fine. I could tell by the tightness in her voice.

"It's not Diego," I replied.

She was quiet for a moment, and I worried she

would send me away. She had the right—I shouldn't have let her be caught off guard like she was. Sending a text giving her a heads-up wouldn't have been the end of the world.

I wasn't single anymore. There were other people to consider.

The door slowly opened, revealing Des in a black silk robe she pulled tightly around herself. She looked up at me, only for a moment, before looking back down.

If we were under different circumstances, I might have paid more attention to the way the silk revealed her curves. Wondered what was underneath the robe. But all I could focus on was bringing a smile back to her face.

"Des." I dipped down to meet her eyes, but she only looked away. "Natalie surprised me today and brought Jade to the set to practice our song. I've already told Natalie she needs to find a way to break the news to Jade that I will not be performing the duet with her."

Finally, she gifted me with her eyes, so I continued. "I'm really sorry I didn't get a chance to tell you. I should have. Jade and I just went out to lunch, and she's cool. The whole time I was thinking how I wished you were there with us. You would have liked her."

Des seemed to relax, if only slightly. "I knew there had to be something."

"*You're* my girlfriend, and Jade knows that."

Des tensed right back up. "What?"

"She kind of guessed, and my face gave it away."

"Jude," Des said, standing back up and pacing. "I asked to keep it between us."

My chest tightened. Just when I thought I was fixing things... "Jade won't tell anyone. She understands the need for privacy."

"You barely know her," Des said. "How can you just trust her so blindly?"

I felt like a little kid again, being chided for taking one too many candy bars from my grandma's cabinet. I had enough of people telling me what to do; I didn't need it from Des too. "I can choose who to trust. Especially when it comes to news about a relationship that I am also in. Why does it need to be such a big secret anyway?"

"You need to trust *me*," Des said, skirting my question altogether.

"That's it?" I asked. "The only girls I've ever

known who wanted to keep a relationship a secret were cheating on their boyfriends."

Her brows drew together, and I knew I'd said something stupid before her voice rose and her hands began gesticulating. "Cheating? How would I even have a chance to cheat? I'm always on set or with my brother!"

"I'm sorry! I didn't mean you're cheating. I just..." I took her hands, holding them in my own. "I don't want to keep it a secret. I'm so happy to be with you and... I don't understand why it has to be so complicated."

Des looked away from me, then stepped back, wrapping her arms around herself. "Jude, I don't do great at relationships."

My heart dropped to the floor, ready for her to stomp on it. Was this really ending before it had a chance to fully start? Is that why she wanted to keep it a secret? So when she broke up with me, I could at least keep the shame to myself?

"Des, did you read the note?" I asked. I needed her to know I was in this. That I thought she was incredible, and I wouldn't do anything to mess it up.

Her eyes widened. "I put it in my purse, but I didn't get to read it..."

"Can you get it?" I asked.

She nodded slowly, leaving the room to retrieve her bag from where it sat on the table.

When she came back, she held the folded sheet of paper in her hand.

Quietly, she read the poem I'd written out loud.

Destalt

Glittering brown eyes

A smile that could kill

A heart that would never

And a soul more beautiful

Than the sum of all her parts.

J

She covered her heart with her free hand, blinking quickly. "You wrote me a poem."

I nodded, stepping closer, and she finally let me take her hand in mine. "Des, this, us, it's not a game to me. I mean it when I say I want to be with you."

She looked up at me, her big brown eyes full of tears. "I think I need to tell you something."

My stomach clenched. This was the bad news. The thing that defined "too good to be true."

She lowered herself onto the bed, and she looked so small sitting there, her hands in her lap, picking at her long red fingernails. I just wanted to hold her. So that's what I did. I put my arms around her and let her rest her head on my shoulder and said, "You don't have to tell me anything you don't want to."

"I want to," she breathed.

So I listened, terrified of what would come next.

FORTY-THREE
DES

I HADN'T TALKED about Luke since the summer after freshman year. But his memory followed me every day. Came into every relationship with me. And if things were going to work with Jude... he deserved to know.

I took a shaking breath, drawing all my strength that was left after the show. After the angst of the day.

"A while ago, you asked who broke my heart," I said slowly. "His name was Luke."

Jude covered my hand with his, and I focused on the contact, drawing strength from his nearness.

"I met him when I was fourteen. He was a senior at my school, and he paid attention to me." I blinked quickly, rolling my eyes. "It all sounds so stupid now."

"Not to me," Jude said.

So, I continued. "I was at the Academy's end-of-year barbecue with Nadira and Cori. Since we'd just finished eighth grade, we went to the high school one to meet some of our new classmates. He came up to me, singled me out. Called me beautiful. And then he asked me out.

"I was so excited. Luke wasn't just a senior. He was *the* senior. He'd been starting quarterback for the football team, his dad was a bigshot in the investment world, he played basketball, and college scouts from major schools were already talking to him. He was good-looking too, blond hair, blue eyes, and a smile that he used to get out of everything. And he drove this bright red sports car, and since red was my favorite color, I thought it was a sign." I rolled my eyes at my own naiveté. Looking back, I could see it all, the red flags. But then? I was star-struck.

"We started dating over the summer, and it was so romantic at first. He took me out to expensive restaurants where we had to dress up just to get in, and he always told me how beautiful I was. That he'd never seen anything so perfect."

I scoffed. "It was all fine when we were in private. But then the back-to-school parties started, and he started bringing me around his friends. I had to send him pictures of my outfits before we went out to make sure they weren't too suggestive. He said it was so his friends wouldn't get any ideas... but I knew it was because he didn't want me to embarrass him.

"And he sent me a workout routine to do. 'So I'd be healthy' and able to stay with him forever. Then he made comments about what I ate and how I shouldn't be having so much of the food that Mom always served us. I started arguing with my mom about eating healthier and why she always served us junk food."

Tears spilled down my cheeks at the strain my relationship with Luke had put on my relationship with my parents. "Dad wanted to keep me from Luke, but Mom said if they tried to break us up, it would make me want him that much more. So then Mom and Dad were fighting too."

Jude shook his head, his eyes full of sympathy. Of understanding.

"He made me nail appointments at the salon his mother went to and hair appointments too. He liked my hair with highlights instead of brown. He said he wanted me to be my best self, and of course I bought into it. Of course I did. How could I not listen to this guy who everyone loved? How could I ignore all the senior girls telling me how lucky I was?

"And you know the worst part about it? I lost all my friends. He thought Nadira was too nerdy and Cori was too tall and had me sitting at the lunch table with him and all the football players and cheerleaders. And I just couldn't understand why they didn't want to be attractive like I was now with all the new hair and makeup and diet and exercise."

Jude rubbed my hand. "That sounds awful, Des. How did you get out of it?"

I closed my eyes, my voice shaking. Because even after all this time, it hurt. "He cheated on me. Left me for a senior girl—a cheerleader. And when I confronted him about it, he told me I should have *expected* it. I was too fat to keep a guy like him interested for long."

Jude's hands tightened on mine, and his jaw clenched. "He was wrong."

"I know," I said, moving my hand to wipe my eyes. "I finally figured that out. It took a year, an entire year of therapy—at my mom's request—and a year to get my friends back. Twelve months to finally get myself back. And at my last therapy session, I promised myself I would never let anyone make me feel small like that again. That I would always be the prize when it came to relationships, and that I'd never let my head get so clouded with love that I forgot to see what was right in front of me."

"Des." Jude turned toward me, putting his hands on both of my shoulders.

I couldn't meet his eyes. No, I was too embarrassed. I should have known better. Should have seen the signs, but I got swept up in a web, and Luke took everything that mattered from me.

"Look at me," he breathed.

Hesitantly, I did. What I found was genuine care in his dark eyes. He reached up and brushed his thumb over my cheek. "It wasn't your fault."

Those words, in his voice... My voice cracked. "But I..."

"It wasn't your fault," he repeated. And he held me against his chest as I fell apart.

FORTY-FOUR
JUDE

MY EYES WERE HOT, matching the fat tears sliding down her beautiful cheeks.

I hated Luke. I didn't know him, but I *hated* him with everything I had.

I hated that he was a part of her story.

That he made her question her worth.

That he made her afraid to give.

She sobbed into my chest, and I held her, telling her everything I knew to be true.

Des deserved someone better, who saw how beautiful she was and knew that she was never too much or not enough. She was always perfectly enough, exactly as she was.

And I would never, ever take the gift she was for granted.

A knock sounded on the door, and I jerked away from her, looking confused. "Maybe Diego forgot his room key?" I whispered.

Des nodded. "Go wait in the bathroom. I'll make sure it's him."

I nodded and hurried went to the bathroom that so closely mirrored my own. Instead of waiting inside, though, I went to the bedroom door and pressed my ear to the white painted wood, wondering who could be at Des's suite without Diego's warning.

I heard her open the door and say, "Hey, I wasn't expecting you."

Then my dad's voice filtered through the door. "Sorry, I—are you doing okay?"

She sniffed, probably wiping at the tears that had so freely streamed down her cheeks only moments ago. "Sorry, homesick."

"Ah, it must be hard to be away from your parents and siblings."

"It is," she said.

"Can we talk?" he asked.

The door shut, and I realized she'd let him inside. They walked closer to the suite door, and I shied away from it, wishing I really had gone to the bathroom like Des had suggested.

But they didn't come to the room. I heard the scraping of chairs as they pulled the seats away from the table and sat down.

What was my dad wanting to talk to her about without telling me? What business could he possibly have with her?

"Des, I want to let you know how amazing you've been doing on this tour. I know I haven't been in this industry long, but I've seen bands who are at it for years not captivate a crowd the way you seem to do so naturally."

"Thanks, Anthony," she replied. Her voice was warm, and I was sure there'd be a smile just as friendly on her face.

"I wanted to come talk because we've started getting calls from talent agencies looking to represent you, and since Natalie passed, I wondered if you were interested in me passing them on?"

My jaw dropped open into a wide-mouthed grin, and I punched the air excitedly. I *knew* Des deserved to be seen!

"Yes!" Des cried, her voice just as excited as I was. "How can I get in touch with them?"

"The first step would be to set up meetings with them. There are a few in LA and a couple in Nashville. They'd fly you out there, of course, and they're going to pull out all the stops to schmooze you and get you to sign with them."

I thought back to when we'd signed with Song-bird Agency. They'd flown us first class to LA, driven us from the airport to the office in a limo, and even put us up in a five-star hotel. It had been incredible. That treatment, and their history of making stars go big, was why we eventually signed with them.

"I need to check my email!" Des said. "I haven't even been on it in weeks; I've been so busy with the tour and trying to keep up on social media."

"Definitely. I'd suggest a separate email for fans and business opportunities. It can get pretty over-whelming at times."

"Good tip," she said. "Would you mind getting on a call with my parents? We've never really done this before, and I think your advice would be really appreciated."

"Of course," he said. "Send me a few times, and we'll set something up."

I heard his chair scrape across the floor, and he said, "By the way, Jude, I'll see you back in the room."

THE BLOOD DRAINED from my face. "Wh-what do you mean?"

Jude's dad knew he was here?

And where the hell was Diego? He was supposed to be looking out!

Anthony wore an amused smile. "Jude's been walking around with a dopey smile for weeks now, and he never leaves the room on show nights. It was easy to guess."

The door to the bedroom slowly opened, and Jude walked out, his bright red cheeks a dead giveaway.

"We're trying to keep it private," I said.

"I respect that," Anthony said. "Most girls would want to scream it from the rooftops."

"Trust me, I do," I replied. "It's mainly one person I don't want to know."

Anthony's eyebrows drew together, but Jude quickly said, "Vanessa. You know the Fantiagos would be out for blood."

Why was Jude lying about this? I didn't understand, but still, I went along with it. "Yeah, I've had enough press scrutiny for now."

Anthony chuckled. "Get used to it. They might not be in the contract, but the media comes right along with it."

"True," Jude said. He came and kissed me on the cheek, but I stood frozen. I couldn't help but think this was bad. Very, *very* bad. "I better get to bed."

"Agreed," Anthony said. "Goodnight, Des."

Jude reached out and brushed my fingers. "Goodnight."

As soon as the Santiago men left my room, I got my phone and dialed Diego's number. When he answered, I said, "Where are you? Anthony came to our room!"

"I know. I was waiting outside the room in one of those sitting areas when he walked past. I tried to stop him, but he told me he already knew. He said he was okay with it, then gave me twenty bucks, so

I'm down in the restaurant eating cheesecake. Want some?"

"Yes, but that's beside the point! Why didn't you lie?"

"First of all," he said, clearly pausing to swallow, "lying is generally looked down upon. Second of all, he knew. It wouldn't have mattered how much I denied it. I don't think he'll tell Natalie. I mean, why would he?"

"Why would he not?" I asked, walking to the door and grabbing my purse on the way. "His literal job is to manage his son's career. Jude's public image, which includes his dating life, is a huge part of ticket sales."

"Jude knew what he was getting into. You asked him not to tell Natalie, right?"

"Yeah, but I didn't mention the part where Natalie threatened to destroy his career." I got into an empty elevator, feeling the swoop of my stomach before it even began its quick descent. "This is bad, Diego."

"It'll be okay. Natalie would be crazy to ruin her highest-grossing rock star, remember?"

That was the argument our family's lawyer made, but if Natalie suspected she'd be losing Jude anyway come January...

I reached the dining room and saw Diego with several plates of desserts around him. Usually, I tried to avoid sweets on Shantelle's guidance, but tonight, I sat with my brother and cleared all the plates with him.

It had been a good night, and for the first time in a long time, I felt free.

I kept waiting for the other shoe to drop with Natalie. But it had been weeks, and nothing had happened yet. Either Anthony hadn't told her about Jude and me, or she'd been bluffing.

And with each day that passed without her retaliation, I felt better about going all in with Jude than ever before. In fact, everything seemed to be coming together.

My parents and I had meetings scheduled for as soon as the tour was over, and I knew my life was only months, if not weeks, from being everything I'd dreamed it could be.

We still had a month left of the tour, and I cherished every moment spent with Jude. Every second I spent on stage. The only part I didn't like was seeing Natalie.

I typically tried to avoid her at all costs, but she called a meeting for the team and I couldn't avoid it.

We all sat in a conference room in the Phoenix concert venue. Each show brought us closer and closer to home, and I could feel both the exhaustion and excitement in the room full of Jude's team members.

Natalie stood at the head of the long table in front of a projected presentation and said, "I wanted to give a rundown of these last few weeks. I know everyone's tired, but I think we can bring it in strong."

She began working through slides of our last towns and the marketing plan for the release of Jude's latest album, which would come out on the last day of the tour.

Then she flipped to a new slide titled *Recording Schedule*. "Jude, the two days between Vegas and Reno is an incredible opportunity for you to fly back to LA and record this last song with Jade. The studio is booked for two days, so it's going to be a lot of hard work, and you won't get that break we'd hoped for, but this song really rounds out your album, and it will help with sales to have Jade's name attached."

Jude's eyebrows drew together, and he said, "Natalie, I told you I wasn't performing that song with Jade."

"Unfortunately, that's not your decision to make." She flipped to the next slide, but Jude spoke even louder.

"I'm not performing that song with Jade. I'm singing it with Des."

My cheeks felt hot as almost every eye in the room turned toward me.

"Jude, I'm not sure what kind of fat liberation statement you're trying to make to the public, but save it. I have a lot to get to and not a lot of time."

My eyes widened, and it was a miracle if my jaw wasn't on the floor. *Fat liberation statement?* Was she being serious?

Diego said in an even voice, "Watch it, Natalie."

Natalie narrowed her eyes at him. "You watch it, tag-along. I'm tired of dealing with all the arguing and drama that comes with this girl. Jude, you signed on with Songbird to manage your career, but I seriously suggest you manage your hormones before you get a reputation."

"A reputation of what?" Jude retorted.

Which was good because I was about to climb across the table and throw down. Who did this suited woman think she was to make comments about my weight and the "drama" I brought to the table?

Natalie narrowed her eyes and said, "A reputation for being *difficult*."

"Because *that* would be the worst thing in the world," he drawled.

Jude's dad stood up. "Enough. Jude, you're recording with Jade. Maybe you and Des can sing a cover someday on your own time. For now, we have business to attend to." He nodded toward Natalie. "Go on, please. We have things to do today."

Jude's jaw tensed, and a muscle in his cheek flickered. I wished I was next to him to grab his knee and let him know it was okay. We could fight this battle later, when Natalie wasn't in the picture anymore. The last thing we needed was for her to find out why Jude was so vehemently defending me.

He slowly sat back in his chair, but I had a feeling this wasn't the end.

FORTY-SIX
JUDE

I WAS PISSED, and my dad knew it. We walked back to my studio in silence, but as soon as the door was shut, I let into him. "How dare Natalie talk about Des like that." I paced the floor. "There was absolutely no need to say anything about her weight."

"You didn't need to argue with Natalie either," Dad said. "She's so set in her ways, nothing you could say would make a difference."

I gaped at him. "So I was just supposed to stay silent?"

"Maybe if Natalie knew you two were dating, she'd tread more lightly?" Dad asked. "You two have been so secretive about everything."

"She shouldn't need to know we're dating to treat Des with common human decency," I spat.

"Can't you just tell her?" Dad asked. "Honestly, I think it would be great for your career to make your relationship public. It would be every girl's dream come true, and you were the one who gave it to them."

I stalled my path across the space and looked at Dad. "We told you Des doesn't want it out."

"But why?" Dad asked. "When I started dating your mother, I wanted everyone to know that I was the guy who got to be with her. Why wouldn't Des want everyone to know?"

"I have no idea," I admitted, finally sitting on the couch.

With a concerned look on his face, Dad put his hand on my shoulder. "Son, in my experience, relationships that have to be kept secret aren't ones you should have."

I raised my eyebrows. "What about you and Francie? Huh?"

Dad's cheeks reddened, and he sputtered. "What Francie and I—it isn't what—"

"What?" I said. "Don't like the shoe on the other foot?"

Dad cleared his throat. "I asked Francie on a

date for when we get back to LA. It isn't fair to date her on the road."

I grinned, momentarily forgetting our argument. "You asked Francie out?"

Dad fought his own smile. "Yes, and she has agreed, so I'd appreciate it if you stop using that as a distraction from what I'm trying to say."

I sobered. "What exactly are you trying to say?"

"If a relationship needs to be a secret, it shouldn't exist in the first place." He took a deep breath and tilted his head. "There are reasons why a girl keeps a relationship a secret. And none of them are good." Dad patted my shoulder. "Think about it."

That was the problem. I couldn't *stop* thinking about it. All throughout the show, I wondered why Des would keep us a secret with no real explanation. The media had said she used boys and threw them away, but I'd thought it was all made up to sell another tabloid. What if there was merit to that? Even a little bit?

What if Des was dating me in secret so when we

broke up in secret she wouldn't be known as the girl who broke my heart?

The thought of her ending things with me and turning those beautiful eyes on someone else, of her lips kissing another guy. It made me want to puke and punch something at the same time.

As soon as we got on the bus, I sent her a text. We didn't have time for a private, face-to-face conversation, and I didn't have time to stew on this and wait.

Jude: Why can't we tell Natalie we're together? Then she'd understand why I need to sing the duet with you. The media would go crazy about a song written by the two of us, especially if we're in a relationship.

Des: We can't tell her. I can't say why. We just... can't.

Jude: Why? I hate these secrets.

Des: I do too.

Jude: Is there someone else?

Des: How could you even say that? Do you really think that's who I am?

Jude: I just don't understand, and you're not telling me. I feel like I'm fighting this battle on my own.

Des: What battle?

Jude: For the duet!

Des: Just sing it with Jade. It doesn't have to be a fight.

Jude: What? No.

Des: Why not? Would it really be the end of the world? We can do a cover later, like your dad said.

Jude: You're the one who was accusing me of being a sellout just a few months ago! Are you really asking me to compromise on this for the sake of money?

Des: It's not about the money.

Jude: Then what is it?

Des: Can you just trust me? I'm doing this to protect you.

Jude: Protect me?

Des: Yes.

Jude: From what?

Des: I can't say.

Jude: This is driving me crazy! Is this how our relationship's going to be? So many secrets?

Des: No! Of course not, Jude. I never want to keep anything from you.

Jude: But you are.

Des: I don't have another choice.

Jude: We always have choices. And I didn't choose a relationship like this.

Des: But you did. I asked if we could keep this from Natalie, and you agreed.

Jude: Natalie WANTS me to date you! She told me so at the beginning of the tour!

Des: WHAT?

Jude: She said she thought it would be great press.

Des: You're kidding me.

Jude: I'm not.

Des: She's bad news, Jude. You can't trust her. With anything.

Jude: I know that. But that doesn't change the fact that you're keeping things from me. I don't like that.

Des: I'm sorry.

Jude: An apology doesn't count unless it comes with a change in behavior.

Des: I'm doing the best I can.

Jude: It's not enough. I need honesty.

Des: I am being honest.

Jude: Transparency then.

Des: I... can't.

Jude: Then I guess that's it.

Des: That's it? Are you breaking up with me?

Jude: What else am I supposed to do?

Des: Don't say that.

Jude: I can't love someone who wants to keep me

their dirty little secret. Especially at the cost of my career.

Des: I'm protecting you!

Jude: You keep saying that, but from what?! I have Jago on me 24/7. What more protection do I need?

Des: You have no idea.

Jude: You're scaring me.

Des: It's not forever, Jude. Please, just a few more months.

Jude: The song will be out by then. And I'm not recording it with Jade. How many times do I have to say that?!

Des: What if I don't want to record it with you?

Jude: What?

Des: What if I don't want to record it with you?

Jude: You've sung it with me so many times on the bus. You inspired me to write it!

Des: And that's enough for me. I don't need to record it too.

Jude: This doesn't make any sense. What's going on?

Des: I want you to be as successful as possible. I don't want to hold you back or hurt you in any way, okay? I feel like it would be so much better for your career to sing it with her. You can always say onstage that you wrote it for me.

Jude: So you're protecting me from... your lack of fans?

Des: Exactly.

Jude: What does Natalie have to do with all this?

Des: Well, if she knew we were in love, she'd have us sing it together, right?

Jude: Exactly!

Des: So she can't know until AFTER you record it with Jade and the album releases, okay?

Jude: You're crazy. You know that?

Des: I'm crazy for you. :) Thanks for understanding. I think Jade will be great.

Jude: She's not you.

Des: I know. Are we okay?

Jude: Of course.

Des: Jude... It will all be better. Just wait for January. Okay?

Jude: Okay. Goodnight. <3

I locked my phone, but I didn't go to sleep. I stared at the text thread over and over again. Des may have put forth a confident front, but if her words told me anything, it was how much she cared. She was willing to sacrifice a role in my album, one that would reach millions of fans, to help my career grow.

But just like I told her, I wasn't a sellout. At the

beginning of the tour, I promised to prove it to her, and now I knew how I could.

Everyone should know that I loved Des. Because when you care for someone that much, you don't keep it a secret. You can't.

ON THE WAY TO REHEARSAL, I whispered to Jude, "Find me after the show? I want to talk to you about something."

"Of course," he said with a concerned look. "Are we okay?"

The fear in his voice almost undid me. It took all I had not to squeeze his hand and kiss his cheek right there in front of everyone. "We're perfect."

His smile was back, and when he flashed it on me, it was like everything came alive. I'd never felt this with a guy before. They had always been fun to hang out with, a good distraction from whatever was stressing me out at school, but never had they been comforting. Inspiring. Adoring. No, that was only Jude.

He'd gone from being a cute rock star to so much more, and I needed to tell him about Natalie's threat at the beginning of the tour, even if it meant breaking my NDA. Especially since she'd been luring him into a trap since day one of the tour. That woman could grow horns and start walking around with a pitchfork and I wouldn't be surprised.

We went about our routine that was now so ingrained we all worked together like a well-oiled machine. Each show was still exciting, but I felt more confident. I could work to make myself better instead of fighting to thrive in the unknown.

I gave it my all during my part of the show. As Jude performed onstage, I smiled over at Diego and saw him grin back. We were both proud of Jude. Not only was he my boyfriend, but he was Diego's friend too. None of my boyfriends had even met my family since Luke, but this was real. Jude and I were connected now more than ever.

Jude grinned at me from onstage and said into the microphone, "Des, can you do me a favor?"

I smiled at him and walked onstage, owning my four-inch heels and the way the fringe on my dress swung with my hips. The crowd cheered for me as I did. "Of course, Jude! How can I help?"

"I have a new song that's getting added to this album as a surprise bonus, and I want to show it to these lovely girls." And when I tell you my eardrums almost burst from the noise. "I need someone to sing it with."

My chest tightened. What was he doing? Angelina screamed the same thing in my ear.

I tried to calm myself as I walked the rest of the way to him and said, "Sure thing." Maybe he really was just teasing the song and needed me to help him out. After all, Jade wasn't exactly on tour with us.

And wasn't that one of the biggest unspoken rules of the performance? *What Jude says goes.* I couldn't tell him no. Not onstage and definitely not in front of all the Fantiagos in the audience.

He hooked his guitar strap over his shoulder and looked me in the eyes. His were black and shining under the spotlight that stayed on us.

Through my earpiece, I could hear Angelina repeating, "WHAT ARE YOU DOING?" But Jude ignored her and said, "Are you ready, love?"

If *swoon* was a sound, you could hear it from the fans.

"I'm ready," I said, smiling back.

Behind him on the giant screen, I could see a

close-up of the two of us. My curled hair. My smile. And the way Jude had eyes *only* for me.

From offstage, I heard Diego's whoop for us. I smiled more.

This was every girl's dream.

I just hoped it didn't turn into a nightmare.

Jude played the opening notes, and I closed my eyes, trying to let the fear slide off me, trying to focus on the music and the beautiful boy singing to me instead of the woman who wanted him destroyed.

"*When I kiss her, I'm going to do it right,*" he sang.

I opened my eyes, seeing Jude bathed in the spotlight's glow. "*When I kiss him, I want to see the light.*"

"*Stars in the sky burst within her eyes.*" He reached out and cupped my cheek with his hand. "*When I kiss her, I want to feel it all.*"

I held his hand to my cheek. "*When I kiss him, I'll be ready for the fall.*"

Together, we sang, "*When we kiss, it'll be everything or nothing at all.*"

With Jude singing to me so sweetly, the crowd fell away, and it was just him and me, singing the lyrics meant for us.

As the song drew to a close, the roar of cheers

became louder, and I looked at the audience in awe, seeing the way they reacted to the music Jude had written right in front of my eyes.

He was incredible.

Jude turned away from me and grinned at every person in the audience, as though he could make eye contact with each one of them. "What do you think?"

As if it were possible, the cheering grew even louder. I could see tears streaming down the cheeks of the people closest to the stage.

Jude had been right. He'd written the song for *us*. It broke my heart that he'd have to sing it with Jade. It just wouldn't be the same.

Jude walked along the front of the stage, touching outstretched hands as the cheering died down. Then he stepped back and glanced at me before turning back toward the crowd. "I have a confession to make."

The crowd became so silent, I could hear Jude's steps on the stage.

Could almost hear the strangled way my anxious heart was pumping.

"I've been listening to Desirae sing before every show for the last year."

My jaw dropped open. "What?" I breathed.

Jude said, "Her voice inspired me so much that I would sit with my earbuds in and listen to her sing, hoping I could be just as authentic in my own performances."

I covered my chest with my hands, feeling like my heart was going to burst.

"And then I asked my agent to have a meeting with her... We all know how that went."

The audience booed, and I let out a teary laugh. How had that soul-shattering rejection been only a couple months ago?

"I knew she could sing and saw she was beautiful from the videos, but as she came on tour with me, I discovered how incredibly brave, quick-witted, and naturally talented she is. I've been inspired by her every day."

The crowd, and I, were silent.

"Every day, I've fallen in love."

My lips fell open, but the audience gasped for me. Jude said he *loved* me?

He came to me, intertwining my fingers with his. "I want the world to know, I'm yours."

I stood frozen, caught between the boy I loved, the thousands of fans who'd be out for blood to see Jude's heart broken, and the one person standing offstage I knew was intent on destroying Jude's career and ruining *my* life.

For once, I didn't know what to say. There wasn't a single word flowing from my brain to my mouth. I couldn't think up a cute quip or a one-liner to fix it all.

So I said what was true:

"I love you."

In front of a stadium full of people.

In front of Natalie.

Jude hugged me tight, rocking us back and forth. I allowed myself to smile, to enjoy it.

But as he let me down and asked me to sing the last song of the night with him, I couldn't help looking over my shoulder. Natalie stood in the wings, a murderous grin on her face.

DES LOVED ME TOO.

She loved me.

It was real.

My whole body exhaled as she said the words, like all the fear and worry I'd been holding in had been for nothing. My dad had been wrong. Des wasn't hiding our relationship because she was embarrassed or pursuing someone else. She had been worried about holding me back.

If the fans' reaction tonight had been any indication, they loved seeing me with Des. They loved hearing us sing together. If they found out I was singing that duet with someone who wasn't my girlfriend, they would lose their minds. They'd be out for blood.

Natalie would have to let me sing it with Des.

There would be no other option.

I sang a happy song with Des for the last one of the show, one about what happens when wishes become reality, because that's how I felt. Holding her in my arms... I knew every dream had come true.

When we walked off the stage, everyone in the crew was clapping us on the back. Hugging us. Congratulating us. Everyone except for Diego.

He pushed me square in the chest, sending me stumbling back. "What the hell?"

Jago was immediately on Diego, holding back his arms and walking him away from me, but Diego didn't fight back. He only sent a glare at me. "*She told you she wanted it private,*" he growled.

I looked around for Des, but she wasn't anywhere in sight. "Where is she?"

"Her studio." Diego shook his head, shaking free of Jago. "I'm going to pick up the pieces."

Jago let him go.

Confused more than ever, I made to follow him, but Dad took my shoulder. "We don't have time now. We have to get to the meet-and-greet."

I wanted to chase after him, ask Diego to explain, but Dad was right. If the Fantiagos had to wait, I had no doubt they'd break down the barricades and find me themselves.

We went together to the tables where I signed merch and posed for photos, and there were about three reactions I got from the fans on the news of Des and me.

A)They were so excited I'd fallen for someone who looked like them.

B)They were pissed I was now off the market.

C)They were happy for me for finally finding love.

But all of them *loved* the new song and couldn't believe it would be on the album.

It was great, really, but I couldn't help the sinking feeling in my gut that was only getting worse. *What had I done wrong?*

And then someone said, "Why did her brother shove you?"

The buzz grew throughout the line of fans, and I drew my eyebrows together. I asked the girl closest to me, "How did they know about that?"

She held out her phone showing a video of Diego pushing me and yelling something indiscernible. It was posted in the Fantiago social media group by Fan No. 1, Vanessa Cooper herself.

"That's not what it looks like," I said quickly, although I had no clue myself. I'd never seen Diego angry like that except in the meeting when he told Natalie to stop bashing Des. Even then, he'd been pretty level-headed.

He must have thought I'd done something bad. Really bad.

Had I?

How could I have? I just told the girl I loved that I loved her.

To hell with what everyone thought about Des and me. I didn't care what happened as long as we were together, and Des shouldn't either.

I could hear Dad on the phone behind me, probably talking to Samantha to figure this out, but I couldn't wait to get done with this signing so I could do the real damage control. I needed to talk to Des and Diego.

The next hour seemed to take five instead, but finally I was done, and I ran through the concert venue to get to Des's studio. Jago kept pace beside me, not trying to stop me, but I knew he'd hold back Diego and get me out of there if things got bad.

Not that they would. I just needed to get them

to understand how great this was. Des and I could be a real couple now. Hang out on the couch in the bus with her legs draped over mine. Go on real dates at fancy restaurants. Kiss without the cover of closed doors.

I reached her studio and knocked right below the sign of her name surrounded with lights. "It's me," I said.

Des opened the door far enough for me to see Diego scowling from the couch. "Come in."

Jago made to go in with me, but I said, "I'm fine."

He seemed conflicted, looking between Diego and me.

"I'm *fine*," I repeated.

"If you need me, there's nothing stopping me from busting down this door."

I nodded. I knew Jago would do it.

I went inside the room, locking the door behind us for good measure. Des, the person I thought would be just as happy as me, seemed distraught. Her eyes were puffy. "Have you been crying?" I asked her, taking her face in my hands. "What's wrong?"

"You shouldn't have done that," she said, her voice breaking. "I asked you to keep it from

Natalie."

"Why?" I asked. "Enough with the secrets. Just tell me what's going on."

She opened her mouth to speak, but a key turned in the lock with the heavy sound of metal sliding against metal.

And then Natalie was in the room.

She looked just as severe as ever with her hair tightly pulled back and her sharp cheekbones catching every shadow in the room. But there was a slight smile playing over her lips too. Instead of being comforting though, it was ominous.

"What are you doing here?" I demanded. "I'm trying to talk to my girlfriend."

Des sucked in a breath behind me.

Natalie only smiled wider, her teeth glinting dangerously. "Why don't you tell him yourself, Des? I'm assuming you haven't broken the terms of your NDA?"

She shook her head.

"What's going on?" I asked, desperate now.

Natalie seemed frustrated, but not enough to take away from her obvious joy at Des's and my discomfort. "I sold the song to Jade," Natalie said. "We just signed the papers. It's a done deal."

My mouth fell open. "What? You can't sell my song—it's my original work."

"Which I am able to negotiate and manage as I please," Natalie said smugly. "It's written in our contract."

My song, the one I'd poured my entire heart into, wasn't even my own? It was like she'd stabbed me in the chest with a jagged knife and twisted.

"Don't worry," Natalie said. "You'll get a good chunk of the money. But I do believe Jade will perform it with someone else. They won't sit on it for long—we all know it's a chart-topper."

"Why would you do this?" I demanded. "You're hurting yourself too! You know it would explode if Des and I sang it together. The fans loved it tonight."

Natalie shrugged, unbothered. "I told Des what would happen if she pursued a relationship with you."

My eyebrows drew together. Des knew Natalie would sell my song? "Explain."

Natalie narrowed her eyes, coming so close I could see the individual pores on her face. "I don't like working with clients who betray my trust and make me look a fool. I will make these last four months of your contract miserable, Jude Santiago, and then I will make sure every agent in LA, Nashville, and anywhere in between knows *exactly* what kind of client you are."

Then she turned on her heel and walked out.

FORTY-NINE

DES

NATALIE WALKED out of the studio, locking the door behind her, and Jude turned to me. Hurt and confusion and *so many questions* were laid bare in his eyes.

Before I could speak, Diego said, "She tried to tell you, Jude. You should have trusted her."

But I held up my hand to him. "Diego, I need a second with Jude."

Diego hesitated, not wanting to move. "Are you sure you're okay?"

I nodded, lying. I was anything but okay.

Natalie had taken a song Diego had poured his heart into. He'd given that heart to me onstage. And now it was crushed, mangled. I could see it in his eyes.

Diego got off the couch and brushed my shoulder before leaving the room. With the heavy sound of the shutting door, Jude finally spoke.

"Des, tell me that's not true," he said, his voice breaking.

I closed my eyes, feeling hot tears squeeze between my lashes. They rolled down my cheeks, down to my throat that ached with pain. With shame.

"Des," Jude repeated.

I opened my eyes, but immediately wished I hadn't. He was corroding with betrayal, with pain I'd placed on him.

"That's what she pulled me aside to talk about that first day," I admitted, each word feeling like razor blades on my tongue. "She said she would destroy your career if I dated you."

His lips parted and he scrubbed his hand over his face, tears of his own sliding down his cheeks. "You've known this entire time."

It wasn't a question.

I didn't reply.

"You knew you could take *everything* from me, and you let this go on anyway."

"My parents' lawyer said it was an empty threat, but I was careful anyway, Jude. I tried to tell you we had to keep it a secret. You said it was okay."

He cut me off, slicing his hand through the air. "It's not consent if I don't know the risks too."

His words were a punch to the stomach. Not because they were mean. But because they were true.

"Jude, I'm sorry."

He shook his head, not even looking me in the eyes anymore. "You can't make that decision for me. It's not just one song; it's my whole career. My entire life. Don't you get that?"

I nodded. "Of course I do."

"No, you don't!" His voice rose. "No, you don't! You have an entire life at home, Des. You have parents who would give anything for you and a brother who would defend you no matter what and siblings who look up to you and friends you can always count on! I don't have that. My dad is my manager. My friends ditched me when I got rich. My grandma lives in Winslow. My mom killed herself before I even knew her. Music is my life. It's *everything*. It's all I have. And you knew that, Des! You knew that! But you took it anyway."

Tears flowed quickly down my cheeks, and I

moved toward him, desperate to let him know how sorry I was. How much I loved him.

But he stepped away, a look of disgust growing on his face. "Don't come near me."

"Jude, I—"

He shook his head. "I thought I loved you, but I could never love someone who would play with everything I have like it's nothing."

Then he turned and put his hand on the doorknob. "I need to fix this mess."

The door shut behind him, but I knew he was gone before he ever left the room. I collapsed onto the floor, not even making it to the couch, sobbing with loss, with heartbreak, with anger at Natalie, who'd been so willing to play with our lives. But mostly, I was angry at myself.

I thought I'd come so far since Luke, but I felt like a lost freshman girl all over again, seeing the love of my life throwing me away like the trash I was.

I wanted no part of myself right now. The realization of what I'd done made me nauseous. I'd been listening to my heart, thinking about what *I* wanted, but I'd never considered that Jude deserved to know what he was risking. How *selfish* could I be?

I wanted out of my skin. I wanted to jump in

the shower and scrub myself raw. I wanted to vomit up everything I was until I was an empty shell.

But there was no hiding from myself.

Diego came into the room and held me, rocking me against his chest.

But I didn't even deserve that.

There was only pain, and I let it consume me. Let it eat every part. I deserved each ache, each tear, each crack in my fracturing heart.

FIFTY

JUDE

I STUMBLED TO MY STUDIO, physically feeling the hurt rising, swelling, threatening to pour over. Jago held my shoulder, keeping me upright as I yanked open the door with clammy hands. I made it inside before I slid down the wall. It was like Des's words had reached into my chest and grabbed out my heart, taking flesh, bones, muscles and all.

I had put *everything* I had into that song, given my heart to her, and now I had *nothing*.

I beat the side of my balled fist on the wall, reveling in the ache. That pain was so much more bearable than the one ripping through my chest.

I wanted it to go away. To stop hurting. So I kept banging my fist until the hurt was all I could feel.

A knock sounded on my door, and I ignored it. What were they going to do? Drag me out of here?

They'd have to, because I was never leaving, never moving. Never showing my face again.

How could I?

I'd humiliated myself in front of thousands of fans, had my life's greatest work sold out from under me. There was no coming back from that.

The knock turned into a bang, and my dad yelled, "Jude, I want to help. If you won't let me in, I will kick this door down!"

Maybe I really was just a child, because when my dad offered his help, I realized I wanted it. He wasn't just my manager; he was the one person in my life who'd never walked away. He wasn't perfect, but I didn't need perfect. I needed present.

I got to my knees and pulled the handle to release the lock, my hands throbbing. It popped open, and soon Dad was on his knees, pulling me to his chest.

I held on, digging my fingers into his back through his suit jacket. "Natalie took it," I choked out. "She took my song."

"I know." Dad ran his hand over my hair, cradling me like I was a baby instead of a man his size. "We'll fix it, okay? We'll get our lawyers on the phone and figure this out."

I pulled back, my eyes raw. "Is that even possible?"

He finally saw my hands and covered his mouth in horror. "Jago! Get a medic!"

My eyes darted from him to my hands, seeing the purple bruising already flowering across my skin.

Dad took my wrists, forcing me to look at him. His dark brown eyes were almost black, and his brow was creased with concern. "Jude, I'm going to tell you something my father told me after your mother passed away. Good guys win in the end. If you haven't won, it's not the end."

I didn't have it in my heart to believe him, but that promise was all I had. "Dad, I can't see her again."

"Who?" he asked. "Natalie? We can't really—"

"Desirae."

Dad's eyebrows drew together. "Natalie put her in a hard position, son. It's not—"

I ripped my hands from his grasp and beat the floor. "I don't want to see her again." It would only be a reminder of the betrayal I'd endured at the hands of the only girl I'd ever really loved. "Rent them another bus, put them up in hotels; I don't care how much it costs. Just keep me away from her."

"If that's what you need," he rushed out. "We can get them off the tour if that's what you want."

I shook my head. Whatever scraps had been left of my heart knew it wouldn't be right, to give Des her dream and then take it away. I hated that I cared so much after what she'd done to me, but it wasn't going away even with the pain blooming in my hands.

"Okay, I'll figure it out. We'll have an emergency meeting with Samantha tonight and have our lawyers working around the clock until they figure this out. Worst-case scenario, we'll buy Natalie out of the contract."

"How much would that cost?" I asked.

"Too much," Dad said gruffly. "But it would be worth it. I'm going to have Jago take you to the bus after we get your hands looked at. We'll get Des and Diego a hotel room, and we'll go from there. It's going to be okay."

I didn't give a reply, and Dad didn't wait for one. He just kissed the top of my head and held me until a medic rushed into the room, carrying a tote.

He and the medic spoke, and I did what he

asked, taking pain medicine and holding my hands out to be wrapped. Somewhere in the back of my mind, I registered them saying I didn't have any broken bones. Just bruising and swelling. But I was already gone. Watching myself from the outside of my body.

Soon, Jago was leading me out the door to the bus and carefully locking it behind us. I went straight back to my room and shut the door. I knew Dad was calling a meeting and there were things to take care of, but I just wanted to shut down my mind. To escape.

So I closed my eyes, put a pillow over my head, and fell asleep.

I CURLED into Diego's side, letting my baby brother hold me together as everything in me fell apart. I never should have agreed to kiss Jude. I should have stuck to the plan all along: growing my career and focusing on my music.

Devon had been right in his interview. I used guys and threw them away when I was done with them. But the way Jude had looked at me when the truth came out... it made me feel worse than garbage.

I wanted to take it all back, but I couldn't. Natalie had sold Jude's incredible song. All because of me.

A knock sounded on the door, and Diego got up to check who was there. After peeking through the crack, he pulled the door open, revealing Angelina.

"Hey," she said gently, "I've got instructions to take you two to a hotel. Your bags will be there when we arrive."

"What's going on?" Diego asked. Probably because he cared what happened to us.

Me? They could toss me in a dumpster out back, and I'd be exactly where I belonged.

Angelina said, "I'm not one hundred percent sure. I just have orders to take you to a hotel for the night before we continue on the tour. I'm pretty sure Anthony and Samantha will be calling Des tonight." Angelina looked from Diego to me, waiting for questions but not getting any. "The car's waiting. Let's go."

We walked together through the echoing hallways, and I hoped beyond hope I could see Jude. I had to let him know how sorry I was.

Instead, we passed no one. We walked by the tour bus with all the blinds closed, got into an inconspicuous black car, and drove away.

It struck me then that I'd been counting all my firsts on this tour. My first time onstage. My first interview. My first kiss with Jude.

But I should have been paying attention to my

lasts instead. I had a feeling I wouldn't share a stage with Jude ever again, and that broke my heart even more.

When we arrived at the hotel, Angelina helped us check in and dropped us off at a suite. I'd half expected to be put up in a one-star, roach-infested motel for what I'd done, but I knew Jude was better than that. His heart was too big to treat someone like dirt. No matter how much they deserved it.

Just as promised, our bags were on the beds—all of them. Not just our overnight bags we kept in the closet on the bus.

Diego linked his hands behind his head, looking pained. "I'm sorry for shoving him, Des. I never should have—"

I held up my hand. "Don't apologize. You're the best brother in the world." I swallowed, trying to keep from breaking down again. "This is all my fault."

"It's Natalie's," Diego argued, gesturing wildly with his hands. "She's the one who got exposed for being *la bruja* and was set on making you the bad guy. I don't understand why Jude can't see that."

"Her guilt doesn't prove my innocence," I replied, sitting on the edge of the bed by my red luggage. I'd used to think it was so pretty, but now the bright color seemed to scream at me, reminding me of why it wasn't stowed safely on the bus.

Diego shook his head. "You know how Jude is. He needs some time to be by himself and cool down, but he'll come around."

My phone went off with a new message alert, and I hurried to get it from the pocket of my leggings, hoping it would be Jude. Instead, it was a text from his father.

Anthony: Samantha and I are working on a media plan. She will be by the hotel in the morning to prep you for the rest of the tour.

My eyes misted as I read his words, and I pointlessly tried to wipe away the tears.

Looking over my shoulder, Diego said, "That's good news, right? There's a rest of the tour for you. And they can't take away your meetings with agents."

I looked up at him, thankful for the way he was trying to comfort me, but knowing I didn't deserve it. "I'm going to take a bath. I'll see you in the morning?"

Diego nodded, then kissed the top of my head and walked away.

I was alone.

Normally, I hated being alone. I wanted to be

surrounded by friends and family and love. But today? I didn't think I deserved it. And no matter how much I hated to admit it, I was mad at everyone too. Why were they pushing me to get in a relationship with him? Shouldn't one of them, at least, have pointed out how wrong it was to risk his career without him knowing?

I'd counted on them for a perspective I didn't have, and they'd failed me.

But most of all, I'd failed myself.

I'd watched Jude write that song, seen how much of himself he put into his career, witnessed the struggle he faced to have his voice heard amongst a crowd of seasoned adults. And I'd jeopardized it anyway.

I went to the bathtub, tears streaming down my cheeks, and turned the water as hot as it would go. Steam poured from the water and clouded the room, filled my lungs and clung to my skin.

When the bathtub filled, I dipped my toes in, letting the burn sink deep into my skin, letting the pain hit me from the inside out.

But no matter how much it hurt, nothing killed me like the look in Jude's eyes when he said he *thought* he loved me.

WHEN I WOKE up in the morning, someone was in bed with me.

I startled awake, but my mom rolled toward me and brushed my hair back, quietly saying, "Shh, shh."

I instantly relaxed, scooting closer to her. She held me, and more tears flowed from my aching, puffy eyes.

"It's okay," she whispered in English and then in Spanish. "It's okay, baby. We're right here."

"We?" I asked through sniffles.

"Your father and me. We came as soon as Diego called us last night."

"What time is it?" I asked.

"Almost eight."

"The meeting," I said, sitting up. "We were supposed to meet with Samantha, and—"

"Honey," Mom said, taking my face in her hands. "We have another thirty minutes before you need to be awake. It starts at half past nine."

I slowly nodded and asked, "Can you turn on the lights?" It was so dim with the blue-gray walls and blackout curtains.

Mom got up and turned on the light, then pushed part of the curtains back. Bright morning light diffused through the sheers, illuminating the room. There was a damp towel scrunched on the floor by the bed. My bag had been left open with clothes I'd pulled out to find my big sleep shirt and shorts. I didn't even want to think about what I looked like right now, having crawled into bed with wet, tangled hair.

Mom came back and sat on the edge of the bed. She was wearing a flowy black dress with long sleeves, and her shoes said she meant business. She'd come to fight for me. "Honey, Diego told us what happened. I'm so furious at *la bruja*. She's not just horrible. She's evil. *Malvada*."

I couldn't help but agree.

"And I'm so glad that Diego was here to take

care of you. Can you imagine if you'd been alone last night?"

I couldn't. I would have been on a taxi to the airport begging for the first plane ticket home. In fact... "Mom, should I just go home?"

Her eyebrows drew together. "Why on earth would you say such a thing? You did nothing wrong."

"I had a relationship with Jude, knowing what Natalie was threatening. Even if the risk was small, I never should have taken it."

"And a girl so young should *never* be put in the position you were. So many adults would have stumbled in your place. If Jude can't understand that you did the best you could and learned from your mistakes, he needs to think more clearly."

A voice I hadn't heard before sounded outside the room, and I drew my eyebrows together. "Mom, who else is here?"

"We brought our lawyer," she said.

My mouth fell open. He flew out here with them at the last minute? "Oh my gosh, how much did that cost?"

She kissed my forehead, surely leaving a red lipstick stain. "A mother protects her child. No matter the cost."

I hugged her tight, breathing in the delicate scent of her perfume. "I missed you so much."

She held me back. "Sometimes the sky feels too far from the nest."

We stayed that way for a moment, and then Mom pulled back, pressing her fingertips to the corners of her eyes. "Why don't you get ready? I'll wait for you with your father."

I nodded and took my bag to the bathroom, trying to care enough about my appearance to make myself look good. I had no idea what was coming in this meeting. Would Jude and I have to break up in public? That would be a disaster.

The Fantiagos would eat me alive if they knew I broke Jude's heart. No amount of security would keep them from coming onstage to protect him— and destroy me. With a cold feeling in my chest, I realized I could be in very real danger.

I hurried through the rest of my routine, straightening my hair and putting on tinted moisturizer and mascara. Then I wore a nicer shirt and dark jeans, along with a pair of heels, and walked into the living room.

My dad immediately took me in his arms, his mustache scratching my cheek as he placed a kiss there.

"Thanks for coming, Daddy," I said.

"Of course." He kept his arms around my shoulders as he reintroduced me to our lawyer. "You remember Manuel? He's going to take good care of you."

Manuel was a big man, taller than my dad and a foot wider too. As I shook his meaty hand, I wasn't upset at all about him going to bat for us.

"I've gotten Diego's version of events, but can you tell me what happened last night?" he asked.

I nodded, and Mom guided us toward the table. Diego and I sat beside each other, Mom and Dad standing beside us, as we broke down every horrifying event for Manuel. He asked for some clarification on certain points, but when we were finished, his frown was deep.

"I'm not sure what the terms of Jude's contract were, but it would have to be pretty tightly knit for her to be able to sell a piece of IP without even a signature."

Now that he said it, that did seem strange. "She said she was in charge of how his IP was managed."

"She probably knows more than I do, but it sounds fishy to me." He clasped his hands together on the table, leaning forward. "The main thing you need to know is that you have done nothing wrong, and you have nothing to worry about."

He'd meant it to be reassuring, but I had plenty of worries. Namely Jude and whether or not he could ever forgive me.

Mom rubbed my shoulders. "It's time to go. Are you ready?"

Not even close.

FIFTY-THREE

DES

WE WALKED downstairs to the main level of the hotel, no one saying a word. My breaths wouldn't come fully, as if they knew I should be holding on to something. On to the way things were.

The conference room was down an empty hallway on the hotel's main level, and when we got there, the door was open.

I searched the space, hoping to see Jude, but only Anthony and Samantha were in the room.

They both stood to greet us, and I desperately searched their eyes for some kind of sign. Anthony was expressionless, but Samantha gave me a compassionate look that I held on to with everything I had. Someone on Jude's team cared, and that meant the world to me.

Anthony took in our group. "I wasn't expecting everyone to be here. I'm so glad you could join us."

Mom narrowed her gaze, but Dad extended his hand and briefly shook Anthony's. "This is our family's lawyer, Manuel Riviera."

Anthony measured up Manuel and said, "There really wasn't a need to involve an attorney."

Manuel replied, "I'll be the judge of that."

We sat around the table, and Anthony cleared his throat. "Well, we're all up to speed on what Natalie did yesterday. Unfortunately, our contract obligates us to continue working with Songbird until January. With only ten shows left, we think it's best to complete the tour with Jude and Des being seen together as a couple."

Samantha nodded. "We all know how devoted the Fantiagos are, and if they perceive Des has hurt Jude in some way, we'd be hard-pressed to find a security detail strong enough to stop them in those numbers with all the excitement of a concert underway. We believe it will take minimal effort to continue the act of a relationship, as long as Des plays up how much she loves him before the show and Jude makes comments about being taken while he's onstage."

Before anyone could speak, I asked, "What does Jude think about this?"

Anthony answered, "He's willing to do what's best, for his fans."

Another stab through the heart. None of this was for me. It was just who Jude was, thinking about everyone else before himself.

My mom said, "What if Desirae disagrees? I think it's hardly fair for her to show so much compassion to a boy who so quickly wrote her off."

Anthony bristled. "Considering Jude's very understandable reaction, this is a more than generous offer. Meteor has offered multiple times to come back on tour, after seeing Jude's response to Natalie's treatment of Desirae, and it would be no problem to bring them back for the last leg of the tour."

Everyone in the room turned to me, waiting for my response, but I only had more questions. "What are you guys doing about Natalie? She can't take that song."

Anthony's defenses seemed to fall away, revealing just how tired and worried he was. "Our legal team is combing over the documents, looking for some loophole, anything that will get Jude out of this contract with her. Since papers have already been signed on the song, it would be really hard to get it back from Jade unless she willingly agrees to give it back to him. Unlikely, considering that song cost a *very* pretty penny."

Manuel leaned forward and said, "Would you mind if I gave the contract a look, pro bono? I've worked with a lot of IP before, and an extra set of eyes could only help, right?"

Anthony rubbed his temples. "I'll have my team fax it to your office. Can I have your card?"

Reaching into his jacket pocket, Manuel retrieved a card and slid it across the glossy table.

Samantha folded her arms tightly around herself. "I'm furious at Natalie. She's had it out for Desirae since the beginning of the tour."

"What do you mean?" Manuel asked.

Samantha launched into an explanation, starting with Natalie's rebuttals to have me join the tour, despite the fact that Samantha thought it was an incredible idea. She talked about Natalie surprising me on a live interview with the head of the Fantiagos, someone who would clearly want to see me taken down.

Manuel asked, "Do you have any proof? Text messages? Voicemails?"

"Yes," Samantha said, drawing her eyebrows together. "Why?"

"I need to get back to my office and look over that contract to confirm, but there may be a way to fix this," Manuel said. He slid another card across the table to Samantha. "Text me screen shots of those messages and send me any audio you have. The more the better."

Dad asked Manuel, "What's going on?"

"There's typically something called a 'good faith' clause. If Natalie failed to perform her duties in Jude's best interest, it may be grounds to terminate the contract. She may be able to make a case that selling the song was in Jude's best interest, but if we have proof of her working to destroy Desirae's, and therefore Jude's, reputation then it may help Jude out of the contract."

Anthony's eyes shined with tears. "I hope you're right. Let me step out of the room so I can give our legal team a call." He left the room, shutting the door behind him, and Samantha gave me a compassionate look.

"How are you doing, Des?" she asked.

Tears formed in my own eyes, and I shook my head. "Not great."

"It sounded brutal," she said, "for both of you."

Diego said, "It was horrible. And the things Jude said to her..."

"They were all true," I said sadly.

Samantha tilted her head, tenderness in her eyes. "We'll figure this out. And in my opinion, Natalie did all of us a favor. Now we know who's truly on our team and who isn't."

"Absolutely," Dad agreed. "We're all on your team, Desirae."

I looked up at my dad, trying to smile but crying again, because all I could think about was Jude and his realization that I wasn't on his team like he'd thought I'd been.

FIFTY-FOUR
JUDE

DAD CAME INTO THE ROOM, and I tried to pretend to be asleep.

I'd woken around three the night before, and no matter how much I tried to go back to sleep, my mind wouldn't let me. My heart ached too bad, and every time I closed my eyes, all I could see was Des saying she loved me.

It had been a lie.

The most beautiful lie.

I glanced at the alarm clock and saw it was nearly noon. We needed to leave soon to be on time for the next show. Not that I had any freaking clue how I was going to perform. I'd sang with bronchitis before, but even that pain came nowhere close to how I felt now.

Dad sat beside me on the bed, rubbing my shoulder. "Jude, Jude."

I opened my eyes and sat up, not bothering to carry on the performance, accepting that this new pain was my life. If it would get better, I didn't know how.

"We have a new lead on something," Dad said. "There might be a part of your contract that could let us get rid of Natalie."

"What? What is it?" My heart leapt, despite my fear of getting my hopes up for something impossible.

"There's a part of your contract. A good faith clause. They're looking at it right now, but Natalie might be fired by the end of the night. When she sues us—which she probably will—we'll be able to show how she was trying to use Des to sabotage you. Isn't that great?"

Des's name was like a punch to the gut. A kick to the kidneys. But I nodded anyway. "What about my song? Can we get it back?"

I saw the answer in his eyes before he spoke a word. "I'm sorry, son, but short of Jade giving it back or selling it back to us... I don't see it happening."

I swallowed down the jagged lump in my throat and nodded. "What about..." I couldn't even bring myself to say her name.

"She agreed to our plan. Two weeks and then she's out of your life—if you want her to be."

Dad acted like we'd won today, but I'd lost so much that mattered to me. I closed my eyes, feeling the heat of fresh tears under my lids. "I think I need to get some more sleep."

"Sure, son." Dad patted my shoulder and left the room.

I didn't sleep. Not for an hour, not for a minute.

I hid in the dark room like I did best.

And when we arrived at the venue and I sat in my makeup chair, Gentry said, "You look like crap."

"I look how I feel," I replied, sitting back and staring at my phone.

"Brooding star doesn't look good on you today," she said.

"Chatty makeup artist isn't a great look for you either," I retorted.

She raised her eyebrows with a small smile and got to work.

Luckily, Dad had taken every step possible to keep Des away from me. Her makeup artist went to her studio, her wardrobe was brought there too, and we even warmed up in separate locker rooms.

But when she was onstage, there was nothing I could do to keep her voice out of my ears. It worked its way through my mind and straight into my fractured heart, vibrating the pieces further and further apart.

And the lies. They fell so smoothly from her lips as she spoke them to thousands of people.

She said things like, "How excited are we to see *my* handsome man on stage?" Or, "One of the things I love about Jude is his authenticity. When he comes up here, he's giving you all of himself. And it's incredible."

And then she said, "Let's hear it for the love of my life! Come out here, Jude!"

Dad patted my back and said into my ear, "You can do this."

I couldn't.

But I had to.

I walked onstage to fanfare, forcing a smile on my face that hurt every part of me. And I walked to stand beside Des, not daring to make eye contact with her. "Isn't she lovely?" I asked.

The crowd cheered, adoring her just like I used to. Just like I wished I could now.

And then I said, "I'm not sure how I could ever measure up to a *performer* like her, but I'll try."

Des replied, "You know I'm not acting when it comes to how I feel about you."

For the first time, I met her eyes. They were full of pain, but what right did she have to feel hurt? I was the one she betrayed. I was the one handing over my heart on a silver platter, only to be gutted and ripped apart.

She had no idea what this pain felt like.

How much I hated the fact that I still loved her.

"Let's do a throwback," I said, facing the audience again. "I may be in love with Des, but the Fantiagos will always by my first love. You got me to where I am tonight, and I'll never forget that."

I walked to the edge of the stage, picking a girl who was exactly the opposite of Des. She had pixie blond hair and light blue eyes. Her body was so small and petite, it was beyond easy to lift her onto the stage. She was exactly the kind of girl who had never caught my eye the way Des had.

And as the band began playing my classic serenade song, I focused only on the girl who could have been any of thousands in the crowd. It was only out of the corner of my eye that I saw Des walk offstage and fall into her brother's arms.

WE HAD two days to spend in Las Vegas before our next show, and only eight performances left. I'd never been to Vegas before, and I knew I should have been seeing the sights, but I couldn't. There just wasn't enough energy left in me.

After a lot of urging, I finally convinced Diego that he could leave me alone in the room so he could go out. There was a long hike he wanted to do, and Jago had agreed to meet him.

Besides, I needed privacy to do what I'd been putting off.

I needed to call my friends. They'd been texting me like crazy since news got out about Jude and me dating. They were all so happy for me. But now I had to disappoint them too.

I pressed dial on a group video call and walked to the window, taking in the view. I could see jagged mountains in the distance and the parking lot below. The tour bus was parked there, along with Vanessa's car and trailer.

If she knew what was going on between Jude and me, she'd be over the moon excited along with royally pissed.

My friends' voices ripped me out of my thoughts, and I looked down at their faces on the screen.

Nadira said, "We thought you'd forgotten about us now that you had a super-hot and famous boyfriend!"

I let out a half cry, half sob. "It's such a mess, guys."

Cori said, "What did he do? I don't care how much security he has. I'm coming, and I'm bringing a shovel."

I laughed, but it only hurt, and I clutched my chest. "Stop making me laugh."

"Des," Faith said, "tell us what's going on."

I wrapped my free arm around my middle and sat on the edge of the bed. "I messed everything up," I began, telling them the horrible story of how Natalie had gotten the revenge she'd warned me of.

Adequately horrified, Adriel said, "Tell me Jude is suing her! This can't be legal."

"His lawyers are working on it, my lawyer's working on it, and there might be something to get him out of the contract with her, but I haven't heard anything about it." I blinked quickly, trying not to completely fall apart. "But Jude feels like I betrayed him, and I did."

Faith frowned deeply. "You betrayed him? Natalie's the one who did all of those horrible things, not you."

"Yeah, but she threatened me, and I dated him anyway."

The girls tried to argue, but I cut them off. "For once, I need to be down on myself. I made a mistake."

Cori said gently, "Beating yourself up won't make him forgive you."

"Then what will?" I asked, "Because I'm dying inside with the guilt of it all."

"He has to decide that," she said. "And he's going to have to decide if he'd rather hold on to his anger or be with you."

At this point, I knew what he was deciding. I'd seen it in his eyes on-stage. The way he'd sang to that girl was clear: he wanted nothing to do with me or anyone remotely like me.

I understood his message, loud and clear.

Never again.

No matter how much I loved him.

No matter how many times I promised to do better.

No matter the regret I felt.

He was never going to have his heart broken by me again.

"What am I supposed to do?" I finally asked my friends.

They were quiet for a moment before Faith finally said, "We do the best with what we have. And when we know better, we do better."

I knew better now, and it was time to put that knowledge into action.

After I hung up with my friends, I wiped at my eyes, flipped through my contacts, and pressed call.

And to my surprise, he answered.

FIFTY-SIX
JUDE

NATALIE HAD BEEN SURPRISINGLY quiet since her act of terror. Samantha told us that she'd gone back to California. Probably on her broomstick to warn Songbird's legal team about the storm we were preparing to rain down on them.

Dad and I went down to the conference room in the hotel for an early morning virtual meeting with our lawyers. According to Dad, they'd been working nonstop to find a loophole in the contract, and they were going to brief us on what they'd discovered.

My hands shook with anticipation. I hoped it would be good news, but I'd also hoped Des and I would sing my song together. Now, we'd probably never sing together ever again, my song or otherwise.

Dad worked at his laptop, connecting to the video call, and soon the screen filled with a room of men wearing unbuttoned dress shirts and loosened ties. By the amount of coffee on the table and the state of their clothes, it was clear they'd been working around the clock to get the best outcome for me. Something about that made my shoulders relax, if only slightly.

Allen, the lead of our legal team, said, "I think we have some good news for you."

My lips parted as the words registered. "I'm getting my song back?"

"Thanks to Manuel's tip, we found a section of the contract that essentially says the contract only stands if Natalie is acting in the best interest of her client. Judging by the ways she was working to tarnish Jude's reputation through Desirae De Leon, we have rights to terminate the contract. Unfortunately, anything she's done up until this point is within her legal right because the contract was still intact, even if she did it with malicious intent." His expression was apologetic, but the truth hurt all the same.

Dad said, "What about the label? Does this affect our relationship with them?"

"That contract is still in place. Natalie's portion

of the royalties will now be diverted to Jude's new agent. Our team is prepared to take on those tasks in the interim."

"Thanks, Allen," Dad said.

I sat back in my chair, taking the blow. It was good news to be free of Natalie before she could inflict any more damage, but the cost of my song would be a permanent reminder to guard my heart. Especially when it came to girls as beautiful, fierce, and fun as Desirae De Leon.

Dad said, "We'll let you get to work on the termination letter. Please be sure to remind Natalie that we will pursue every legal avenue available when it comes to defamation and libel."

"Absolutely," Allen said.

Dad turned to me. "Anything to add?"

It was subtle, Dad including me in the conversation, but it was one of the first times he really let me have a true seat at the table.

"It sounds good to me," I said, leaning forward. "Thanks for your work."

Dad added, "Let us know when you've sent it so we can have Samantha ready on PR."

Allen nodded. "Have a good day, gentlemen." And then he signed off.

Dad turned toward me, a bittersweet expression

on his face. "It's better than nothing. And maybe we can have them get in touch with Jade to see about buying back the song."

"Do you think she would do that?" I asked.

"Maybe," Dad said. "How much it will cost us is another question altogether."

Dad clapped my shoulder. "Grandma should be arriving in half an hour or so. Want to grab juice or something at the breakfast bar and wait for her?"

"Wait, Grandma's coming?" The news was sunshine on a storm cloud day.

Dad nodded with a small smile. "I thought you might want to see her. And I missed her myself."

My smile came easier than it had in previous days. "Yeah. I'll be out there soon. I need to make a call before she gets here."

I could see the questions in Dad's eyes, but he simply said, "I'll be there. Security is waiting outside to walk with you."

As the door closed behind him, I got out my phone and looked through the contacts, finding her name. I stared at it for a moment.

Maybe calling her would be a terrible idea.

But I pressed call anyway.

FIFTY-SEVEN

DES

THE PHONE RANG several times before his voice came on the line.

"Didn't think I'd be hearing from you," he said bitterly. "After all, I probably deserve a thank you for all the media attention you've gotten for being 'sex positive.'" It had been a minute since I'd heard his voice, since we'd spent hours making out and going to parties and watching movies together.

The hatred in his voice threw me. It seemed to be coming from a different guy. "That's not why I called."

"Why did you then?" He seemed on edge, defensive.

"I wanted to talk to you," I said.

"I'm surprised a star like you has any time for me. Aren't you banging Jude now?"

It was an insult, a punch to the gut. "Devon, please."

He took a deep breath. "What?"

I sighed, holding the phone between my cheek and my shoulder so I could rub my temples as I paced the room. "Devon, did I hurt you?"

He was quiet for a moment. "What?"

"Did I hurt you, by breaking up with you?" I asked, afraid to hear the answer. All that time I'd thought we'd just been having fun, but now? I wasn't so sure.

His tone completely changed, going from prickly to weak. "I mean, yeah. I thought we were good together, and then you just dropped me."

I pressed my lips together, sitting on the edge of my bed. "I didn't realize you were so serious about me. I thought we were just a casual thing."

"It started out that way, but damn, Des, you have to know what kind of girl you are."

"What does that mean?" I asked.

"It means, you're the kind of girl a guy falls for, even when he isn't meaning to." He seemed frustrated at himself, exasperated at me for not knowing.

But I couldn't control his feelings, only what I'd done. "I'm sorry for not being clearer in my intentions. I promise I never meant to hurt you."

He was silent for a beat. "I appreciate that. You, apologizing."

We were both quiet for a moment, neither of us really knowing what to say. My throat ached, and my eyes stung with unshed tears. This was such a mess.

I'd gone from not wanting to break my own heart to being careless with the hearts of others. That was never what I wanted. But that was the result of my actions. And the worst part? I missed out on love *and* friendship with the guys I dated.

"Is everything okay?" he asked.

My voice shook. "Not really, Dev."

"What's going on?"

"I messed up. And I don't think I can fix it."

My heart ached thinking of Jude. We hadn't known each other that long, but he understood me, my music, in a way so few people did.

And he got me to open up my heart to real love for the first time since Luke. This time hurt so much worse.

Now I was out on my own, away from the

comfort and safety of my bedroom, where my mom could fix everything with a *tres leches* cake.

"Some problems aren't meant to be fixed. They exist to remind us of what we've learned and where we came from."

I blinked back tears. "You're right." But it still hurt.

He heaved a sigh. "I'm sorry too. For everything. I shouldn't have yelled at you when we broke up, and it was crappy of me to talk to the press like that. It was just my first time being interviewed and my feelings were hurt and—"

"Don't worry about it," I said. "You did kind of help me launch a speaking platform on my first tour as a singer."

He chuckled. "Leave it to you to make lemonade out of sour grapes."

"That's not the phrase," I said.

"It is now." He laughed. "So… friends?"

"Not really. But I hope we're not enemies."

"Not anymore," he replied. "And keep climbing the ladder. I want to tell my future children I got with a famous singer."

"So crass," I said.

He snickered. "Goodbye, Des."

"Goodbye, Devon."

I hung up, feeling tears coming down my cheeks. But this time they were lighter, freer, a release instead of grief.

I was learning, every single day; I was becoming a better version of myself.

And I hoped beyond all hope that Jude would see that.

And maybe he'd forgive me too.

FIFTY-EIGHT
JUDE

AFTER A FEW RINGS, Jade answered, a smile in her voice. "Hey, Jude! I should have called you myself to thank you for the song. I can't believe you decided to get rid of it."

I curled and uncurled my fingers, watching them on the table. "Actually, Jade, I didn't. My agent sold it out from under me."

"What?" she asked. "She carried on and on about how she wished you would keep it and put it on your album. What's going on?"

My knuckles were white from clenching my fists. "She lied to you, Jade. That's what's going on."

"Oh, Jude, you can't be serious."

"She was mad that Des and I were dating, so

she got back at me." I pushed away from the table, pacing around the conference room.

"*Were* dating?" Jade said. "You seemed so smitten when we had lunch. What happened?"

My throat felt tight, so I swallowed, hard, trying to get that ever-present lump to go away. "Apparently, Natalie had threatened Des that she would do something bad to me if we dated, but she dated me anyway."

"I can't believe your agent would do that to you guys." Jade sighed. "Jude, I wish I could sell you the song back, but my agent is salivating over it. She's looking for people to sing it with me as we speak since Natalie said you weren't interested anymore. Unless… would you sing it with me?"

The sheer irony of it brought a twisted grin to my face. "I'd love to."

"We can still perform it at the last show of your tour, right? I already had my schedule cleared for it."

I smiled, shaking my head in disbelief. "That would be great. I'll see you then."

"I'll see you then. And Jude?"

"Yeah?" I asked, pausing in my route around the room.

"You wrote this song about her, didn't you?"

My voice broke. "Yeah."

"I hope you can work things out with her."

"It's a little late for that," I said. "I'll see you next Friday."

"It's a date."

I hung up the phone and took a deep breath. I wanted to hide in this room, to avoid all the pain I'd gone through in the last couple days. But I was done hiding. If I had people around me who could take down a powerful agent like Natalie, I could deal with my own feelings. Instead of going out to the breakfast bar, I called Dad and asked him if he would come back to the conference room.

Within minutes, he was back, a concerned look on his face. "Is everything okay?"

"I called Jade, and she said she couldn't sell the song back, but that she'd sing it with me."

A grin split Dad's features. "Jude, that's amazing!"

My lips lifted for a moment. "Yeah, but that's not why I called you in here."

The concerned look was back in two seconds flat. "What's going on?"

I gestured at a chair, and Dad uneasily sat down. "I want to talk about Mom."

Dad's chest rose and fell, and he laced his fingers tightly. "What do you want to know?"

I took a deep breath, feeling shaky myself. "Did Mom have postpartum depression?"

His features crumbled, and he nodded. "I should have known, Jude, but back then, especially in small towns, they didn't talk about mental health like that. I talked to a doctor a couple years ago, and he said lots of women have the same struggles after giving birth. Especially after fighting infertility for so long."

Each new piece of information hit me like a ton of bricks. "Why didn't you tell me you spoke with a doctor?" I asked. "I've been worrying this whole time that there was—" My voice broke. "I thought there was something wrong with me."

"Oh, Jude." Dad rose from his chair and walked around the table to kneel beside me. He took my face in his hands and looked me square in the eyes. This close, I could see the worry lines around his eyes. The touch of gray at his temples. "I don't want you ever, for a second, to think there is anything wrong with you. Your mother, she dreamed about you, she prayed to have you. When she was pregnant with you, she'd sit on the couch, rubbing her belly and speak so sweetly to you."

Tears pooled in Dad's eyes. "She loved you more than life itself. She would have been an incredible mom, but PPD got in the way."

My own eyes stung with the release of a fear I'd held on to for so long. "Dad, why didn't you tell me?"

"You never wanted to talk about her. I thought maybe if we went to the cemetery together, we could discuss it then, but..."

I'd hidden away from anything hard. My voice was thick as I said, "Thanks for telling me now. I know how much you've missed her."

He nodded, wiping at his eyes. "You never get over your first love."

The truth behind his words hurt me. But I pushed on anyway. "I'd like to hear more about her, someday."

Dad hugged me tight. "I'd love that."

And for the first time, I could honestly say, "Me too."

Dad's phone began ringing, and he glanced at it. "Your grandma's here."

"We should go give her a warm welcome." I sniffed, wiping my eyes. "Or at least a wet one."

With a chuckle, Dad put his arm around my shoulders. "Let's go."

FIFTY-NINE
JUDE

SHE ARRIVED in the hotel carrying the Louis Vuitton purse we got her for her birthday and flipped her giant Fossil sunglasses atop her permed hair. As soon as she saw me, she hurried to me and gave me a big hug and kiss. It was almost enough to bring me to tears.

"Do you get more handsome every time I see you?" she asked, holding my face in her hands. Then her expression became worried. "Have you been crying?" she looked at Dad. "Has he been crying? Oh my gosh, you've been crying too!" Her murky brown eyes darted between us. "You two better explain."

Dad smiled tearfully at me. "We talked about his mom."

Grandma covered her heart, hugging both of us again. "I'm so happy for you two."

It never struck me to be happy about it, but maybe I should have been. For all the things my mom took from me, she gave me something bigger: my life.

And for Dad, he'd been her first love, the one he said he never got over, even after nearly twenty years. I never really thought how it must have felt for him to carry that burden, and her memory, alone.

I glanced over at him, and it could have just been my imagination, but he looked free too.

"Come sit," Grandma said, shuffling us to a bench in the corner of the lobby. "I want to get off my feet for a bit before we go out."

Security walked with us, giving us just enough space for some semblance of privacy.

Grandma looked around and said, "Where are Desirae and Diego? I thought they might be going out with us since their family isn't around."

Dad and I exchanged a glance. "They're busy today," Dad said.

Grandma set her purse on the floor beside her feet and folded her arms across her chest. "I did not drive from Winslow to Flagstaff with cars lined up behind me, and then get on an airplane to this godforsaken town to be lied to by my *only* son and grandson. There may be plenty of sins happening in this city, but lying to me won't be one of them."

I shook my head, smiling despite myself.

Grandma lifted one penciled eyebrow.

I glanced around, just to make extra sure no one was paying attention to us. "Des and I broke up."

Grandma's face fell, and she hugged me again. "Oh, honey, I'm so sorry. What happened?"

I pressed my lips together. "It's a long story that ends with a broken heart and me getting a new agent."

Grandma asked Dad to explain, since she wasn't getting enough out of me. Dad gave her the details while I tried not to feel her sorry eyes on me. I felt bad enough for all of us.

"Now that that's done," I said, "I'd rather focus on enjoying the day with you."

"Of course," Grandma said gently. "I think I have just the thing."

And man, did she come through. Even though we weren't at her house, surrounded by baking supplies, she still managed to stuff me so full of food I couldn't feel anything but my bloated stomach.

We went to a scratch kitchen for brunch, a cookie restaurant for dessert, and now we were walking down the aisles of a chocolate shop. I held two boxes for Grandma to take home, and Dad had a tray of caramel apples wrapped in iridescent cellophane for "road snacks" as she called them.

"Do you think Diego and Desirae want anything?" she asked.

Dad and I gave each other a look.

"What?" Grandma asked. "Just because you're upset with them doesn't mean they don't like chocolate."

Dad gave her an exasperated shake of the head, and I said, "I'm sure they'd appreciate that."

I had no idea what they'd been up to today. I pictured them going out and exploring the city. I could see Desirae going to the Eiffel Tower and eating a fancy dessert in the Paris restaurant.

But the worst part of it was that Des would be fine, just like she always was when the cards were stacked against her. She never failed to find a way to make the best of something or flip a situation in her favor.

I admired that about her.

And now I was jealous of her.

Because I knew she would go on to do amazing

things and meet some other incredible guy while my heart always ached for what could have been.

But I put on a smiling face for Grandma. And at the end of the day, when it was time to drop her off at her hotel room, she gave me a big hug and a chocolate and told me everything would be alright.

For a second, I let myself believe her.

DES

A FEW KNOCKS sounded on the door, and since Diego and Jago were tearing through a massive order they'd gotten from room service, I went to see who it was.

When I looked through the peephole, I couldn't see anyone. Figuring we'd gotten another room service delivery, I undid the safety bolt and opened the door to see Mama Santiago herself.

She stood a proud four feet, eleven inches tall and looked absolutely fabulous in her brightly colored outfit with a flowing shawl.

Worry quickly replaced my happiness at seeing her. She loved her grandson more than anything, had practically been a mother to him. Did she hate me for breaking his heart?

Before I could say anything, she crossed the threshold and gave me a hug.

I stiffened, then slowly relaxed into her embrace that felt so much like family's.

"I heard everything," she said. "I'm so sorry you were put in that position."

I blinked quickly, trying not to cry. I usually wasn't a teary person, but Jude had changed all that. "I feel so guilty," I admitted.

From the living area in our suite, Diego called, "Who is it?"

Mama Santiago yelled back, "Only your road trip grandma!"

The sounds of video games on the TV immediately stopped as Diego and Jago came our way. They both gave Mama Santiago long hugs and let her dote over them. She licked her fingers and adjusted Diego's curly hair. She squeezed Jago's biceps and said he was stronger than ever.

Then she sat at our table and said, "Now, what are we going to do about Des and Jude?"

Diego clapped his hands together, sliding into a chair across from her. "Now we're talking!"

"Yes!" Jago said. "We've been trying to come up with a plan all day!"

I stood in place, stunned by their admissions, by

Mama Santiago's willingness to fight for my relationship with her grandson, after everything that had transpired between us.

She leaned forward, tapping her manicured nails on the glass tabletop. "I'm thinking we have to find a way to get Jude out of his own way. He's always so lost in his head."

Jago nodded. "That's what I was saying to Diego. If he gets out of the pain, he'll see that Desirae's hurting too, and nothing like this will ever happen again."

I stepped forward, feeling guilty about all the plotting occurring behind Jude's back. He had every right to be upset with me. And he didn't have to forgive me, no matter how invested people were in our love story. "It was Jude's heart that was broken," I reminded them. "If he never forgives me, I wouldn't blame him at all."

The three of them were quiet for a moment. Then Mama Santiago got out of her chair and walked to me. Her brown eyes were full of compassion as she put a weathered hand on my cheek.

"Maybe you're right. He doesn't have to forgive you, but you need to forgive yourself for what you did while you were becoming a better version of you."

My eyes stung, and I reached up, holding her hand to my cheek. "I'm so lucky to have met you."

She smiled, the laugh lines deepening on her face. "I consider myself lucky to have met such a strong-willed, kind-hearted, beautiful girl. And I hope you know that no matter where you go, you'll always have a grandma in Winslow, Arizona."

"Love you, Mama," I said, giving her a hug.

She hugged me back. "Have a great night, sweetheart." She turned back to the boys. "I think it's time for me to head to my room."

Jago said, "I should probably get some sleep too."

Diego said, "I'll walk you to your room, Mama Santiago. It's getting late."

The three of them left me in the suite alone, but I didn't feel quite so lonely as before.

No, I was standing with the younger version of me, thanking her for all she'd done to get me here.

Then I sat in my room with a piece of paper and started writing.

SIXTY-ONE
JUDE

I LOOKED over the breakfast menu the next morning, wondering if I'd ever be hungry after all
Grandma had fed me the day before.

She and Dad were out shopping for a replace-
ment part for her CPAP machine, so I'd taken my
time getting around and making my way down to
the hotel restaurant. Maybe I was also hoping Des
had already eaten so I wouldn't run into her.

Unfortunately, I found something just as
unpleasant.

"Having trouble deciding what to order?"
Vanessa asked.

I looked up from my menu, seeing her sitting
just a couple tables over. *Great.*

"Just taking my time," I said. "I thought you were staying in your trailer?"

She laughed. "Where you stay, I stay, silly."

Okay, that wasn't creepy at all.

"Speaking of," she said, "where's Desirae? Aren't you two obsessed with each other or something?"

"She wanted to sleep in," I lied.

She tapped the corner of her menu. "That's interesting, because she was here an hour ago."

My cheeks instantly flushed. I hated lying almost as much as I hated being caught in one. "Right. She got a snack, and now she's sleeping."

"Snack." Vanessa snorted, and it rubbed me the wrong way.

I hated that I still felt so defensive about Des. That I wanted to fight every battle for her—I always had. I'd meant it when I said she made me want to be a hero. But I shoved that feeling away and refocused on my menu.

A waiter came and asked me what I wanted, and I pointed at something without really taking it in.

"What if we did a live video together?" Vanessa persisted. "The Fantiagos would love feeling like they were eating breakfast with *the* Jude Santiago."

I glanced longingly toward my security detail, wishing we hadn't allowed Vanessa so much access to me on tour. That arrangement would definitely be something to address with Samantha and my future agent.

"I'm trying to recharge," I said. "This has been my only 'vacation' for like three months."

She laughed. "Being driven around by Francie and waited on hand and foot must be so hard."

My eyebrows drew together. Vanessa hadn't ever come at me like that before. "What's your problem?"

"What's my problem?" she asked, setting her menu down. "I've been following you around for *years*, Jude. I learned how to drive a trailer for you! I've been taking online classes for college with satellite internet, which, let me tell you, isn't that great. All so I can be closer to you and maybe one day you'd see me and see that I'm special." A small muscle above Vanessa's right eye began twitching. "But then Des shows up and you're all of a sudden *in love with her*? It's not fair!"

Her voice echoed off the marble floors, and my security guard began walking closer.

"Maybe you're just a crappy boyfriend,"

Vanessa said. "That's why Des is never around you! Or maybe she's not your girlfriend at all."

I hated my face. My stupid expressive face. Because at that moment, Vanessa's eyes flew open. "You're not dating her for real, are you?"

Just then, my security guard arrived and began carrying Vanessa away, kicking and screaming.

I got out my phone and started a group call with Dad and Samantha. "Hey, um, I think we've got a problem."

I NAPPED for as long as I could after grabbing breakfast, but around noon, my phone went crazy with new notifications. From DMs on social media to text messages, people were asking me if I was really dating Jude Santiago. Or if it had all been fake.

There was even a long YouTube video with film from each of our interactions onstage and a very in-depth dissection of our body language throughout the duration of the tour.

We were in hot water. And it didn't take the trending hashtags to tell me that. Although, there were several.

. . .

#Juderae4ever
    #hesavailable
    #DIEdes
    #breakfastgate

Not to mention the crazy theories and rumors that were spinning out of control in the Fantiagos' online group.

Some girls were thrilled that Jude could potentially be back on the market.

Plenty more wanted my head on a silver platter because Jude could do no wrong, and therefore the failed relationship *had* to be my fault.

Or maybe the worst of all: people suspecting that Jude had only dated me to get extra publicity for his new release. Because, in their eyes, a guy like Jude could never have liked a plus-size girl like me.

Somewhere down the rabbit hole of my notifications, I saw I'd missed multiple calls from my parents, friends, and Samantha.

I sent a quick text to my family group chat, letting them know I was okay. Then I texted my friends, promising to call them later. And finally, I called Samantha back.

She answered after a single ring and said,

"Thank God, you're awake. We're sending a security guard to come get you."

"Where are you taking me?" I asked. Were they kicking me out of the tour now?

"Jude's room," she said. "We're doing damage control."

I felt weak. Jude's room? I hadn't seen him since the last concert, and that had been pure torture.

Samantha hung up, and I rushed out of bed, doing my best to look like I hadn't been lying in bed all day.

Diego was out with Jago on another hike, thank goodness, but I still called him in case no one had gotten through to them with the media crisis.

"Hey," he said as soon as he answered. "Are you okay?"

"You heard?" I shoved my head through the hole in my shirt while talking to him on speakerphone.

"Yeah, Jago and I are on our way back now. Apparently, they're having a séance in Jude's room."

"How can you be joking right now?" I asked, hopping around to get my leggings on.

"If this tour's taught me anything, it's that you have to learn to laugh or this business will eat you alive."

Diego wasn't wrong. "Be safe on your way back, okay? I'm not sure if anyone will recognize you, but it's better safe than sorry. I don't want the Fantiagos to beat you to a pulp because you're related to me."

"We'll be careful," Diego promised. "See you soon, sis."

We hung up, and I hurried to the bathroom, fixing my hair the best I could with dry shampoo and a lukewarm straightener.

A loud knock sounded on the door, and I could only assume it was the guard they sent to retrieve me.

I hurriedly swiped a mascara wand through my lashes and went to the door, grabbing my purse on the way. The guy I saw through the peephole wore all black, was muscled as all heck, and even had on aviator sunglasses.

He knocked again. "Samantha sent me."

I opened the door and said, "Let's go."

He led me to Jude's room, which was five floors away from mine. I tried not to be hurt as I wondered if that was intentional or not. We used to always stay on the same floor at least.

When we got there, he took me to the main living area where Jude, Anthony, and Samantha sat at a glass-top table identical to the one in my room, papers spread before them.

"You made it," she said, coming to get me.

Jude didn't even look up, determinedly facing the paper he held in his hands.

She walked me to the table, saying, "We are doing *major* damage control. Sentiment on social media is eighty-nine percent negative and media monitor shows—"

"Wait," I said, "I don't understand the jargon."

"Right." She took a breath. "Most posts on social media are negative—trending toward blaming Jude for dating you as a publicity stunt. Album sales are already down, and some people are planning to boycott him."

I covered my mouth, horrified that my actions were still wrecking his career. "Oh my gosh, I'm so sorry."

Samantha shook her head. "Let's remember who the real orchestrator of this chaos is."

"Exactly," Anthony agreed, although his son stayed very audibly silent.

"So what are we doing to fix this?" I asked.

"We're doing an exclusive interview with Winnie."

My eyebrows flew up. "Winnie? She tried to *slaughter* me last time I was on her show!"

"Exactly," Samantha said with a sharp smile. "No one would accuse her of airing a fluff piece."

"What are we going to say?" I asked. "Are we going to fly there?"

"She's agreed to a remote interview. The plan is to position you and Jude as happier than ever. We'll say that Vanessa's accusations, the source of the rumors, are nothing more than lies spread out of jealousy."

I glanced toward Jude, wondering what he thought of all this. If the idea of pretending to be happy killed him inside as much as it did me. "What do you think?" I asked.

Jude lifted his chin and said, "I think it's a good idea."

I nodded, bracing myself for the torture of what was to come. "Tell me what to do."

Samantha nodded. "The interview's in an hour."

SIXTY-THREE

JUDE

NO PART of me wanted to pretend to have feelings for Des. Because what I felt was real, and it hurt like hell. Every part of me wished a relationship full of love and trust could be true.

I hated that my love for her had been so twisted—like our relationship was some kind of show. I had hoped my fans would know me better, but this was just a reminder to be careful who I let get close. Vanessa had used her access to me as a chance to get my affection. And when she was disappointed? I got hurt.

For the next hour, I went over the talking points Samantha had printed out for me, trying not to focus on the beautiful girl sitting across the table from me.

There was a makeup artist working on her complexion, but if you asked me, she didn't need any makeup. I loved her natural look just as much as I loved her fully-done on-stage hair and makeup.

The longer I sat across from her, the more trouble I had remembering what she'd done that had been so bad. I missed her. Missed being able to talk to her about things I never told anyone else.

I missed holding her hand in mine, feeling the softness of her skin and smelling the spicy sweet scent of her perfume.

And this interview would just hurt me that much more, just remind me of what I couldn't have.

Samantha positioned us in front of a camera setup and made sure our chairs were scooted close together.

"Put your arm around her," Samantha said.

And I did as she asked, feeling all the heat I'd felt that first day we filmed a sizzle reel for social media. Des's perfume took over all my senses, and I closed my eyes, trying not to get swept away by her all over again.

I knew firsthand how easy it was to get crushed in the end.

The camera guy counted down, and I flashed a

smile at the camera, becoming Jude Santiago, sexy, practiced rock star, not Jude Santiago, nineteen-year-old, heart-broken boy.

Des tilted her head into my shoulder like she was exactly where she was meant to be. It killed me, because I'd thought the same thing not so long ago.

Winnie showed up on the TV in my room, and she said, "Jude, Desirae, I'm so happy to have you here! Look at you all cuddled up together! Looks like we're going to find out if it's all for show or not!"

Samantha pointed at her smile, reminding us to turn up the brightness. This couldn't fail. My album needed to succeed or finding another agency might not be the simple process we thought it would be.

"Hi, Winnie," I said. "I'm so thankful for you having us on to address some of these crazy rumors! And honestly, I'm just glad I get to show off my girl." I kissed the top of her head, realizing I was getting to do what I'd hoped for that day that I told Des I loved her.

I was showing her off to the world, proclaiming her as mine.

What a cruel, ironic joke.

Des smiled up at me and then at the camera, saying, "It's great to see you again, Winnie!"

"It's not just me," Winnie said. The camera panned to Vanessa, who was on the physical set.

I wanted to cuss or maybe kick a chair, but I quickly recovered in case they were still showing my face.

"Tell us what you've seen of these two the last couple weeks of the tour," Winnie said to Vanessa.

Making her eyes wide and innocent, Vanessa crossed her thin legs and said, "It's been crazy. Jude and Des never interact offstage, going to separate studios, and even riding in separate cars between shows. Des and her brother have been staying in hotels while Jude stays on the bus with his dad. Very confusing for a couple claiming to be in love."

Samantha held up a whiteboard with the words PROTECTIVE PARENTS written on it.

I chuckled and said, "Ever since we shared our feelings for each other, my dad's been super protective. He doesn't want any 'hanky panky' going on during the tour. His words, not mine."

Des giggled beside me, and it sounded so fake. It struck me then that I knew the real her. Knew when she was acting.

She hadn't been acting before, with me.

Winnie narrowed her eyes. "If your dad is so

'protective,' why did you have a clandestine lunch with Jade?"

The screen filled with a photo of Jade and me together in a restaurant at a table only big enough for two.

"That photo doesn't show my security guard in the background," I said. "You know, it's all about the angles."

Winnie smiled. "It's almost like he wasn't there at all, right?"

Her studio audience oohed and cackled in response.

"And what about the shove Des's brother gave you after your 'confession'? Not the sign of a supportive brother. More like the reaction of a brother who didn't appreciate his sister being *used* by a powerful celebrity."

"He's just as protective of me as Jude's dad is of him," Des said quickly. "In my family, we're there for each other, no matter what."

"Is that so? How, then, have you been able to sleep with half the college boys on the western seaboard?" Winnie asked.

"Hey!" I said, shifting as if I could hide Des from the camera, from Winnie's slut-shaming words. Samantha started writing in a hurry, but I wasn't waiting for her. "You do not talk to Des like that."

Winnie only laughed. "Jealous, Jude?"

I ground my teeth together. "Winnie, if you're going to treat Des like this, the interview is over."

"Then I suppose we'll have to use the rest of this segment to postulate," Winnie said. "There is plenty of evidence we can go over, showing that you and Des have had no relationship outside of the one you presented onstage. Including this voice recording we have from the agent you recently fired."

Crap.

Crap.

This was bad. So bad.

Natalie's voice came over the speakers, saying, "Thanks for calling me, Winnie. We've always loved working with your show and the credible stories you bring forth with journalistic integrity."

Integrity? Like Natalie knew anything about that.

"Unfortunately, my relationship with Jude Santiago became rocky as soon as Desirae De Leon became involved. He asked me to take a meeting with her, and when it became clear he was only using her to get ahead, I decided to decline representing her, for her own safety, you know."

Winnie replied in the recording, "That is true. We never got to hear your perspective of what happened in that first meeting. Only an angry video Des posted on her own YouTube, followed by Jude's publicity stunt, bringing a full-figured girl on tour with no real singing experience."

No experience? Had they not seen the hundred-plus videos she'd recorded on her channel? She told me she'd been practicing and performing for as long as she could remember! And I could tell she was more practiced than me during that first warmup with Shantelle!

Natalie's audio continued on air. "Jude decided to part ways with me after I expressed my concerns about his quote/unquote relationship with Desir-ae." The recording ended, and Natalie's photo filled the screen.

"There you have it," Winnie said. "A quote from one of Jude's closest sources on the situation at hand."

"You want a close source?" Des asked, fire in her eyes. "How about me?" She narrowed her gaze at the camera. "From the second I've been on tour with Jude, he's been nothing but a perfect gentleman. He is kind and caring and the most considerate person I've ever met. And as you so eloquently put it, Winnie, I've met many."

Winnie didn't even break a smile. "Speaking of the many boys you've been with, we have a special guest. Luke, why don't you come onstage?"

ALL THE BLOOD in my body rushed to the floor, and I very nearly passed out as he walked onto the stage. He looked just as I remembered him. Tall and fit and blond and perfectly dressed. He easily could have stood in a line of rock stars and super-models and fit right in.

While pieces of me I hadn't even known were broken rained inside me, Winnie said, "Everyone, I'd like you to meet Desirae De Leon's first boyfriend, Luke Okeson. He's currently a senior at Upton University, where he's quarterback on the football team, an all-American athlete, and has a 4.0 grade point average!" The crowd cheered for him, and Winnie said, "You might say Desirae knows how *hit above her weight!*"

"Des," Jude whispered. "Are you okay?"

It sounded like his voice was coming from so far away.

Winnie smiled at Luke like he was made of pure media gold. "My, my, aren't you handsome! Tell us about your relationship with Desirae."

Luke smiled that perfect smile that used to melt my heart and take my breath away. It still did one of those things. I could hardly breathe. My head felt so hot.

"Well, Winnie, just like Jude Santiago, I got swept away by that pretty girl. Of course, she weighed about a hundred pounds less when I met her."

My mouth fell open. Was he seriously commenting on my weight?

Jude whispered, "*Breathe*, Des."

Luke continued talking. "I met her at a freshman barbecue, and she was so eager back then. She came right up to me and started flirting with all she had." He chuckled. "So, I thought I'd give the girl a chance. You know, go on a date or two."

"It turned into more than that," Winnie said. "Didn't it?"

Luke acted all abashed and rubbed the back of

his neck. "You know how Desirae is. She took me under her spell, and before too long, I couldn't get enough of her. She was my high school sweetheart. We went to parties together, dances together, she wore my jersey to the homecoming game. I fell in love."

The studio audience "awwed", and I could feel bile rising in my throat.

"How did it end?" Winnie asked.

"You know Desirae. Nothing's good enough for her. I wasn't good enough for her."

Winnie's stunned face filled the screen. "You're telling me this fine scoop of vanilla ice cream wasn't good enough for *her*?"

Luke regretfully shook his head. "I just have one thing to say to you, Jude." He leaned forward, his hands on his knees, and the camera did a closeup on him. I hadn't seen his face this close since I was fifteen years old. Since he was breaking my heart. "Jude, man, if you really are getting with her, you aren't her first." He winked. "And you *definitely* won't be her last."

A gasp went through the studio audience and sounded on camera.

Jude got up from our chair and put his face right in the camera. "Take her name out of your mouth, you worthless piece of crap." His fists shook at his side. "You want to know why I fell in love with her? It's because she's perfect, exactly as she is. She doesn't need to lose weight or change outfits or act differently to be worthy of my love. Because she has it."

His jaw clenched and unclenched. "And do you want to know why I invited Des on tour in the first place?" Jude asked. "*I* was the one who wanted Natalie to take the meeting with Desirae. I've been listening to her YouTube channel for a year, wondering when she'd get discovered, and then I realized I could be the one to help her."

He looked at me for a moment, his deep brown eyes holding mine for the longest amount of time since the night he told me he *thought* he loved me.

"Natalie dismissed her because of her looks, and I didn't want to work with someone who was so shallow, and honestly, *blind*. Desirae is the most beautiful girl I've ever seen. She caught my eye from the first moment I saw her, and she's held it every moment since.

"In fact," he continued, "the very fact that everyone is so ready to assume our relationship is fake or she has me under some 'spell,' rather than accept the fact that someone like me could be genuinely attracted to someone like Des shows how messed up our society is. You think just because she's got some extra weight she's not beautiful? That she deserves any less than the absolute best? Look in the mirror and see the ugly in yourself. Because when I first saw Des, I couldn't find anything I didn't like."

Jude's chest rose and fell with his emotion, and even Winnie was silent for a moment.

"And Luke? If I was onstage right now, I'd punch you in the face like you deserve. Winnie, did you ever do the math? He dated Desirae when he was a *senior in high school*. She was a *freshman*. What stance does your journalistic 'integrity' have on emotional abuse and statutory rape?"

She quickly said, "There you have it, an exclusive, live interview with Jude Santiago himself and Desirae. Is she really his girlfriend? You'll have to decide for yourself! Next week, we'll be covering…"

The cameras came off, and the camera guy began packing up. Samantha clapped her hands together, tears shining in her eyes. "That was amazing. I couldn't have asked for anything better."

Anthony nodded in agreement. "That was great work, you two. We'll have to see how the chips fall online."

I looked over at Jude, his jaw was tight, and it felt like all that intensity had mirrored its way to my own heart. "Thank you," I said slowly, "for saying all of that… It means a lot to me."

Jude looked up to me, his brown eyes tortured. "I meant every word."

Then he got up, walked to his room, and closed the door.

WE DROVE three hours to Winslow on the way to our next show to drop off Grandma. We thought that would be easier than her taking an airplane back home. Plus, it gave us some extra time to sit and talk.

For part of the trip, she sat up toward the front with Francie, getting to know the woman my dad was beginning to look at so tenderly. They laughed, too. It looked like they would become fast friends.

But as we approached my hometown, Francie waved Dad up front. After speaking for a moment, Dad came back to me and said, "We're stopping by the cemetery, but don't worry. I won't ask you to come with me. I just... want to say hello."

I nodded and was silent as I looked out the

window. This town was so familiar. I'd spent most of my life here as a regular kid, living in a small two-bedroom apartment with my dad and visiting my grandma every chance I got. I'd gone to public school, taken guitar lessons from someone whose preferred performance venue was a campfire.

And somehow, *somehow*, I'd ended up here.

People paid hundreds, if not thousands of dollars, just to hear me sing. They spent extra to see me.

I'd met a girl and fallen in love with her. Fallen flat on my face.

And still, the only people I really had were my dad and my grandma.

I'd spent as long as I could remember being angry at my mom for leaving me. I couldn't put myself in her shoes and imagine why she might want to end her life and leave us all behind. And in a lot of ways, I still didn't understand.

But one thing I *did* understand was getting everything you thought you wanted, and still having a deep sense of sadness.

When I was a kid, putting videos up online for my grandma to listen to, part of me had wanted to be discovered. Part of me wanted to believe I could be the one in a million to become famous.

But now that I was famous... it wasn't enough.

I wanted love. I wanted my mom.

The bus slowed outside the cemetery and pulled to a stop. Dad got up and walked to the front of the bus, stepping outside. Francie and Grandma sat together, looking out the window toward my dad. Out my own window, I could see him walking alone toward Mom's grave.

The flowers he'd left a few months before were still there, along with the ceramics and other decorations he'd placed throughout the years.

Whatever shards were left of my heart painfully turned.

My anger hadn't hurt my mom. She was already gone. But it had hurt my dad. He'd walked to the cemetery so many times, carried his grief and his memories, alone.

I couldn't imagine what that pain must have felt like for him. But I wouldn't let him carry it alone anymore.

I got out of my seat and walked toward the front door. Francie opened it wordlessly. Mama Santiago brushed my hand as I walked by, but stayed silent.

As I stepped outside, the cool evening breeze

chilled my skin. Something about tonight felt different.

Buffalo grass crunched underfoot as I walked toward my dad where he knelt by Mom's grave. His hand was on the cross, as always. His eyes turned toward the ground.

Until he heard me.

He turned to look at me, and his lips parted. Even as I approached him, he didn't say anything. He didn't need to. I was the one who needed to speak.

I put my hand on Dad's shoulder, my throat feeling tight. "I'm sorry, Dad."

His lips trembled before he took me in his arms and held on tight.

"I'm sorry," I breathed again.

He pulled back, taking a deep breath, and wiped at his tears with his thumbs. "I'm happy you're here now."

He looked back toward her grave, and I read her headstone for the first time I could remember.

Marisol Santiago
  An incredible wife, mother, and friend.

.   .   .

My vision blurred with tears before I even made it to the years that marked a life cut far too short.

"I want to know about her," I said, my voice thick with emotion. "What was she like?"

Dad gave me a watery smile. "Where do I even begin?"

DES

MY PHONE RANG too early the next morning, but since it was my mom, I had to answer it. She'd been so worried about me the night before and even stayed on the phone with me until I fell asleep, just to be there for me.

I rubbed the corners of my eyes, if only to help me wake up, and answered her call. "Hello?"

"Honey." She sounded relieved to hear my voice. "Have you heard the news?"

My eyebrows drew together. "What news?" The media had surprised me throughout this tour. I still couldn't believe Winnie had brought Luke to Philadelphia for that interview. Seeing him had been like a punch to the gut. I braced myself for what Mom had to say.

"The college Luke attended just released a statement. They're kicking him off the football team and taking away his scholarship."

"What?" I sat up, kicking off my covers. If I hadn't been awake before, I certainly was now.

"They put out a press release. It says, 'After reviewing the claims made against Luke Okeson, we have come to a decision to release him from the football team and strip him of all honorary titles and scholarships. Okeson's actions on national television are in direct violation of our code of conduct. Our university expects its students to uphold the highest level of integrity and takes claims like those made against Okeson seriously. May this serve as a reminder to all of our students that humans are to be treated with human dignity.'"

I sat back on the bed, stunned to silence.

"What do you think?" she asked nervously.

"I... I can't believe it. Just because of the interview?"

"He said some truly awful things, and Jude was right to call him out for his behavior."

Tears slid down my cheeks. When I'd been a freshman in high school, I'd felt so powerless against Luke. Even when my parents found out what was going on, it was too late for Emerson Academy to rebuke him. It was like Luke had always gone on to live a carefree, happy life, even after taking away so much of me. And judging by the confident way he'd walked onstage, the careless way he mentioned my weight... this might be the first consequence he's ever had.

"Talk to me," Mom breathed.

I wiped at my eyes, even though the tears kept coming. "I can't help but think that if he did it to me, he's done it to other girls too... Maybe this will make him see that he's done something wrong."

"I hope so," Mom said. "And now girls everywhere know what he's capable of, without you even saying a word."

I let out a choked laugh. I felt vindicated. All this time, I'd been so ashamed of what Luke put me through, but I never needed to be.

Luke had shown the world who he was.

And Jude had helped everyone, including me, see who I really was.

"Des?" Mom said.

"Yeah?"

"I might not have told you yet, but I want you to know I'm proud of you. I was worried about you going on this tour, thinking you were my little girl who needed protection."

"And now?" I asked.

A soft laugh came through the line. "Now, I *know* you're a strong woman. It's all the bullies, the Lukes and Natalies of the world, who need protecting from you."

Her words brought a smile to my face. "You're the strongest woman I know, Mom. No matter where I go, I'll always want to be like you. I love you."

"I love you too."

DAD STOOD in the bus with me and put his hands on my shoulders. "Last day of the Summer of Santiago. Are you ready?"

I nodded emphatically. So much had happened, and I wasn't even close to fully processing.

Vanessa was officially off the tour. Natalie was gone. The rumors about Des and me died down. The college Luke attended had stripped him of his honorary titles and kicked him off the football team. And we signed a deal with Jade to have me be the male half of the duet on the song I wrote.

It wasn't the same as owning the song myself, but after the ordeal I'd been through, I was just happy to be a part of it.

In fact, I considered this the best and worst tour

of my life. There were high ups and low downs, and I'd made it through every single one. On the last day of the tour, I couldn't help but feel proud of myself for making it through days that felt impossible.

After tonight, Des would go back to her life, I would go back to mine, and we wouldn't have to see each other ever again. We'd tell the media we drifted apart after not seeing each other every day. Easy enough. If I didn't spend too much time thinking about it.

Dad rubbed my arms and said, "Let's get this show on the road."

I nodded and we got off the bus, walking past the fans into the concert venue. I signed autographs as I could, held hands, smiled, and finally walked inside.

But my dad had a surprise waiting for me.

My grandma stood with a bouquet of blooming lilies and said, "Congratulations!"

I grinned, going to hug her. "I didn't need all these lilies when I have a Rose in front of me!"

She chuckled. "You are too sweet." Then she looked quizzically at Dad and said, "Where did he get that from?"

Dad laughed. "Not me." He glanced at Jago

and said, "Will you two walk him to the studio? I have some matters to attend to."

They agreed, and I held out my arm for Grandma. She looped hers through the crook of my elbow and held on. Jago and I slowed our pace to match hers, and it really was like stopping to smell the roses.

This was a venue in LA where I'd performed dozens of times now, but this would be the last time of this tour. Of a summer that had changed my life. How different today would have been if Des and I could have walked these halls together, moments away from living the future together we'd dreamed up in late-night text messages.

When we got close to the door with my name surrounded in lights, Grandma said, "That was really sweet, what you said for Desirae in that interview."

I blinked, a fresh well of pain rising in my chest. Jago was great at protecting me from screaming fans. A broken heart? Not so much.

Grandma continued, "I'll be in the lounge, but I can't wait to cheer you on from backstage tonight." She gave me a big hug. "Can I give you some advice?"

My eyebrows drew together. "Of course, Mama. Anytime."

She took my hand in both of hers, looking down at them for a moment before meeting my eyes again. "I'm nearly eighty, and I still make mistakes. I'm learning every day."

I studied her for a moment. "You may not be perfect, but you've been exactly what I needed."

She smiled, patting my cheek with her hand. "Remember that, okay?"

I nodded, confused, then watched as she walked away. Once she rounded the corner, I opened the door to my studio and Jago shoved me in, closing the door swiftly behind me.

Then my eyes took in the person sitting in front of the mirror.

Oh, hell no.

I turned around and yanked on the handle, but the door wouldn't budge. "Jago! What are you doing?"

"You two need to talk!" he yelled back.

I slapped my recently healed hand on the door. "Let me out or so help me, I'll fire you, Jago! Don't think I won't!"

Then Diego said, "It's been long enough! I miss my best friend, and my sister misses her boyfriend!"

I let out a sigh. They'd ganged up on us. "I'm going to call my dad."

Jago said, "He already knows."

I growled, kicking the door and instantly regretting it. These canvas shoes proved next to nothing by way of protection from metal doors. I hopped on one leg, holding my hurt foot, then slowly let it down, remembering who was in the room with me.

Des was still in front of the mirror, but instead of looking at me in the reflection, she had her eyes down on her lap.

She sniffed softly. "I'm sorry," she said. "I didn't know they were planning this."

Feeling guilty, I said, "Really?"

She nodded. "This is a nicer room than usual, though. Roomier. I should have guessed."

"That's because it's my studio," I retorted. I wasn't angry, not really. But this was just like salt in the wound. "Didn't you see the name on the door?"

"It had my name on it when I came in."

I shook my head, thinking back to the "advice" Grandma had given me. She had been in on this stunt too. "Why would they get an idea like this? Did you lead them to it?"

She leveled her gaze at me. "Of course not. I told you, I respect your decision."

How could she be so calm about this? Just being in the same room with her, smelling her perfume, was ripping what was left of my heart out of my chest, strand by freaking strand.

"Why then?" I asked. "Why?"

She gave me a gentle smile. "Probably because Diego misses you."

"No. Why did *you* do it?" My voice shook, making up for all the lack of emotion in hers. "Why did you risk my career like that when you knew how much it meant to me? Why did you risk *our* future?"

DES

MY LIPS PARTED as I looked at Jude and heard the rising volume in his voice. He'd been so cold toward me, so emotionless. "I didn't know you even cared about our future anymore."

His face contorted into layers of pain I hadn't seen since Natalie's confession. "Of course I care. Of course I do. Our relationship was the first thing I'd really looked forward to in a long time. You were the first person I let myself get that close to. You're the one who told me about PPD. And you clobbered me, Des. You freaking destroyed me without so much as a second thought."

I shook my head, hurt at his oversimplification of my actions. Did he really think it had been so easy for me? "Do you want to see my text messages?

All the conversations I had with my friends about how much I liked you but how I couldn't come near you because of what Natalie said. Do you want to call my parents and ask them about the fees we paid our lawyer to see if it was safe for me to like you? Do *you* know what it feels like to have someone tell you they'd wreck their most lucrative client's career? Would you believe her if you were in my situation? It was *stupid* for her to do what she did."

"So you didn't believe her?" Jude asked skeptically. "Why risk it? Why not tell me?"

"I had an NDA!"

"That didn't keep you from telling all of your friends," he said quickly. "You didn't trust me."

I looked down at my lap again. At my brightly painted nails that looked so perfectly smooth compared to the jagged edges of my heart. "Maybe I didn't trust you. I was afraid to love you, Jude, but I did it anyway."

I shook my head, knowing this wasn't where I wanted to go with him. "Look, Jude, it's not your fault. You're completely right. I never should have risked it without telling you. Every day since Natalie did what she did, I've gone over each second, wishing I could have just waited until January. Even with the risk that you'd fall for someone else. I've gone over every moment, thinking of all the times I could have handled it differently, and the truth is, I could have. I could have done so many things differently. I wish I would have.

"But the thing is, I can't go back in time. I can't change the past." My voice cracked on that truth. "All I can *be* is sorry. And all I can *do* is better."

A muscle in his jaw ticked, but he didn't stop me, so I kept going.

"I wish you would give me another chance so I could prove how much better I would do. I miss you like crazy, and I know Diego does too. You were so much more than my boyfriend. You were our best friend."

His eyes met mine then. "I can't forget what you did."

"Me neither," I admitted, my throat tight. "Do you remember the video that started all of this?" I thought back to the video I'd posted, and it seemed like I was a different person now—so much different than that hot-headed girl afraid of missing out on her dreams.

Jude simply nodded.

"I was so wrong, Jude, about everything. You aren't a sellout, not even close. I've seen you go up against big shot executives and fight battles with your dad and love your fans like no one I've ever seen. No matter what happened with us, I'll never stop being amazed by you, Jude Santiago."

His lips formed a shaky smile, and he said, "You're the amazing one. After everything Luke put you through, after all the crap you've put up with from the media... you still put your heart on the line. I'm not that brave."

My lips trembled, because this felt an awful lot like goodbye. "I'm going to miss you."

His eyes shined. "I'll miss you too." And then he did the most incredible thing. He hugged me. Not as a lover, not as a friend. But as two people who shared an incredible part of their lives.

It had changed us forever, even if it couldn't last.

SIXTY-NINE

JUDE

I STOOD OFFSTAGE BY JAGO, Mama, my dad, and Jade, listening to Des sing onstage for the last time in my life. Diego was feet away from us, but he may have been a lifetime away for how distant he felt.

Tears formed in my eyes as I watched her sing with all her heart. As I thought of all I'd gained and lost in such a short span of time.

She finished her song and began speaking over the slow strumming of the bass player. "Joining the Summer of Santiago tour has been the biggest blessing of my life." Cheers ripped through the audience, and as they died, she continued.

"And I know there are girls in the audience right now. Girls like me who are bigger than other girls. Who have to shop in plus-size sections. I bet, just like me, you've been told your entire life that you don't deserve to fall in love. I bet you've been told that people will treat you worse because of your size or that reaching your dreams is impossible because you don't fit society's expectations." She shook her head and screamed, "Screw those expectations!"

The cheers got even louder.

"You need to know, deep in here"—she clutched at her chest—"that you are worthy of every good thing in this life. Not because of anything you do or how much makeup you wear or the kinds of clothes you buy." She paused, looking into the eyes of everyone she could. "You are worthy because you *are*."

The noise reached a feverish crescendo, and she continued, louder than before.

"Jude Santiago has taught me so much about music, life, and love. But one of the best things I've learned from him is how to pour my heart into the creation of a song. So, if you'll let me, I'd love to sing my very first original song for you."

My lips parted. Desirae had written her own song?

I found myself anxious to hear the first chords,

the notes, the way her heart would pour through her vocal cords.

She began singing, and Grandma reached for my hand, squeezing it tight. She may have been the only thing keeping me upright.

I was afraid of something real,
    Fearing a heartbreak I couldn't heal.
    Sharing shame with the highlight reel
    Standing in the rain and waiting for the kill.

And damn if those brown eyes didn't kill me.
    Damn if those sweet words didn't take me away.
    Damn if my heart didn't get lost in translation.
    Damn if my fears weren't real.

I gave all of myself
    Put it all out like it wouldn't kill me
    Then I stood in the rain and I realized
    Oh I realized
    That I was stronger
    Braver
    Truer

Than I ever suspected.

I was smarter
Wiser
And taller
Than anyone knew.

And the only thing that could kill me
Was giving my heart to you.

Yeah I'm stronger than I was before
Yeah I've laid down and cried on the floor
Yeah I've poured every bit of myself into dreams I
thought could never come true.

But still the thing that will get me.

Is crying, and singing, and begging, and wishing, and trying,
and hoping, and thinking, that somehow,
This song could lead me
Right back to before.

.   .   .

Phone lights shone in the swaying audience as Des sang the last of the song and the music faded into clapping and roaring. The camera panned over her friends in the audience holding signs that said WE LOVE DES DE LEON!

They had cupcakes painted on their cheeks and glitter on their eyes, and they looked so proud of Des.

Just as proud as *I* was of Des.

I covered my mouth with my free hand, feeling wetness on my cheeks. Her song, her lyrics, had brought me to tears I wasn't expecting. And my heart ached, feeling her words, digesting my grandma's advice, and wondering why in the hell I let Natalie get in the way of me and the woman I *loved*.

Des's voice shook as she said, "I was so scared to share that with you, but sometimes we need to do things that scare us to reach our dreams."

The cheers practically vibrated my core.

Sometimes we need to do things that scare us to reach our dreams.

Giving my heart to Des, again, was the scariest thing I could think of. But there wasn't a way to get to my dreams of being with her without risking it all.

Without thinking, I jogged onto the stage, slowing only as I stood before her.

Her big brown eyes looked up at me, so full of questions.

And there was only one way to answer.

I kissed her, in front of all those people. I held her and let my heart come out through my actions.

Because Desirae De Leon was the woman I loved. And I was done getting in my own damn way.

SEVENTY

DES

I HELD Jude's cheeks in my hands, letting the microphone fall to the stage floor. I had to feel him, to know this was real.

He searched my eyes with his own and, over the thundering applause, said three words that healed everything inside me that had been broken. "I love you."

Tears streamed down my cheeks, but I didn't care. I kissed him, savoring the taste of his lips, the tenderness in his embrace, and the impossible reality that Jude Santiago was giving me another chance.

He held my hand and led me off the stage as the lights dimmed behind us. Right there in the wings, he held me tight, kissing me again.

This time, when we broke apart, Diego hugged him too, taking him from me and swinging him around. As soon as Diego let him down, Jago high-fived Jude, and Anthony and Mama Santiago hugged him together. Even Angelina was smiling ear-to-ear. It was the biggest off-stage celebration we'd had since day one of the tour. The perfect way to end the best and worst summer of my life.

And then Jude came back to me, kissing my lips again. "Go on a date with me?"

I laughed, happiness bursting out of me. "We have a concert to finish!"

"Oh yeah," he said, laughing and kissing me again. "As soon as the signings are done?"

"Of course," I replied. Happily ever after couldn't come soon enough for us.

He squeezed my hands and jogged away from me onto the stage. He picked up the mic that had fallen on the floor and said, "Isn't she amazing?!"

The crowd roared, and I laughed happily. Diego hugged me to his side, congratulating me. As Jude began singing, Mama Santiago wrapped her arms around my waist. "I knew he just needed to get out of his own head! That song was lovely, dear."

I smiled at her. "You're so wise."

"And stubborn," she added. "That helps."

Then a person I'd only ever seen on television appeared, standing next to me. "Jade?" I breathed. I'd heard from Samantha that she'd be here, but I still hadn't quite believed it.

She was taller in person than I thought, standing at least five or six inches taller than me. She had to be five-nine, like Cori. At least. And she was beautiful, in an edgy way, with electric-blue streaks dyed into her white-blond hair and contrasting with her black lashes.

But her smile was even brighter than her hair. "I'm so happy for you and Jude. And you were so inspiring up there! I think you have real potential, Des."

"Thank you!" I stammered. Maybe I wasn't quite used to being around famous people yet.

"We need to jam sometime," she said.

My mouth opened and closed. "Um, yes, anytime."

We stood next to each other, chatting as Jude went through his set, casting smiles my way every now and then. And then he said, "Thanks to a change in plans from my former agent, I'll be singing 'First Kisses' with Jade! She's here tonight to give us a little preview!"

Jade grinned at me, then jogged onto the stage

with Jude.

Everyone in the crowd went wild, and I knew if I'd been in the audience, I would have felt like I'd hit the jackpot with a surprise performance from Jade.

Jude began playing his guitar, singing the first aching lyrics, but Jade put her hand over his, stopping his music.

On the big screen, I could see him giving her a confused look, but she simply shook her head. "This isn't right," she said, her mic picking up every word. "You and Des deserve this moment."

It was almost too good to be true. But she walked directly to me, taking my hand and leading me onstage to stand across from Jude.

So overwhelmed by it all, I looked at Jude, mouthing, "Is this my life?"

He smiled in return and said, "It's ours."

I stuck my surfboard into the sand of our private beach and sat back against it. Back in May, I'd expected to travel a bit over the summer, maybe hang out with my sister for her last few months at home before she hit it big. Instead, I'd gotten an inside look into the music industry and a best friend out of the experience too.

Ignore the fact that he was currently making out with my sister in the water instead of taking a surf lesson with me like we'd agreed to, and it was a pretty cool deal.

I had a week before my senior year began and just a few months before Des started her first tour as a headliner.

After that final show, Jude signed with Jade's

agent, and Des signed with an outfit out of LA that seemed beyond dedicated to get both her voice and her body-positive message into the world.

It made me think—if my big sister—the same one who couldn't wake up before nine in the morning—could accomplish all that and fall in love… what *and who* were waiting out there for me?

I couldn't wait to find out.

Dear Reader,

The next book in this series is Diego's story, Curvy Girls Can't Date Surfers. I have a HUGE, crazy goal of hitting the NYT Bestsellers List with this book, because I want to see fat representation on one of the biggest bestsellers lists in existence. I'm hoping you will help me.

All you have to do is preorder a copy of this book for less than a dollar and tell your friends about the Curvy Girl Club.

I promise, an amazing story is coming, and you will love every single page.

Lots of love,

Kelsie Stelting

Preorder here.

Use this QR code to learn more about
Diego's story!

Want to see the Curvy Girl Club 2.0 get back together again? Read "Waldo's Diner," a FREE short story of Des telling her friends some MAJOR news!

Use this QR code to access your free short
story!

AUTHOR'S NOTE

More than two years ago, I was at an author's conference, thinking about this series. I was dreaming about the girls and the kinds of lives they would live. I imagined how the stories of big girls getting their dream guys would resonate with readers. I hoped it could be the thing to launch my career as a full-time author.

So many of my dreams came true times ten.

That's one of the reasons why Des is so special to me. She is so audacious and unapologetic about her pursuit of big dreams that most people would consider impossible. She doesn't let anything hold her back either. Not once was did she see her size or her past as an obstacle—she used them to help others along the way.

I used to think of my weight as something that would hold me back. When I was serious about sports, it was the thing keeping me from the next level. When I wanted a guy who didn't like me back, it had to be because of my weight.

While writing this series, I realized my weight (and even my struggle with it) is my superpower. Because of my size, I relate to so many girls and women who've had similar struggles. This extra weight has let me write stories that help others feel seen and valued and worthy of love exactly as they are.

I am *thankful* for my experience as a plus sized person.

No, it hasn't been easy to live in a bigger body in a society that values thinness so highly. I've cried about weight, gone on tons of diets that didn't work, felt uncomfortable in public, worried about fitting in an airplane seat, and more.

But damn has being bigger brought so many incredible gifts into my life. (You, my sweet reader, being one of them!)

I wonder if there's been something holding you back in pursuit of your big audacious goals?

What if the thing holding you back is secretly

your superpower, waiting to be used for the good of everyone around you?

I can't wait to see what happens when you put it to use. Message me. Email me. Post it online with the hashtag #CurvyGirlsCAN. I'd love to see you shine.

ACKNOWLEDGMENTS

First, I would like to thank you, sweet reader, for picking up this story, and making it through every page. Just by reading this book, you've done more for me than you can ever know. I love that we can share these words and characters with each other.

My family is so supportive of my writing, and I'll forever be thankful for them. Especially when I'm an emotional wreck because I'm writing the dark moment. All your extra love means the world!

I have an amazing team behind me for the production of each book. Tricia Harden is the dream editor. I adore working with her, and I always know the girls are in good hands when I send them to her! Najla Qamber has consistently given me beautiful cover designs, and I love seeing and being inspired by them! My mom, Jennifer Hoss, has been a huge help with making sure orders are shipped and taking on audiobook production so I have more time to focus on stories like this one. Plus, my brother, Tucker Hoss, has been helping out with great content on my site! I love having their support!

My sensitivity readers, Christina Silva, Alejandra Guadalupe Garcia, and Capriana Flowers gave me such amazing feedback and helped make sure Des and her family were well represented. I'm so thankful they volunteered and care enough about this series to dedicate their time and talents!

My dear friend Sally Henson has been such an amazing sounding board throughout the story creation process and just in life in general. She's the best cheerleader and friend a girl could ask for.

Kelsie Stelting: Reader's Club has always been the coolest place on the internet. All the beautiful humans in that group make being a writer so much fun! I love having them as readers and friends.

GLOSSARY

LATIN PHRASES

Ad Meliora: School motto meaning "toward better things."

Audentes fortuna iuvat: Motto of *Dulce Periculum* meaning "Fortune favors the bold."

Dulce Periculum: means "danger is sweet" - local secret club that performs stunts

Multum in Parvo: means "much in little"

LOCATIONS

Town Name: Emerson

Location: Halfway between Los Angeles and San Francisco

Surrounding towns: Brentwood, Seaton, Heywood

Emerson Academy: Private school Rory and Beckett attend

Brentwood Academy: Rival private school

Walden Island: Tourism island off the coast, only accessible by helicopter or ferry

Laughlin: Small country between England and Scotland formed in the early 1900s.

MacColl: Capital city of Laughlin where the royal family resides.

MAIN HANGOUTS

Emerson Elementary Library: Where Rory tutors Anna, open to students K-7

Emerson Field: Massive park in the center of Emerson

Emerson Memorial: Local hospital

Emerson Shoppes: Shopping mall

Emerson Trails: Hiking trails in Emerson, near Emerson Field

Halfway Café: Expensive dining option in Emerson, frequented by celebrities

La La Pictures: Movie theater in Emerson

Ripe: Major health food store serving the tri-city area

Roasted: Popular coffee shop in Emerson

JJ Cleaning: Cleaning service owned by Jordan's mom

Seaton Bakery: Delicious dining and drink option in Seaton where Beckett works

Seaton Beach: Beach near Seaton – rougher than the beach near Brentwood

Seaton Pier: Fishing pier near Seaton

Spike's: Local 18-and-under club

Waldo's Diner: local diner, especially popular after sporting events

APPS

Rush+: Game app designed by Kai Rush and his father

Sermo: chat app used by private school students

IMPORTANT ENTITIES

Bhatta Productions: Production company owned by Zara's father

Brentwood Badgers: Professional football team

Heywood Market: Big ranch/distributor where everyone can purchase their meat locally

Invisible Mountains: Local major nonprofit - Callie's dad is the CEO

Dugan Industries: Owns and manages Brentwood Marina, along with other entities. Owned by Ryker Dugan's father, Trent Dugan.

Always Anika

New at Texas High

Abi and the Boy Next Door

Abi and the Boy Who Lied

Abi and the Boy She Loves

The Pen Pal Romance Series

Dear Adam

Fabio Vs. the Friend Zone

Sincerely Cinderella

The Sweet Water High Series: A Multi-Author Collaboration

Road Trip with the Enemy: A Sweet Standalone Romance

YA Contemporary Romance Anthologies

The Art of Taking Chances

Two More Days

Nonfiction

Raising the West

Kelsie Stelting is a body positive romance author who writes love stories with strong characters, deep feelings, and happy endings.

She currently lives in Colorado with her family. You can often find her writing, spending time with family, and soaking up too much sun wherever she can find it.

Visit www.kelsiestelting.com to get a free story and sign up for her readers' group!

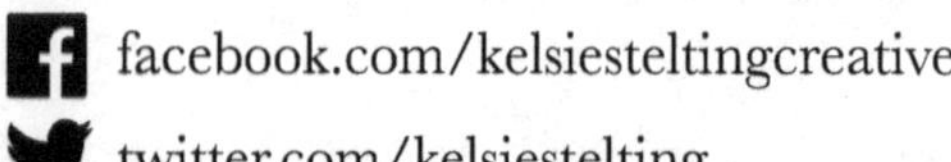